PRAISE FOR THE DAN CONNOR MYSTERIES

"R.J. McMillen's mastery of description and amazing ability to create enriched metaphors adds so much to this chilling mystery. This is a book to read in the comforting light of day" —Judy King, author of *Living at Lake Chapala*

"A pure pleasure to read." —Roberta Rich, author of *The Midwife of Venice* and *The Harem Midwife*

A DAN CONNOR MYSTERY

BLACK TIDE RISING

R.J. McMILLEN

TouchWood
Editions

TouchWood Editions
touchwoodeditions.com

LIBRARY AND ARCHIVES CANADA CATALOGUING IN PUBLICATION
McMillen, R.J., 1945–, author
Black tide rising / R.J. McMillen.

(A Dan Connor mystery; 2)
Issued in print and electronic formats.
ISBN 978-1-77151-123-0

I. Title. II. Series: McMillen, R.J., 1945– Dan Connor mystery; 2.

PS8625.M56B53 2015   C813'.6   C2014-908213-4

Editor: Linda L. Richards
Proofreader: Vivian Sinclair
Design: Pete Kohut
Cover images: Spooky forest, Pr3t3nd3r, istockphoto.com
Jogging-away silhouette, Illustrious, istockphoto.com
Native American eagle (detail), LeshaBu, istockphoto.com

| Canadian Heritage | Patrimoine canadien | | Canada Council for the Arts | Conseil des Arts du Canada | | BRITISH COLUMBIA ARTS COUNCIL |

We gratefully acknowledge the financial support for our publishing activities from the Government of Canada through the Canada Book Fund and the Canada Council for the Arts, and from the Province of British Columbia through the British Columbia Arts Council and the Book Publishing Tax Credit.

The interior pages of this book have been printed on 100% post-consumer recycled paper, processed chlorine free, and printed with vegetable-based inks.

1 2 3 4 5 19 18 17 16 15

PRINTED IN CANADA

To Jesse, Shelley, and Virginia, with love.

ENLARGED SECTION OF VANCOUVER ISLAND, BRITISH COLUMBIA, CANADA

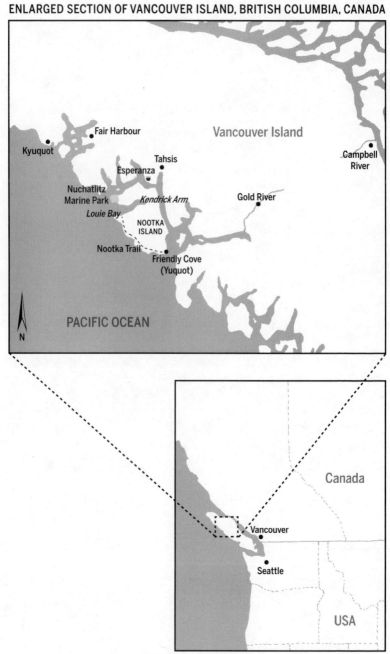

ONE

The chisel slid into the soft wood as easily as an eel slips through water. He had known it would. The carpentry instructor inside the joint had taught him well and had praised his ability to use tools. He wasn't used to hearing praise, but it had felt good. After he was released, he found a hardware store a couple of blocks from the halfway house they put him in, and over the course of three or four weeks he stole a whole box of woodworking tools—although woodworking wasn't what he planned to use them for.

He'd spent long hours honing the edge, first sharpening it with a file, then whetting it on water-stones, each one finer than the one before, coaxing each molecule of metal into perfect alignment. It would have cut into a living ironwood tree had he needed it to, but this was cedar: soft, porous as a sponge, grayed by age and rain and sun. The totem had been lying here for decades, cradled by the sand and the seagrass. It still held its form; the intricately carved figures of eagle and bear, deer and salmon, all wrapped in the coils of a lightning snake, but its substance was decaying back into the same soil that had nurtured it all those years before.

He pushed the chisel in again. The blade tore into the bear's snout, slid down into the gaping mouth, and stabbed into the striped coils of the snake. It gouged and ripped, dug deep, its path traced by the pale glow of new yellow cedar exposed to the air for the first time, and against the surrounding darkness of the night the snake seemed to shiver.

The man cursed as more and more new wood gleamed up at him. He had been so certain this was the place, but there was nothing. Nothing but weathered wood smudged with faded patches of blue, green, and red paint. He searched his memory, sure of what he had heard but wanting to hear the words again. Pat and Carl had been in the dining room of the house they had broken into, huddled over a table. They had sent him out to the kitchen on some pretext or other—they always did that. Sent him to get wood. Sent him to get beer. Sent him to get food. Whatever. He knew it was because they thought he was too stupid to be included in their fancy plans. They said he was unpredictable. Had too short a fuse. It had pissed him off at first, but then he had decided to just play along. Why not? He was going to get the last laugh anyway. They'd find out soon enough just who was stupid.

So he had gone out to find coffee, but some trick of sound in the empty house had brought him every word.

"We gotta hide it, man. The cops know. They followed us here. That was them we saw up at the hotel. They're lookin' for us, but even if they find us, they got nothin' if we don't have the stuff."

"So if they can find us so easy, they can find this shit too."

That had been Carl, always the downer. Not quick like Pat. Pat was the brain.

"We can take it out to the cove. Hide it there. Nothing there but the lighthouse and the church. No one's gonna find it there."

He had known right away what cove they were talking about. He had taken them there. It was called Friendly Cove on the charts, but the Indians called it Yuquot. "The place where the winds blow from many directions" or some such shit. Had to be there. It was the only place around with a lighthouse and a church, and the Indians that had once lived there had all left and moved down to Gold River years ago. Even the houses were gone. Only one left there now, and that was often empty.

"How the hell we gonna get to the cove? That boat only goes a couple a times a week and the cops'll probably be watchin' it anyway. We ain't never gonna get on that."

Carl again. Asshole.

"Water taxi. Get it to take us out to that fishing lodge where the old cannery used to be. We can walk over, easy. Walk over, hide the stuff, then walk back. Who's gonna know?"

It had been quiet for a few minutes then, and he had made a show of slamming cupboards and clattering dishes so they wouldn't know he was listening.

"So where the hell would we hide it? Like you said, there's nothin' there."

"There's plenty of places. How about the old cemetery? All those graves have stones or markers or something. We could put it somewhere there."

"I dunno, man. I don't wanna be diggin' up graves and shit."

That was Carl again. They should've put that miserable bastard in a grave.

"So we can use the church. Plenty of places in there too. They got all those poles in there now. That carver guy made 'em. Took out all the religious stuff and carved a bunch of totems instead. Gotta be some real good places to hide it there."

"It's May. They're gonna have a bunch of tourists there now, man."

Bloody Carl. Nothing was ever right for him and he always made sure you knew it.

"They take 'em over on that supply boat and drop 'em off. They got cabins there and everything. Goddamn people all over the place. They'd see us for sure."

Carl again. The man could find something wrong with a million dollars if it fell out of the sky in front of him.

"Yeah, maybe."

Even Pat sounded down now. Hell, talking to Carl could bring anybody down. It stayed quiet for a minute or two, and he was about to go back and join them when they spoke again. He had been almost at the door, so he heard Pat's words clearly.

"That's it! The old totem. We can shove it up the bear's snout. No noise, nothing. Just wait till there's no one around and push it in. No one will look there."

3

He would have waited to see if there was anything more, but they yelled for him and told him they had to go out. Told him to wait there and they'd be back in a couple of hours. Yeah, right. The only ones who would be there in a couple of hours were the cops. He was the fall guy. The gofer. Too stupid to be trusted. Those assholes were planning on taking off and leaving him to face the cops alone. Well, he'd show them!

Five minutes after they were gone he was out of there. He'd given them a few hours, and then he'd gone down to the wharf and stolen a runabout. He could get the stuff for himself and they'd never know. So who was the stupid one?

Now he stood back and looked around him. Maybe there was another totem. A second bear. Shit, there were bears on every goddamn totem he'd ever seen. This was an Indian village—or at least it used to be. Sure to be more totems. He moved the narrow beam of his flashlight farther up the bank. There! What was that? Looked more like a bundle of old clothes than a totem, but it was worth checking out.

▶ **TWO** ◀

▶ A following sea pushed *Dreamspeaker* up the west coast of Vancouver Island, the swells lifting her stern as they passed beneath. Dan Connor stood barefoot at the helm, letting his body move with the rise and fall, the soles of his feet transmitting the surging power of water forced up from a depth of eight thousand feet by the steep face of the continental shelf. It was everything he had hoped it would be, and he was enjoying every single thing about it: the challenge; the sense of accomplishment; the high he felt just being out here, alone, on this vast ocean.

He was a big man, a couple of inches over six feet tall, with a lean, rangy build and a face that showed the marks of both a year on the water and recent grief. Time on the boat had bleached his dark hair and darkened his light skin. Grief had added shadows to his eyes and lines to his face, but out here, with the morning breeze fresh in his face, time and grief were both suspended.

He had left Barkley Sound as the first pale light of dawn seeped into the night sky, excited by the looming prospect of the trip up the "outside" and eager to reach his destination. Nootka Island had held him enthralled for years, ever since he had sailed past it on his father's fishboat the first summer he had been allowed to join him. Now, as the early rays of sunlight glinted off the wave crests, patterning the ocean with shafts of light, he watched the remembered names of childhood scroll past—Ucluelet, Amphitrite Point, Tofino, Clayoquot Sound,

Estevan Point—each one as familiar as an old friend yet suddenly new again.

He had stayed at the marina in Victoria longer than he had planned. It was late May, and soon it would be summer. The winds of winter that howled into the inlets and bays and coves of the west coast of Vancouver Island, twisting the stunted trees into misshapen and grotesque forms, and tossing unsuspecting boats aside like so much flotsam, were calmer now, and only light gusts teased the cool morning air.

To port, Dan could see the Pacific Ocean stretching out to the horizon. To starboard, the solid mass of Vancouver Island slid steadily southward, its rugged peaks silhouetted against the early-morning sky, while the treed slopes still held the darkness of night. A mist had formed, and it writhed and twisted near the shore, now hiding, now revealing the foaming surf. Dan hoped it would lift by the time he reached Nootka Island. He wanted to anchor in Friendly Cove and visit the lighthouse and the lightkeeper he had spoken to as a child, but he also wanted to see the cove itself, and he knew that out here on the rugged west coast of British Columbia, mist could easily turn into a heavy fog that lasted for days.

He checked the radar and GPS and altered course, feeling the motion change as he rounded Estevan Point and entered Nootka Sound. *Dreamspeaker* was a heavily built boat, a converted fish packer nearly sixty feet long and over seventeen feet wide, with a solid wooden hull. He had done the last of the conversion himself, equipping her with every piece of modern navigation gear he could think of, but she still needed a careful hand on the wheel.

Dan slowed the engines and nudged the big boat deep around the curving headlands of the cove, keeping an eye on the depth sounder as the bottom shelved beneath him. At thirty feet he pressed the anchor release and waited for the slight change in movement that told him the anchor had settled on the gravel. Now he could let the wind and water do the work of settling the boat.

He went back to the galley and poured himself a cup of coffee before returning to the wheelhouse. In front of him, the land rose in a gentle sweep to a low crest. The trees had been cleared in the center portion of the crest, and in the open area a tiny white church huddled close against the tree line on the western side, while a square white house sat boldly in the center. Lower down, a smaller building, also white, nestled into the bank, just above a sandy beach that was mostly covered by driftwood. That was all that remained of the village he had seen in his grandfather's old photographs, taken many years ago when there had been a cannery operating a short distance away up the coast. They had shown a cove studded with wooden houses, smoke drifting up from the chimneys, children playing, and people standing in doorways as they stared toward the camera.

The boat swung toward the wind and his view changed. Now he was looking at the lighthouse complex high on a rocky islet to the west, and the red railings of the government wharf below. A metal walkway, glinting in the morning light, spanned the gap between the buildings and Nootka Island.

It felt good to be here. In some strange way it felt like coming home, although he had only been here once before, as a child on his father's boat, and he had never been ashore.

He felt the motion change again and moved the transmission into reverse as he let out more anchor rope. A final surge of power from the big diesel engine to dig the flukes in, and he felt the boat lift as the anchor set hard. He was done. Time to go ashore.

▶ The mist that had wrapped the bay through the night was lifting, trailing gauze fingers through the seagrass. Dan pushed himself up from the log he had been sitting on and ambled along the beach. He moved with an easy grace acquired from years of judo practice, but he picked his way carefully along the shore: new driftwood had arrived with the recent storm, and the twisted roots and branches formed a treacherous maze. Most of it was faded gray by months or even years in the ocean, drifting in the currents, but here and there the gleam of newer wood added a counterpoint of light.

The storm had carried heavy rains, and the new-washed bay gleamed in the morning light. Dan looked over toward the lighthouse. It would have been good to share this moment with Claire, but she was still back in Victoria, over 170 miles away by land and a good deal more than that by water, and she would be busy for days yet, finalizing the details of the contract she had signed with Fisheries and Oceans Canada to study sea otters. Dan wouldn't be able to reach her until later that day, when she had finished with her meetings, and she wouldn't be leaving for their rendezvous in the tiny village of Kyuquot, another hundred miles north, until later in the week.

He had met Claire last year, when the jagged wound left by the death of his wife, Susan, was still so raw he had wanted to scream every time he thought of it, so tender that even the idea of ever having another relationship would have seemed sacrilegious. But the wound of Susan's murder was healing, slowly scabbing over with time and distance, and Claire was part of that healing. Their relationship had deepened over the previous winter, although he knew neither of them was ready to make a serious commitment.

Dan made his way along the shore and headed up to the lighthouse to introduce himself to Gene and Mary Dorman, the keepers of the light. He had first spoken to them years ago as a kid of ten, spending the summer on his father's fishboat. It had been the first time he was allowed to use the radio, and he had been nervous, wanting to impress his father, wanting to prove that he was capable of being the first mate his father wanted him to be, but worried that he would screw it up. He had checked the list to see which channel he should use, turned the big knob on the radio until he reached it, lifted the microphone out of its holder, pressed the transmit button, and carefully repeated "Nootka Island light" the requisite three times, just as he had heard his father do. When the answering voice boomed out of the speakers, he had been so surprised he actually dropped the mic. He smiled at the memory. The details of the conversation were lost in the haze of time, but those simple actions were etched on his mind.

It was hard to believe the same two people were still there almost thirty years later, but they were. He had called up the lighthouse a few days ago, and Gene had answered in that same rasping voice. Told him to drop in for a cup of coffee when he arrived. Dan was looking forward to meeting both him and his wife in person.

He remembered the light, too, although he had only seen it from out in the ocean as he and his father motored past. It sat on the highest point of a small island lying off the entrance to the cove. To Dan's ten-year-old self, it had seemed like something out of a storybook, the light winking out its endless warning in an unvarying pattern of long and short flashes, the black rocks glistening with ocean spray and the waves foaming below. He'd seen photos of it since, but all of them were taken from inside the cove, and the different angle made it impossible for him to reconcile them with his own memory. Now, finally, he was here, where he could fit all the pieces together.

He followed the beach to the wharf and then took a winding path up the rocks to the end of the walkway. The door of the lightkeeper's house was open, and as he approached he heard voices. It sounded as if Gene and Mary already had company, although there were no other boats in the cove.

A slim, wiry man with a sun-wrinkled face, iron-gray hair tied in a ponytail, and a quiet smile answered his knock and beckoned him inside.

"Come on in. I'm Gene. You must be Dan. We seem to have a bit of a problem here, but maybe you can help."

He led Dan into a bright, old-fashioned kitchen where a man and woman sat at a wooden table, watching his approach. Gene introduced Mary, his wife, and Jens Rasmussen, the assistant lightkeeper.

"Jens is the one with the problem," Gene said as Dan reached across to shake the other man's hand. "He says his wife, Margrethe, is missing."

Jens's eyes moved from Dan to Gene and back again.

"Gene says you're a cop?" he asked, his voice soft and hopeful.

"Used to be. Been a couple of years now," Dan replied.

A look of disappointment flashed across Jens's face before he dropped his eyes back down to the table. He had the high cheekbones of his native Scandinavia, and straight hair so blond it was almost white.

"Did you see her last night, Jens?" Mary's voice was gentle. "Maybe she got up early and went for a walk?"

Jens shook his head. "She never gets up early," he said, his voice tight with worry. "She's a night owl. Stays up till two, three o'clock and then sleeps until almost noon. I was down in the shed and she brought me a cup of tea around two o'clock this morning. We sat and talked for a while, and then she said she was going up to bed."

Mary watched him for a couple of minutes, then looked across at Dan, a quick smile of apology lighting her face.

"I'm sorry. I'm forgetting my manners. Can I get you a cup of coffee? Just made a fresh pot a couple of minutes before you arrived."

Dan returned her smile. In some inexplicable way, she was his idea of the perfect lightkeeper's wife: dark hair twisted into a careless knot at the back of her neck, a little gray starting to show on her temples, dressed in old jeans and a faded wool sweater. A plain, no-nonsense type—except for her huge, brightly colored earrings and the bracelets that shone from her wrists. An artist, maybe. Someone who would have no problem spending time alone.

"Thanks. That would be great."

He looked back at Jens. The man was obviously distraught.

"Have you checked the cove?" Dan asked. "Are there trails she likes to take—or maybe a boat she could have taken out . . ."

"She hates boats!" The man's raw cry tore through the air as he covered his head with his hands and leaned his forehead down onto the table. "She hates boats," he repeated softly. "I should never have brought her here."

Dan shot a glance at Gene. Was there more going on here than simply a missing woman?

"Jens and Margrethe only arrived here a couple of months ago," Gene said, reading the question in Dan's glance. "Jens was the light-keeper at the Point Atkinson light over in West Vancouver, but they automated it and put him out of a job. He applied for the assistant job here when old Walter retired."

Hmmm, thought Dan. Point Atkinson was on the mainland, at the outer, western edge of Vancouver Harbour. Jens and Margrethe would have lived right in the city—and in the high-rent district at that. Shops. Cars. Restaurants. Movies. Wouldn't have needed a boat there. So maybe Margrethe liked the bright lights—but there weren't any bright lights around here. There was only one other house in the cove.

"Does she like living here?" Dan asked.

There was no answer, and Dan looked over at Mary, who was standing by the stove. She shrugged and glanced at Gene, who simply spread his hands. No answers there either.

"She says she does." Jens's voice, when he finally answered, was still soft. Remote. Unsure. Whatever else might be going on, Dan figured the man was genuinely worried.

Mary brought the coffee over and sat down again. "Drink your coffee, Jens. Then we'll go down to your house. Maybe she's come home and is wondering where you are."

She pushed a cup toward him, and when he didn't respond, she took his hands and wrapped them around it, urging him to drink. He gave her a wan smile, but didn't look any happier.

▶ They didn't have far to walk. The assistant's house was just steps away, across a cement pad that connected both houses to the light itself. The whole place looked like a postcard. The square wooden houses, both painted white below red metal roofs. The matching light tower, topped by a red housing for the constantly turning lens. The blue ocean beyond, stretching out to the distant horizon, and, to the east, the perfect curve of the cove itself, with its fringe of golden sand.

It looked idyllic, but Dan figured the reality would undoubtedly be something different. Living on a remote island on the edge of the Pacific would not be for everyone. Maybe Margrethe had simply decided she couldn't take the isolation anymore. But she couldn't simply walk away. She would have needed a boat—and Jens said she hated boats.

The inside of the house was much like the one they had just left: simple but functional. There were only five rooms including the bathroom, each with minimal furniture, but clean and neat and obviously cared for. It took the four of them less than a minute to determine that Margrethe had not returned, but that was long enough for Dan to take in the disturbed bed, the clothes hanging neatly in the closet, the hairbrush and makeup bag sitting on the vanity, and the cups that had been rinsed and placed beside the sink to drain. If Jens's wife

11

had decided to walk away, she might have left her clothes—probably would have—and she might even have rinsed out the cups before she left, but Dan didn't know any woman who would leave her hairbrush and makeup behind.

"Is there anything missing, Jens? A jacket, maybe? Boots?"

Jens looked at him for a moment, a kaleidoscope of emotions flashing across his face, and then he turned, walked back to the doorway, and opened a closet. He stared into it for a minute, then turned back.

"Yes. Both."

So it looked like Margrethe had left the house voluntarily sometime in the early morning, but had planned to return.

"When did you notice she was gone?"

Dan realized he had taken over all the questioning, and it seemed Gene and Mary were happy to let him do it. Maybe he still wore that cop persona people talked about, even after a couple of years away. Something to think about. He didn't know if he liked the idea. He didn't feel like a cop anymore, although there were still times when he missed the job.

"I was working down in the generator shed most of the night," Jens replied. "I came up here around seven this morning and made myself a cup of tea. I don't know what time I went to the bedroom. Maybe seven thirty, maybe eight. But she wasn't there."

Jens's voice wavered. He was near tears, maybe near collapse. Mary went over to him and put her arm around his shoulders.

"Come on, Jens. We'll find her. Come on back up to the house and I'll make you some breakfast. Gene and Dan can go down to the cove and see if she's there."

She cast a meaningful look at Dan and Gene as she nudged the distraught man past them. They were almost out the door when Dan thought of another question.

"Did you pull the bedding down, or was it like that when you went in this morning?"

Jens turned and stared at him. "I didn't touch it. I guess it was like that." He frowned. "I never thought about it."

"That's okay. Go on with Mary. Gene and I will take a look around."

► THREE ◄

► The lazy sweep of the cove spread out in front of the two men as they crossed the walkway, a peaceful scene with no sign of movement anywhere.

"You want to take the church?" Gene asked. "I know the family over at the house pretty well. Probably better if I go talk to them."

Dan nodded. He was an outsider. He didn't want to have to explain what was happening or what he was doing here. It would take too long and bring up memories and issues he didn't want to deal with.

"Sounds good. I'll call you if I find anything. Otherwise I'll meet you down at that shed over there." He nodded toward the beach.

"It's not a shed, it's a studio," Gene said. "Sanford does his carving there. You'll see some of it up in the church. House posts and crests mostly. It's amazing stuff."

Dan nodded and the two men headed off in separate directions, Gene to the house and Dan to the church.

Like Jens's house, the church was empty—if you could call a space filled with exquisitely carved poles and figures empty. All the religious paraphernalia had been removed and the building was now occupied by a host of stylized and mythological creatures: a thunderbird over the door, an owl, perhaps a wolf, certainly a bear on the house posts. Killer whales arched over what might have once served as an altar and, twining everywhere, were the coils of a snake. Dan didn't have time to take a close look, but he saw enough to know he wanted to come back and check it out. His hobby was—or had been, because he hadn't done any lately—wood carving. The hold of his boat was full of gnarled and twisted driftwood waiting for him to pick up his tools and bring the shapes held within the wood to life. He didn't have a rich cultural heritage to draw from, but the wood spoke to him nonetheless. He would like to be able to share his passion with someone as creative and adept as this carver obviously was.

But that was for later. Now he had a more urgent task, and it didn't take long for him to see that there was no sign of the woman. No sign of anyone, in fact. The place was silent and lifeless, except for the carved figures standing as sentries, and those seemed to have a life of their own.

Dan walked back out into the sunshine and met Gene coming up the path from the house.

"No one home," Gene said. "I think they must have gone over to Gold River. Probably won't be back for a couple of days." He shrugged. "The house is locked but I looked in the windows. No sign of anyone or anything there."

That left the studio on the beach where the figures that occupied the church had been created. Gene said the carver, Sanford, was the son of the family that lived in the house.

They headed down toward the water, eyes scanning the ground for any signs that might show them where Margrethe had gone, but there was nothing. Like the house, the studio was locked and empty, the wide windows that formed the major part of every wall providing a clear view of a partially carved log laid out across two stumps. It was beginning to look as if Jens's wife had simply walked out of the house and vanished.

"Any ideas?" Dan asked.

"Nope. Doesn't make any sense."

"Maybe she went out and slipped on the rocks. Fell into the water."

Gene shook his head. "She was damn near as scared of the water as she was of boats. Maybe more. Never saw her outside on the beach unless she was with Jens. Can't figure out why they ever came here."

"Did Jens ever talk about it?"

"Jens? Hell no. Jens isn't much of a talker. He's kind of like me—spent most of his life on the lights, but in his case they were all close to the city. Don't think either one of them really thought about whether they liked boats or how they would handle being out here in the middle of nowhere."

"Think Margrethe might have just walked away? Got tired of it all?"

Again, Gene shook his head. "Where would she walk to? And in the dark? Alone?"

Dan nodded. He had asked himself the same questions. "So how about Jens? How is he handling the isolation? Think he might have reached breaking point?"

"Jens?" Gene looked at him in amazement. "Not a chance. He loves it. He's a weather guy. Studied meteorology at university before he went on the lights. Margrethe might have some issues with living out here, but the two of them are real good together. She's as quiet as he is, although in her case it's probably because she's got a bit of a hearing problem. She's not deaf, mind you, but she doesn't hear all that well, so she keeps pretty much to herself. She cooks half the day. Sends bags of cookies and bread and buns and stuff up for Mary and me—not that I need it." He glanced down at his stomach. "Anyway. Rest of the time she reads or weaves. Got some kind of loom thing over there. Makes all kinds of shit—scarves and towels and stuff. We've got a bunch of those up at the house too. And Jens putters. He fixes things and makes stuff down in the workshop. Spends hours there. They're happy together."

The two men stood together looking out over the cove, trying to come up with something that would make sense. The woman had to be somewhere. She couldn't have vanished into thin air.

"What's that over there?" Dan noticed the gap first. Not really a gap. More of a space in the wide stretch of seagrass that formed a barrier between the beach and the shallow bowl of the cove and rustled in the breeze.

"Where?" Gene followed his gaze. "Hey, that's odd. That's about where the old totem is. Been there for years. But I've never seen the grass laid down like that. Looks like it's been trampled or something."

"Maybe you had better wait here a minute, Gene," Dan said. "I'll go check it out."

"Sure," said Gene, a note of wariness creeping into his voice as he realized the reason for Dan's caution. "No problem."

It wasn't just a gap. It was more like an open wound, the grass flattened in a wide swath and a deep gouge in the sand where the ancient pole had been dragged from its resting place. The eyes of an eagle still stared sightlessly up at him from the grayed cedar, but its beak had been ripped away, one wing was broken off, and the snout of the bear had been hacked open to expose a core of new wood. Below that, the striped coils of a lightning snake the bear had once held in its jaws were slashed in two places and lay off to one side.

The damage was recent, the exposed wood still a bright and glowing yellow. Dan stared at it in puzzlement. He had stopped believing in coincidence a long time ago. This had to be linked with the woman's disappearance, but how? He looked back at Gene and beckoned him down.

"What the hell!" Gene was stunned. "Who would do this? And why? Doesn't make any sense." He shook his head. "This is going to upset a lot of people."

Dan looked at him. "You think there's any way Margrethe could have done it?"

"Margrethe?" Gene looked at him in horror. "Hell no. She loves it! Loves all the stuff Sanford does. Even asked him if she could use his designs in her weaving. I'll show you some of the stuff she's done. It's good."

Dan looked back down at the exposed wood. "When was the last time you saw this?"

"Me? Damned if I know. A while, I guess. I don't come down here that often, but Mary walks the beach almost every day. You can ask her." Gene started to leave, then turned back. "You should ask Sanford too. He comes over here all the time. It was one of his family that carved it way back. Can't remember the year, but it was a long time ago. It's been part of his heritage ever since he was born." He shook his head. "Sure going to be pissed off."

The two men looked down toward the water, silently scanning the beach for any sign of footprints, but the tide was coming in and the driftwood made it difficult. Behind them, up on the hill, a ray of sunlight lit the steeple of the church like the finger of God pointing the way home.

"Damn," said Dan. "We sure could use Walker here."

"Who the hell is Walker?" asked Gene.

"What? Oh, sorry. Didn't mean to talk out loud. Walker's just a guy I know. Lives up north around Hakai Pass somewhere. He helped me out last year when Claire and I ran into some trouble. He's the best tracker I ever met, and he knows the tides and currents like—well, like a fish!"

Dan noticed Gene staring at him intently. "What?" he asked.

"He Native, this Walker guy?"

"Uh, yeah. He is. Why?"

"Big guy?"

"Yeah. Guess so."

"His legs all banged up? Can't walk well?"

"You know him?" Dan couldn't believe it. Gene couldn't possibly know Walker. Walker was almost a recluse, living his life in the traditional way of his people at least a couple of hundred miles away. Probably more. Even Dan didn't know exactly where his home was or how to find him. He had run into him purely by chance the previous year when he had tied up at a floating store in Dawson Inlet to take on supplies. A man had hobbled across the float in front of him and Dan had recognized him from his days as a detective. Back then, Walker had been a punk kid living in the city and Dan had been part of a response team that had chased Walker and his friends across a roof after a bank robbery had been called in. Walker had tripped and fallen to the street below, breaking his pelvis and both legs. Dan had spent a good deal of time questioning him while he was in the hospital and had come to believe that, given a chance, this was a kid who might be able to turn his life around. It turned out he had been right. The man he had met the previous year was no punk. He was quiet and confident, spending most of his time on the water, where his damaged legs were not a handicap.

"Can't be the same guy," he told Gene.

"Sure sounds like the same guy," Gene answered. "Paddles a canoe?"

Dan stared at him. "Yeah," he said. "He does. But how the hell do you know him?"

"Well, if it is the same guy, he comes here every once in a while," Gene answered. "His family's related to Sanford's somehow. I think his sister married Sanford's cousin or something. The sister and her husband live over in Gold River, but I guess Walker goes to visit them occasionally. Don't know how he gets there, but he always comes here by canoe."

It was unreal. When Dan had run into Walker the previous year, it had been a coincidence—a very fortunate one, as it turned out, because it had been Walker's knowledge and skills that had helped prevent a major disaster. To have him turn up again here would be simply unbelievable.

But it was Walker they were talking about, and as Dan had been forced to acknowledge, strange things happened when Walker was involved. Things Dan still could not fully explain even though he had experienced them himself.

"I don't suppose he's there now?" Dan felt foolish even asking the question.

"I don't know. I don't think so, but then again it looks like the whole family's probably heading over to Gold River, so if it's a big gathering he might have come in. Guess we'll find out in a few days."

"Yeah. Well, that's going to be too late to help us figure out what's happened to Margrethe. We'd better head back and see if Mary and Jens have come up with anything yet, and if they haven't, you'd better call the police."

Gene nodded glumly. "Guess so," he said. "Although it sure is going to be a mess. The cops are going to call the coast guard, and those guys'll be swarming all over here like ants at a picnic."

Dan looked at him. "Don't you work for the coast guard?"

"Yeah, I guess I do—but the coast guard we usually see are the boys on the supply boats, and we only see them every six months—although once in a while it's a whole lot longer than that. On the real remote lights, you have to depend on them for food and clothing, even water, and I'll tell you something. You spend a whole winter waiting for a supply boat that doesn't arrive and you start to get a little disenchanted with 'em." Gene laughed. "Happened to us a few years back when we were up at Quatsino. Now every time I see one of those damn boats I start remembering a whole winter of eating nothing but Spam and canned peas. Kind of hard to feel a whole bunch of brotherly love after that."

Dan laughed. "I guess I can understand that. Never could stand Spam myself." He braced himself against the top of a log as he worked his way past a mound of driftwood.

Gene snorted. "Yep. Never eaten the stuff since." He glanced back at Dan. "What?"

Dan had stopped and was standing absolutely still, staring at his hand. Slowly he lifted it up and turned it toward Gene. A patch of dark red glistened on his palm.

"Ah, Jesus! That what I think it is?"

Dan raised his hand to his face and sniffed. The coppery smell of blood was unmistakable. "Yeah. It is."

▶ FOUR ◀

▶ It was early morning, the sky still dark and scattered with stars. Off the western shore of Nootka Island, the Alaska current moved relentlessly north, carrying with it everything its progenitor, the Pacific current, had met on its long journey from Japan: logs and plastic, discarded oil drums, bottles and boxes, shipping crates, tsunami debris—and now it picked up yet another passenger. The body was submerged and fully clothed, and it had drifted a little west of the lighthouse on an ebb tide. The current picked it up as it passed and carried it on up the coast until, with the push and swirl of a local eddy, it released it into Nicolaye Channel to drift gently into the embrace of a kelp bed just off the shore of Aktis Island. Only the sea otters that called the kelp bed home noted its presence.

▶ Leif Nielson was sixty-nine years old, and he had spent all sixty-nine of them in the tiny village of Kyuquot on Walters Island, on the northwest coast of Vancouver Island, just south of the Brooks Peninsula. He knew every one of the three hundred or so folks who lived in the two communities surrounding Walters Cove, and all he had ever dreamed about was fishing. He had learned to operate a boat long before he was old enough to learn how to drive a car. Boats were a necessity, the lifeblood of the two villages, and even kids of six or seven knew how to run them. As far back as he could remember, it seemed like all people ever talked about was fishing. Was there going to be a good run of pinks? Were the Rivers Inlet sockeye going to take the inside or the outside passage? Who had caught the biggest chinook? If someone had netted some chum salmon, there would be gutted fish spread out on the drying racks over on the reserve and hanging in all the smokehouses. Celebrations of any kind involved filling a forty-five-gallon drum with freshly netted prawns and cooking them with a steam hose.

But then the big schools of herring disappeared, and one after another the fishboats became idle. A few of the younger men got work on the big seiners over at Port Hardy, or at Campbell River on the east side of the island, but most of them left to get jobs in the mines or with the logging companies or even down in the city. Only the old-timers stayed behind to cater to the tourists who arrived each summer in the fancy inflatables they launched up at Fair Harbour, near the eastern end of Kyuquot Sound. By the time Leif decided to beach his boat, unable to justify the cost of maintaining her, the only job available was guiding for the guests at the fishing lodge. It wasn't the kind of fishing he wanted to do, but it was still fishing, and at least he was out on the water every day. Besides, the guests tipped well, laughed at the yarns he told them, and never left without a salmon.

The lodge had been busy and Leif had worked twelve-hour days for the past week, taking guests out to the fishing grounds in one of the big Lund outboards. Today had been the last day for the biggest group, and they had wanted to get out on the water early. He had been up at four and on the water by five. By the time he brought them back to shore, off-loaded their fish, cleaned and refueled the boat, and then reloaded both the guests and their luggage for their trip back to Fair Harbour, he had another nine hours racked up. He was tired. Tired of helping other people fish. Tired of telling the same old stories. Tired of hearing the same old jokes. Tired of every damn thing. He was too old for this shit. He needed a break and he was damn well going to take one, even if it was just one afternoon and evening. Maybe tomorrow he would feel better.

He steered the boat across the tiny harbor and over to the dock in front of the village of Houpsitas, on the reserve side of the water. He and Archie Jack had grown up together, had fished together, had gotten drunk together. They had both married local girls, the weddings held in the same church in the same year, and they had both buried those same girls after forty-seven years of marriage, in the same church, in the same month, just two years ago. If Archie was around, they could head across the inlet to the old village on Aktis Island. The sea otters had eaten most of the rock urchins the two men loved to eat, but there was a good oyster bed there. It would only take a few minutes to pick enough to make themselves a decent supper, and then he and Archie could shoot the breeze, maybe have a couple of beers, play a game of bones.

He didn't have far to look. Archie was sitting on the dock, his legs dangling over the side, baiting a crab trap.

"Hey, old man. What you doing over here in that fancy boat?"

"Never mind the 'old man' shit. I'm younger than you are," Leif retorted as he slid the dinghy up to the dock.

"Only two weeks and that don't count. Us Indians age better than you white folks. Less wrinkles."

"Yeah, right." Leif's laugh was more of a snort. "You got so many wrinkles you look like one of them dogs from China. What do they call 'em? Shar-pay or something. Wrinkle dog."

Archie's cackle of laughter echoed over the water. "Wrinkle dog! That's good. I like that." He lowered the trap back down, watching as it dropped through the clear water to the bottom. "So what are you doing over here this time of day? Thought you'd be outside, helping those tourists steal our fish."

Leif nodded. "Just finished. Took a load of 'em back up to Fair Harbour. Next bunch don't come in till Monday."

Archie nodded. "Guess they're good for business anyway. Billy James was tellin' me Old Joe at the store had him take four loads of supplies over to the lodge after the freight boat unloaded yesterday."

"Yeah." Leif nodded. "They ain't so bad, most of them. City folks. They just want to catch a few big ones so they can go home and brag about it. Never been out on the outside before. Don't know shit about the ocean, but they mostly know how to fish. Sort of." He laughed.

"Did have one guy who couldn't bait a hook. Didn't matter much, though. He turned green the first big wave we got, and I had to bring him back in."

They sat quietly for a while, listening to the water chuckle under the dock, enjoying the warmth of the day, and then Leif asked, "You want to go over to Aktis and get a few oysters?"

"Sure." Archie never turned down a chance to go out on the water, and Aktis was both his traditional home and one of his favorite places. "You got any beer hidden away in there?"

"Might have one or two," Leif answered. Houpsitas, like all the villages on the reserve, was dry. No booze was allowed, but that restriction didn't include the fishing lodge.

Archie grinned as he lowered himself into the dinghy. "Gotta have beer with oysters. Don't taste the same without it. My ancestors told me that."

"Yeah right," Leif retorted. "I guess they told you to catch crabs with ham too." He had seen the chunk of meat Archie had put into the crab trap.

Archie nodded, his face serious. "Yep. They did." Then the familiar grin returned. "Told me not to let anything go to waste, and them crabs can't tell the difference between ham and a good salmon head anyway."

"Why the hell didn't you eat it yourself?" Leif still missed his wife's cooking and ate mostly out of cans.

"If you'd ever tasted the ham Pearl cooks, you'd probably choose the salmon head." Pearl was Archie's daughter, and her cooking was infamous.

"That bad, huh?" Leif shook his head as he engaged the clutch and sent the little boat surging forward. "Seems like a ham would be a hard thing to ruin."

The whine of the motor cut off any further conversation as the little boat ran through the narrow pass leading out of the harbor and turned into the sound, heading west toward the open ocean.

Leif cut the engine as they neared the shore at Aktis. "You want to try here or should we go 'round the other side?"

"Might as well try here first," Archie answered. "The tide's a bit high, but we should be able to get enough for the two of us." He reached into a locker in the cockpit and pulled out a bucket. "You got any gloves?"

Leif pulled out a pair of heavy rubber gloves and passed them to Archie. "Here. I'll bring us in a bit closer. Those kelp leaves'll hold us in."

Leif might not have noticed the body caught between the fronds of kelp except for the long hair swaying back and forth on the waves, rippling in the angled rays of the afternoon sun. It was floating face down, and the dark shirt was almost invisible under the surface of the water. He cut back the motor as the dinghy drifted closer.

"Whatcha doin'?" Archie asked. "There ain't nothin' there 'cept those damn otters. The oysters are that way." He pointed to his left.

"I don't know. There's something there. Not otters, that's for sure." Leif angled the dinghy to get a better look. "Looks like a shirt or something."

"Where you looking?" Archie twisted his body to get a better look. "Hey, yeah. I see it. What the hell . . ."

"Oh shit!" Leif jerked the transmission into reverse. "Holy Christ. We gotta get out of here." He spun the wheel and pushed the gearshift into forward. "Gotta call the cops. Let them handle it. I'm not touching that." The little boat's nose lifted high into the air and surged forward on its own bow wave. Behind them, the body bobbed in the wake.

FIVE

▶ The sea was already rising, the waves smashing on the rocks below and sending up curtains of spray as Mary led Jens and Dan to the workshop. It had been Dan's suggestion to check it out. He had needed an excuse to get the other two out of the house while Gene made the call to the Gold River police detachment.

"She's not going to be here," Mary said, keeping her voice low so Jens wouldn't hear. "This is where Jens was working last night and she was already gone when he got up to the house."

Dan shrugged. "She might have come back while we were out looking for her and come down here to check." It sounded weak even to him, but there was no way he wanted to be the one to tell Mary and Jens about the totem and the blood. He hated giving bad news. It was the one thing about police work that he dreaded. Plus he didn't know how either of them would react, and right now Mary was doing a good job of keeping Jens calm. They would find out soon enough once the police arrived.

"I guess." She looked dubious. "At least it's keeping him busy."

Dan nodded. "We should check down on the rocks too. Can't do anything on the outside, but we can look down by the fuel storage tanks. She might have slipped or lost her nerve and be stuck halfway down."

"Maybe. Doesn't seem likely, but I guess we have to check everything."

The workshop was empty, and after they had checked it and scanned the rocks below, the three of them returned to Jens's house and stood quietly in the kitchen, looking out through the open door to the ocean beyond. Silence grew like a physical presence, thick and heavy, stretching and coiling to fill the space around them until it muted even the crashing of the waves. It was finally broken by Jens's choked sob. Mary turned to him and grasped his arm.

"Come on, Jens. Let's go up and call the police. They'll figure it out." She pulled the distraught man close and led him back out. Dan followed.

▶ "Already done," Gene told them when Mary explained what she wanted to do. "I could see you hadn't found her and I figured we shouldn't wait any longer." It seemed he too did not want to be the one to tell them the news.

"Okay," said Mary, though she looked surprised.

"Did they say how long they'd be?" asked Dan, offering a silent thank-you to whatever power had allowed him to dodge that particular task. He knew he would have to wait for the police to arrive or face an unpleasant barrage of questions, not only from the guys who responded but also from Mike, Dan's boss when he was on the anti-terrorist squad, and the rest of the group back in Victoria, who would undoubtedly hear about it. On the other hand, he had promised Claire he would meet her later that week up in Kyuquot, and the weather forecast was predicting another storm would move in early the following afternoon. He hoped to beat it by leaving later that day.

Gene shook his head. "Probably take them a few hours. They'll make it high priority, but it's a pretty small detachment. They may have to bring someone over from Campbell River."

Dan fought to keep his frustration in check. Patience was not something he had a lot of, but he didn't want to upset Jens more than he already was. Sitting around waiting, doing absolutely nothing when there were things to be done, would drive Dan crazy—and it wouldn't help him figure out what had happened to Margrethe either. If that was her blood he had found, then there was a lot that needed doing. He knew the police would search Jens's house. It was standard procedure. But if Jens wasn't involved—and Dan thought he probably wasn't—then the search of the cove and surroundings needed to start now.

And he couldn't let Claire down. Their rendezvous might be almost a week away, but the weather on this coast was unpredictable. He cursed under his breath. It didn't seem possible. Just last year, cruising up the inside coast, he had become involved in a search for a missing woman—Claire was that woman—and now here it was happening again. Walker would probably tell him that he attracted these events. Or more likely he would say the events attracted Dan—reached out to him somehow. That was how Walker explained the things that happened in his world, but Dan didn't buy it—although, now that he thought about it, it had certainly seemed that way when he'd been on the police force. They'd called him "Copper" Connor because his watch always seemed to cop the big ones, and that had been fine with him. Why not? It was why he had joined up. But now? His life had changed. He had moved on. This had to be coincidence. But Dan didn't believe in coincidence.

He pushed himself up from the table, feeling three pairs of eyes follow his progress.

"I'm going to go back out to the boat," he told them. "I need to check on her. The tide's dropping, and she's in pretty close." He saw them all nod their understanding: these were people who lived with the sea. "I have to call my partner too. I'm supposed to meet her up in Kyuquot in a few days, and if I don't get out of here today, I might get held up by the weather."

All three heads turned automatically to the barometer hanging on the wall and then moved in unison to look out the window before swinging back to focus on him. Dan fought back a smile. Old habits kicked in no matter what the situation.

"I won't be long, although if the guys haven't arrived by the time I'm finished, I might take another look around the cove," he said, turning to leave.

Only Gene watched him go. Mary was already bent over Jens, comforting him again.

▶ On board *Dreamspeaker* it took less than a minute for Dan to confirm what he already knew: the boat was fine, sitting in thirty feet of water well off the shoreline, bow steady to the wind. And he didn't call Claire. He hadn't planned to. She would still be down on the south end of the island, maybe meeting with the people at the Pacific Biological Station in Nanaimo, or testing out the Boston Whaler she had bought to replace the boat she had lost last year. Dan wasn't happy with her choice. He didn't like the idea of her taking what was essentially a small power boat out on the open ocean of the west coast for the research she planned to do, but he had found out she could be at least as stubborn as he was. Their argument had been short but intense, and he had lost—although making up afterward had eased the sting. He would call her tonight. Let her know there was a chance he might be delayed. He would blame it on the weather. No need to stir up bad memories with stories of a missing and possibly murdered woman.

He made his way out to the aft deck and pulled a length of yellow nylon rope out of one of the lockers. Nootka Island was a popular destination for kayakers and boaters, and the old totem was one of the best-known artifacts there. It was still early in the season, and so far today they had been lucky in not seeing any visitors, but that could change at any time. At least he could rope off the area and preserve whatever evidence was there.

He thought about digging out his shoulder holster and gun from the locked compartment up on the bridge where he kept them, but decided against it. He had no authority even if he did happen upon something, and it would be hard to explain a gun to the police when they arrived. Instead, he slid a leather knife sheath onto his belt and settled it comfortably in front of his hip. Sailors and wood-carvers always carried a knife, didn't they? So what if this one had a six-inch blade honed to a razor-sharp edge?

Dan motored back to shore and pulled the dinghy up on the beach a few yards away from the totem, near the log he had leaned on. It was impossible to see exactly where the blood was, so he carefully traced the path he had taken earlier, trying to keep disturbance to a minimum as he led the rope in a wide arc, wrapping it around the driftwood in an uneven line. The seagrass area was a bigger problem. He had to search farther along the shore to find branches he could break off and drive into the sandy soil, hammering them down with a rock he found on the beach, but at last he managed to create a complete circle of rope, a makeshift police line he hoped would keep out any visitors until the police themselves arrived. He knew he had trampled the grass even more as he created his barrier, but it couldn't be helped, and he thought whoever had desecrated the totem—and maybe killed the woman—had probably come and gone by water, so the tide would have washed away any trace anyway.

He stood back to survey his work and caught movement out of the corner of his eye. Gene was coming down the beach to join him.

"Saw what you were doing and came down to see if I could give you a hand," he said as he stepped down onto the beach to join Dan. "Guess I'm a bit late."

"No problem. How are things up at the house?"

Gene grimaced. "Not too good. I told them the totem had been damaged. Had to tell them something when they saw you stringing up the rope. It really bothered both of them. Guess they know there must be some connection, but I didn't say anything about the blood. Jens has got enough on his plate. No need to make it harder for him."

Dan nodded. "Guess he'll find out soon enough once the police get here." He looked up toward the lighthouse. "Mary still there with him?"

"Yeah. One of us has to be on hand for any calls, and Jens doesn't look like he wants to go anywhere."

"Probably a good idea for him to stay put," Dan agreed. He gestured up the hill. "I thought I might head up there and see if I could spot anything. You're welcome to join me. Won't take long and we can be back at the house before the police arrive."

"Sure," said Gene. "But you might want to talk to him first." He was looking over Dan's shoulder, to where the ocean lapped at the edge of the land.

"Talk to whom?" Dan asked as he turned to follow Gene's gaze. A canoe was gliding silently in toward the shore. It was close enough that he could see the man who was paddling it. A man with long black hair woven into a thick braid that hung down his back. A man whose broad shoulders rippled with muscle as they worked. A man Dan was very familiar with.

"Son of a bitch!" Dan shook his head as he made his way down to the shore. "Gene said you came here sometimes, but I didn't believe him." He reached out to take the line Walker was extending.

"Hey, white man. Thought that was your boat out there. What you doin' out here in Indian territory?"

Dan smiled. Walker had a unique way of both challenging him and making him smile at the same time. "Came here to visit Gene," Dan said, gesturing to the lighthouse keeper. "Guess you two already know each other?"

"Sure," Walker answered. "How you doin', Gene?"

"Fine," Gene answered. "But we've got a bit of a problem. Where's Sanford? He headed back too?"

"Sanford?" Walker looked back and forth from Gene to Dan. "He'll be here in a couple of hours. He and his mom and dad went to visit a cousin over by Esperanza. Why?"

Dan nodded toward the roped-off area. "You need to come and see this."

Walker looked at him for a long minute, studying his face, then nodded. He dug his paddle down into the gravel bottom and drove the canoe up onto the sand, beside a bleached log.

On the water, Walker looked at ease, fit, powerful, with a natural grace. That all changed as he struggled to get out of the canoe. His damaged legs twisted at an awkward angle and seemed barely able to support him. Watching him, Dan was taken back to the time, more than ten years ago now, when he had chased a much younger man across a roof after being called out to a bank robbery in progress. He could still picture the scene: the gap between buildings, the hesitant leap, the windmilling arms, the sickening thud that followed. Remembering that crumpled body, Dan was amazed the man could walk at all. The doctors had worked miracles, but it was Walker's spirit and determination that had fueled his recovery through his long months in hospital and his longer ones in jail.

Walker used the log to pull himself upright, then slowly stepped out of the canoe and worked his way up the beach, using the driftwood for support. With no clear path up to the roped-off area, he had to take the long way round, and it took almost ten slow and painful minutes before he finally reached a place where he could see the desecrated totem.

"Jesus!" he breathed, staring in horror at the mutilated wood. "What the hell happened?"

"We don't know," Dan answered. "We found it this morning. It looks new, but we're not sure. I guess it could have happened yesterday, or even the day before."

"No." Walker shook his head, his eyes moving slowly over the destroyed figures. "This is very new. Maybe only a few hours old." He reached down and let his hand rest gently on the bear's head. "Who would do this?" he asked, his voice tight with grief and anger. "And why?"

The three men stood in silence for a few minutes, looking at the carnage in front of them, and then Dan voiced what he had been thinking.

"Probably the same guy that killed Margrethe."

Gene sucked in his breath. "You think she's dead?"

"I think it's a good possibility," Dan answered. "The blood was pretty fresh, and there's too much for it to be from just a cut finger or something. How else could it have gotten there? Hell, you saw it the same as I did."

"Margrethe?" Walker asked. "That the woman from the lighthouse that Sanford talks about? She weaves his designs or something?"

"Yes," Gene answered. "She's missing. And Dan found blood on one of those pieces of driftwood."

Walker stared down at the jumbled driftwood, then looked back at the totem.

"Damn, white man. You're the strangest lightning snake I ever saw."

"Lightning snake? What the hell are you talking about?"

Walker looked at him, his voice serious.

"His name is He'-e-tlik. He's a friend of Thunderbird. He punishes those who break the moral laws of the people." He gestured to where the severed pieces of a carved snake lay on the ground. "Guess Thunderbird figured this one was lost, so he chose you for the job."

▶ "So tell me about this lightning snake thing," Dan said.

Gene had returned to the lighthouse and Dan and Walker were sitting on the beach, their backs to the water. Dan had suggested it might be more comfortable if they sat on a piece of driftwood, well away from both the totem and the blood, but Walker insisted on sitting on the sand, and Dan knew better than to argue. Walker did what Walker wanted to do.

Walker shrugged, his eyes focused on the sweep of land that rose in front of him. "It's a Mowachaht story. You should ask Sanford."

"Sanford isn't here," Dan said.

"He will be." Walker leaned to the right and ducked his head down low, squinting at something in the distance.

Dan shook his head. This was obviously all he was going to get on that subject.

"So what do you think he'll do when he gets here?" he asked.

Walker shrugged again. "Don't know," he said.

"Is there a ceremony he can perform?" Dan persisted. "Some kind of healing chant or something?" He knew he sounded naïve, even foolish, but the desecrated totem pole bothered him in a way he could not understand. He had never seen it before, but its destruction had created a feeling of deep personal loss.

Walker didn't answer. He had stretched his torso forward, his head low to the beach. Now he leaned back and then sideways, pushing hard against Dan, who was forced to brace himself against the beach.

"What the hell are you doing?" Dan asked, pushing him back. "Is this some kind of weird ritual?"

Again Walker didn't respond. His body moved faster now, weaving from side to side, his head lifting and dipping although his gaze always seemed focused on the same spot.

"Walker, this is . . ."

"There!" Walker straightened and pointed up the hill.

"There what? What the hell are you talking about? There's nothing there but grass and weeds."

Walker turned to look at him and smiled. "You're still the same, white man. You talk too much. You gotta learn to look."

"Look at what? There's nothing to look at."

"They left a trail."

"A trail?" Dan closed his eyes as he realized he was repeating Walker's words. He had found himself doing that the last time the two of them were together and had hoped it would never happen again. It was a sure sign he was out of his depth. What the hell was it about Walker?

"Yep."

"What kind of trail?" Dan asked cautiously as he stared up at the wide, uninterrupted expanse of new grass.

"Move over here." Walker dragged himself a little farther along the beach. "You gotta get the light in the right place."

Dan looked at him for a minute and then moved to the space Walker had vacated.

"Start at the totem," Walker said, pointing. "Then look up the hill. Move like I did, side to side. It makes the angle change."

Feeling more than a little foolish, Dan did as instructed.

"So what, exactly, am I looking for?" he asked.

"Footprints."

"Footprints?" There it was again. The repeating thing. "You can see footprints in the grass from all the way down here?"

"Yeah," said Walker. "Two sets."

"Two sets?" Shit. He had to stop doing that.

"Yeah. One's bigger and heavier than the other."

Dan stared at Walker for a minute, then looked back up the slope. Either the man really was crazy or there was something there. Time to find out. He focused on the top of the totem and rocked his body slowly from side to side, rotating his head and nodding it up and down just as Walker had done. Slowly he moved his eyes higher, letting them skim the surface of the bright-green shoots of new grass that filled the bowl—and there they were. Four indentations. Two deeper than the others, the outlines rimmed by the rays of the sun.

He moved his eyes higher still and saw another set. And then another. A clear trail leading up from the totem, just as Walker had said.

"How the hell did you know they were there?" Dan asked, turning to stare at the man next to him.

Walker shrugged. "I didn't. Just looked and found them."

Dan turned back to look at the tracks. "Hell, I figured it was just one guy. Came and went on the water. That would have been the easiest way." He stared over at the lighthouse, his mind racing. "This changes everything. Two people? A man and a woman?" He looked back at the totem. "So maybe she's not dead. Maybe she had a lover. Set it up to meet him. Maybe the totem was some kind of twisted goodbye."

He was thinking aloud, and even as he heard the words, he found himself shaking his head. It was a possible scenario, but it didn't feel right. And it didn't account for the blood he had found. Could that have been caused by something as innocent as an accident?

"Don't think the guy was her lover," Walker said.

Dan looked at him. "Why the hell not? You telling me you can read the grass like tea leaves or something?"

Walker grinned. It was a grin that could get seriously irritating, Dan thought.

"What?" he snapped.

"Look at the prints," Walker said. "See how the small ones are kind of a bit behind the big ones, and off to the side? And they weave in and out a little bit?"

"Yeah," said Dan, looking again. "I can sort of see that. So what?"

"So the side nearest the big ones is a bit blurred—smeared, maybe. Like she was resisting and he kept dragging her back."

"Jesus," Dan said, still focused on the tracks. "You're kind of stretching it a bit, don't you think?"

"Could be." Walker gave his trademark shrug. "Guess you'll have to go check it out and see for yourself."

Dan turned to look at him. "Not me. I'm off the force, remember? The cops can check it out when they get here."

"Too late," Walker replied.

"What's too late? The cops? Gene called them a couple of hours ago. Gold River's not that far, and they've got a pretty fast boat. They'll be here soon." Dan glanced out across the water and then looked up at the sun. "Lots of light left too."

"Doesn't matter," Walker answered. "That's young grass. Soft. It's already starting to stand up again. There won't be a trail in an hour or so. Maybe sooner."

"Shit!" said Dan.

Walker stayed on the beach. He couldn't walk, but he could give directions, and Dan needed them. As soon as he changed his position and stepped up onto the grass, the imprints disappeared.

Moving slowly, guided by Walker's hand signals, he followed the tracks up the hill until he reached the crest. This was as far as Walker could take him. From here on he would be on his own, and with the land now sloping steeply down to the northwest, he wasn't sure the footprints would still show up.

He took a step forward, following the direction the tracks had led, and saw nothing. The grass seemed different here, tougher than the other side. Maybe a different variety, changed by more exposure to the winds and the salt spray. Perhaps it hadn't held the imprints the same way.

He turned back toward Walker and shook his head. "Nothing," he shouted.

Walker pointed down, then patted the beach beside him.

Of course. Dan needed to get lower.

He sat down beside the last visible footprints and looked across the grass, letting his body sway and his head move. It took time, but suddenly he saw a faint indentation. Then another. They led down to a sweep of gravel edging the open ocean.

Dan followed them until they turned to the right and disappeared into a tide line of seaweed. The same high tide he had arrived with earlier that day had washed the rest away.

▶ "So. Guess that's as far as we can go," Dan said when he was back on the cove side with Walker. "I'll tell the guys when they get here. They can take it from here."

He looked at Walker, who had neither moved nor spoken. "You planning on staying here until Sanford and his folks get back?" Dan asked.

"Yeah. Why?"

"Don't get me wrong, Walker, but you and the police are not a good mix. If you're here, they're gonna have to question you, and as I recall, you don't handle that well. In fact, you tend to mouth off, and that's gonna piss them off. And then they're gonna check your name and find out you've got a record . . . what?"

Walker was grinning at him again. "Come a long way in a couple of years: advising a known criminal to leave the scene."

"Fuck off, Walker. I'm just trying to help here. You don't like talking to them any more than they like talking to you."

"True." Walker nodded. "And you're right. Maybe I'll go find Sanford and his folks. Tell them what's happened."

"Good idea," Dan agreed. "Better make it soon. The boys could arrive any time."

▶ The "boys" arrived twenty minutes after Walker left. They were neither the RCMP West Coast Marine Division nor the coast guard, but a couple of constables from the Gold River detachment, who tied their boat to the wharf and headed straight up to the lighthouse. Gene met them at the door.

"Hi, George. Parker. Figured it might be you two. Don't think you've met Jens yet. He's the new assistant lightkeeper. Came here when Walter retired."

The two men nodded at Jens.

"And this is Dan Connor. He just stopped by on his way up north.

36

He's one of your guys. At least, he used to be. He's been helping with the search."

George and Parker—Gene didn't share their last names and their heavy parkas hid their name tags—shook Dan's hand with the odd mixture of reticence and camaraderie reserved by serving police for those who had left the force.

"You here when they discovered her missing?" George asked Dan. He was a dark, heavyset man with a square jaw, thick neck, and steeply sloping shoulders that suggested he spent a lot of time in the gym.

"No. I arrived here around nine this morning," Dan answered. "That's my boat out in the cove. Came up to the lighthouse to introduce myself to Gene and Mary."

"Huh." George appeared to lose interest in Dan and turned back to Gene. "You checked the cove? Everywhere she might have gone?"

Gene nodded. "Yeah. Dan and I checked the church and the house and studio down there. Mary and Dan checked Jens's place and the workshop."

"You didn't find any sign of her?"

"Not exactly." Gene shot an awkward glance at Jens.

"Sounds like maybe you did find something," George said, his gaze sharpening.

"Yeah, well, not really." Gene was obviously uncomfortable talking in front of Jens. "What we found was the old totem. Someone had dragged it out onto the beach and destroyed it."

"You can't be serious!" Mary stared at him in shock. "You said it was damaged, but destroyed? Margrethe would never do that. It must have been one of those people that were here on the weekend." She turned to George. "There were a bunch of them: kayakers, boaters, hikers from the trail."

Gene shook his head. "The damage is too new. And we found some blood. It was still tacky."

"Blood?" The news was greeted by a chorus of horrified voices. One of them belonged to Jens.

"I'm sorry, Jens," Gene said. "I didn't want to tell you."

"Oh God." Jens collapsed into a chair. "Oh God."

▶ Gene and Dan led the two constables down to the beach and pointed out the mutilated totem and the blood on the driftwood. The constables returned to their boat and used their radio to call back to the detachment and request assistance. Dan shook his head. He knew they were following procedure—they were constables, not detectives—but it meant the trail of footprints would have completely disappeared by the time investigators arrived. It also meant he would have to spend even more time here, unable to do anything practical and surrounded by feelings of fear and grief that brought unwanted memories of Susan surging back.

"I'm going to head back to my boat," he said to them. "There are things I need to be doing."

"You need to stay here until the detectives arrive." Parker spoke for the first time, his voice gruff and his tone officious. He was considerably younger than his partner, with thin, blond hair and a round, pink face that made Dan think he might be on his first posting. "They'll want to talk to you."

"I know," Dan replied. "I was a cop, remember? A detective, as a matter of fact. I'm not going anywhere. I'll come back up to the house as soon as I've finished."

He felt them watching him as he made his way across the walkway and back down to the beach where he had left the dinghy. It didn't bother him. He would have done the same.

Back on board, Dan went straight to the wheelhouse and slid into the captain's chair. He had lied. He had nothing to do—except deal with his memories. The look on Jens's face, the agonized clenching of his body as he listened to Gene explain what they had found, had stirred up feelings Dan thought he had left behind. He would have looked exactly like that the day he found Susan, her body slumped on the dining room table in a pool of blood. He could still taste the grief, smell the emptiness, hear his sobs of anguish. He was back there, feeling the pain twist in his gut, listening to his brain scream. That was what he had run from when he quit the force. That was what had driven him to *Dreamspeaker* and pointed him north into a maze of empty islands and channels he could lose himself in. That is what he thought he had beaten when he met Claire.

And what about Claire? She would be waiting for him to join her in Kyuquot in just a few days, excited to see him, eager to share what she had learned about the otters she loved, ready to share her life and her body with a zest and openness that delighted him. Was it fair to her to share that life and body if he was still tied to Susan?

He came back to the present to find his world blurred by tears he hadn't realized he'd shed. He glanced at his watch as he brushed them from his face. Had he really been here over an hour? They'd be coming to look for him soon, wondering what the hell he was up to. He looked across at the wharf. There was still only one boat—the one the two constables had arrived in—so the detectives weren't here yet. Thank God for that. They'd be really pissed if they had to come and get him.

He went down to the head and splashed cold water on his face. At least the trip back to shore in the dinghy would hide the evidence of his emotional meltdown. Too bad it couldn't take care of the issues that had caused it.

The sound of an inboard engine caught his attention, and he watched through the porthole as an ancient cabin cruiser appeared around the eastern point and headed for the shore. It ran up onto the beach and a young Native man jumped out, almost falling in the sand as he struggled toward the totem. He slowed as he neared the yellow rope and, before Dan could yell a warning, stopped and grasped it with both hands, his body suddenly rigid. He stood there, completely still, for several minutes and then slowly bent his head down until it touched the bright strands of nylon.

Dan figured it had to be Sanford. More grief, thought Dan. More loss. He felt a quick surge of gratitude that Walker had been able to reach the man and forewarn him. It would have surely been even harder if he had come home unprepared.

► SEVEN ◄

► A detective and a forensic specialist arrived a few hours later. As he had done with the constables from Gold River, Gene led them down and showed them the totem and the driftwood where he and Dan had found the blood. By the time they had finished questioning, and searching, and scraping, and bagging, the long twilight of late May had deepened into night.

Dan went down to the wharf with Gene to see them off, then said good night and returned to his boat. He had told them about the footprints, but, as he had expected, when he led the forensic guy over to point them out, they had already disappeared, and he was pretty sure the man hadn't believed him. Not that it mattered. The trail hadn't led anywhere except to the outer beach, and he hadn't wanted to involve Walker by explaining how he had found them. He gave a snort of derision as he thought about it and wondered how many of the witnesses he had questioned over the years had withheld information from him for similar reasons: didn't want to involve a friend; didn't want to sound like a weirdo . . .

He wandered into the salon. There was no way he was going to be able to sleep anytime soon. Too many thoughts rolled around in his head. Too many memories. Too many questions, all of them unanswered. Maybe if he could just concentrate on the questions, he would be able to push the memories back. Store them away until he could deal with them. Yeah, like that was ever going to happen!

He went back to the wheelhouse and tried to call Claire, but there was no answer. He guessed she was probably out for dinner with friends. After all, she was going to be away until at least September, maybe longer, so she would want to say goodbye. He left a message and went back to the salon.

Maybe it was time for a beer and some music: a little jazz to help smooth out the brain waves and get his gray cells working. It had always worked for him in the past. He found *Jazz Samba* by Charlie Byrd and Stan Getz, and let the honeyed sounds flow around him as he made his way out to the aft deck.

It was time to concentrate on the present. What the hell had happened here? It looked like Margrethe had left the house voluntarily, but why? If she hadn't gone to meet someone, she had to have seen something. And it would have needed to be something major to take her outside on her own and down to the beach. This was a woman who was uncomfortable around the water. He hadn't checked the line of sight from the house, but if she had seen someone down by the totem, would that have been enough to pull her out? She wouldn't have been able to see exactly what was going on—not at that distance and not at night, even though there had been a moon—so why would she go? And wouldn't she just assume it was Sanford?

He thought about that for a while, trying to put himself in Margrethe's head, trying to find a scenario that worked, letting the music wheel and dance around him before it drifted out over the dark water, but nothing came to him. He shook his head. The pieces didn't fit. He was missing something. He needed to get back out there, talk to Jens again, check the house and the bedroom window, go down to the outer beach the footprints had led him to and make a wider search . . . but there was the problem. He was no longer a cop, and that meant he was useless. Goddamn it! Back to square one . . .

He turned off the music and turned on the weather channel. Maybe the forecast had changed. Maybe the bad weather had hung up farther north or slid to the east, and he would be able to head up to Kyuquot tomorrow, a little later than he had planned but still in plenty of time to meet Claire when she arrived. He could stop off at Rugged Point Marine

Park, maybe catch a salmon or two. He could even dig out his carving tools, start carving again. He had been away from that for too long . . .

The careful, cultured voice of the weather announcer filled the wheelhouse, and as if to emphasize the words emanating from the speaker, a gust of wind rocked the boat. The weather had indeed changed, but for the worse. The front was moving in faster and would blow harder than was previously forecast. Winds from the southeast, gusting to storm force. Heavy rain squalls. Great. Looked like he was here for at least another couple of days, maybe longer. So much for all those distractions he had been playing with.

He got another beer from the refrigerator and put Sonny Rollins on the stereo. It was going to be a long night.

▶ A noise pulled Dan from a restless sleep. He was sprawled on the settee, the speakers silent and his glass empty. He looked around the salon in confusion. Something had woken him, but he had no idea what. The cove looked peaceful and quiet under a moonlit sky muted by the first thin clouds of the coming weather. There was almost no wind, and the water in the cove was calm, not even a line of foam marking the beach.

He stood up and started toward the wheelhouse, but was stopped in mid-stride by three loud knocks that seemed to come from the stern. He moved back toward the aft deck, bare feet silent on the night-damp wood, and peered over the railing. There was a dark shadow on the swim grid, and he thought he could see something underneath. He leaned to the side to get a better view, and the shadow turned to face him. It was Walker.

"You're a hard man to wake, white man."

"Walker? What the hell are you doing here in the middle of the night?"

Walker's teeth gleamed back at him. "Figured it was a good time to talk."

Dan checked his watch. "It's three o'clock in the morning. This is when people usually sleep." He wasn't sure, but he thought Walker might have shrugged.

"You gonna invite me up?"

Dan laughed. "Why not? I'll put some coffee on."

Walker didn't drink alcohol, and Dan knew better than to offer him any help, so he simply walked back inside and headed for the galley.

▶ "The cops find anything?"

Dan and Walker were sprawled on the upholstered settees that ran the length of the salon, the planes of their faces lit by the faint moonlight seeping in through the windows.

"Nope," Dan replied. "Dusted the totem, but getting a print off that old wood is pretty well impossible. They scraped up the blood. Found a few places I missed. Should get some DNA off that." He glanced at Walker. "They couldn't find the footprints."

"Big surprise."

"You really think she left with someone?" The idea still didn't sit right with Dan, but he had learned to respect Walker's abilities.

"Yeah," Walker answered. "I think she left with the guy who wrecked the totem."

"Doesn't fit," Dan said. "If that was their footprints we saw, how did the blood get onto that driftwood? They were heading the other way."

"Might be his," Walker offered.

"Maybe. But there's no blood on the totem. And if he came and went from the other side—left his boat over there on the outside beach—he wouldn't have any reason to climb over that driftwood."

"He didn't have a boat over there." Walker's voice held complete conviction. "Whole place is a mass of rocks. There's a reef just offshore too. No way he could have come in there."

"So how the hell did he get here?" Dan asked. "And where did he go?"

Silence fell while the two men tried to come with up an answer.

▶ "Bet they're on the trail." It was Walker who spoke first.

"Trail?" asked Dan. "What trail are you talking about?"

"Sanford once told me he had a couple of people come off the trail just about starving to death. Didn't have any gear. Nothing. Said they

43

ate all his food. Had to call the water taxi to come and get them."

"Sounds like a pretty rough trail," Dan said. "Don't think Margrethe would be the type to hike something like that."

"Might not have had any choice," Walker answered.

Dan looked at him. He could see him more clearly now. The long, slow, northern dawn was already chasing the night out of the sky.

"So tell me about this trail," he said.

Walker shrugged. It seemed he knew nothing about it other than it existed. Dan stared at him for a minute, then went forward and switched on the computer. It came to life, the screen casting a pale glow over the wheelhouse as Dan ran a search for trails on Nootka Island. Within seconds, line after line of entries appeared. Dan picked the first one that looked promising. It called the trail "rugged," said it stretched for twenty-two miles between some place called Louie Lagoon and Friendly Cove, and suggested it would take a minimum of five days to hike it from end to end. The next one said much the same but called for six days. It also said hikers would have to scale cliffs and would be miserably exposed, with rain and wind the norm and hypothermia a threat. A third entry said there were waterfalls and fast-running rivers to be waded, and warned that rogue waves and tides posed the greatest hazard. Not a place Margrethe would go by choice. Not a place he would go by choice either, thought Dan, although he had a sneaking suspicion that Walker might have a different view.

He switched the computer off and headed back to the salon. Walker was still sprawled on the settee, gazing out the window.

"You find anything?"

"Yep," Dan answered. "There's a twenty-two-mile trail runs up the coast from here to some place called Louie Lagoon. It's wild, rough, and dangerous. Takes five or six days to hike it and you gotta climb cliffs, cross rivers, and dodge tides."

"You get all that from a book or chart or something?" Walker asked.

"Nope. The computer."

Walker looked at him for long moment.

"You got a computer out here in the middle of nowhere? Now how the hell does that work?"

Dan smiled. "The miracle of modern technology, my traditional friend. Got a satellite dish up on the mast."

▸ The two men sat quietly, each wrapped in his own thoughts, as the day swelled to life and lit the cabin with a soft golden light. Outside, a gull shrieked. Then another. There was the occasional slap of a fish jumping. The lazy drone of a bumblebee. The constant lapping of water against the hull.

"You figure Margrethe's still alive?" Dan's question broke their silence.

"Yeah. Yesterday anyway."

"Jesus! You know those footprints could've been two guys."

"Maybe. But the second set was real small," Walker said. "And light. Didn't leave much of an imprint."

"Shit. If you're right . . ."

"Yeah."

The silence fell again. This time it was Walker who spoke first.

"Can you get the cops back?"

"Don't need to—and I couldn't anyway. They'll send more guys in. Probably a dog team. Maybe ask the coast guard if they can send out a boat to search the shoreline. Might even send out a helicopter. No way they'll listen to me. They don't take direction from the public, and they think I'm crazy anyway after I told them about the disappearing footprints. If I called them up and said I thought Margrethe had been dragged out on the trail by some guy, they'd think I'd really lost it. That's the kind of thing they have to figure out for themselves."

"Yeah. So how about that guy you called last year?"

"Mike?"

"Yeah."

"Mike can't help with this. He's got some pull with the Marine Division, but this isn't something they'd normally respond to—and we have nothing to give them. We don't even know for sure she's out there."

"Gonna feel like shit if she is and she don't make it."

"I feel like shit already, Walker. Her husband's up there at the lighthouse, going through the worst time of his life, and there's nothing

I can do to help. Can't even ask him what she looks like because then he'd want to know why. Think we'd found her body or something."

"Yeah," said Walker as he turned to stare morosely out the window.

"Shit!" Dan broke the silence that had fallen. "There must be something we can do. We can't just leave her out there with some asshole." He stood up and went to stand by the cabin door, staring out over the dawn-flecked water.

"True," Walker said, watching him. "Could leave the asshole out there though. Be kinda good if he ran into trouble." He pushed himself up off the settee.

"Where are you going?" Dan said as Walker struggled toward the aft deck. "You can't go out looking for her. And there's a weather system coming in from the north anyway."

Walker reached the door and peered out. "Yep. Gonna be here soon, too." He turned back and looked at Dan. "I'm going to go talk to Sanford. There's some people over near Esperanza who might know the trail. They know this whole area. Might be able to get them over there."

Dan narrowed his eyes. "These like those kids you called in last year?" Walker had asked a group of Native youth, who were living in a remote camp run by a friend of his, to help him disable a boat whose crew had threatened Claire.

Walker grinned. "Did a good job, those kids. Percy was real proud of them."

"Yeah, Walker. They did an incredible job. Hell, I'm proud of them too. But they didn't have to deal with anybody face-to-face. This guy could be armed. I don't want anyone to get hurt."

"I'll let them know," Walker said, the grin still on his face as he made his way out onto the deck. "They'll be happy to hear you're looking out for them."

Dan shook his head. "Walker, you know what I'm saying—"

"Think you could make it up to Louie Lagoon if you go round the inside?" Walker asked, turning back to look at Dan as he cut him off in mid-sentence.

"What?" Dan wasn't sure he'd heard right. "Why the hell would I go to Louie Lagoon? I don't even know where it is!"

"It's the other end of the trail. Your fancy computer told you. Remember?"

"Dammit, Walker. Are you nuts?" Dan followed him outside and leaned over the stern, watching as Walker used his arms to lower himself to the swim grid and pull the canoe up. "You've got to stop this. Let the police handle it. You can't keep putting your friends at risk. This is not your problem." Even as he was speaking, Dan was aware of the contradiction. Just seconds ago he had been saying they had to do something. Now he was telling Walker it was none of his business.

Walker slid his feet into the canoe, then twisted so his weight was braced on his arms as he lowered his body onto the seat.

"Worked pretty good last time," he said as he untied the rope from the swim grid.

"Ah, hell!" Dan ran his hand through his hair as Walker lifted his paddle over the side. "Okay. Fine. I'll have a look at the charts, see if it's possible, but I'm damned if I know what good I can do even if I get there."

"He's heading that way. It's probably the only place he can go. And we could pick up the Esperanza folks on the way. Save them a bunch of time."

"You're serious, aren't you? You really figure these people can help?"

"You got a better idea? That trail sounds pretty lonely. She might not make it to the other end."

Dan shook his head. He might as well give up now. Walker wasn't going to change his mind.

"Fine. How long do you think you'll be? I'm guessing you're planning on coming along for the ride? At least as far as Esperanza?"

That irritating grin flashed again. "Thought you'd never ask! Might take a bit of time to track the boys down. They tend to move about a bit, but it shouldn't be too long. I'll . . ."

They both turned as the sound of an engine swelled behind the point and another cabin cruiser, this one considerably older than Sanford's, nosed into the cove and made its way toward the float.

"Looks like he knows where he's going," Dan said as they watched the boat slide up to the float. "Must be a local."

Walker nodded. "Might be a friend of Sanford's parents. Looks like he's headed for the house." He dug the paddle into the water and turned the canoe toward the shore. "I'll see what he wants. Sanford probably knows him."

"I'll plot a course," Dan said, his voice resigned. "Then I'd better go up to the light and let them know where I'm going. Don't want them to think I'm running out on them."

"Tell 'em we'll call them from the lagoon. Might be good to have an extra pair of eyes at this end too. I'll meet you back here."

"We?" asked Dan, but he was talking to himself. Walker was already away on the water.

EIGHT

The smell of bacon drifted from the open door of the lightkeeper's house, and Dan heard the clink of plates and cutlery as he approached on the walkway. He hadn't eaten breakfast—or dinner the night before, for that matter—and all of a sudden he was ravenous.

"Good morning," he said as he stuck his head in the door. "Sure smells good in here."

"Hey, Dan. Come on in." Mary was busy at the stove, forking strips of crisp bacon onto a plate. "Would you like some breakfast? There's more than enough."

"Wouldn't say no," Dan answered. "But I'd hate to be the one responsible if you guys had to go back to eating Spam."

Mary laughed. "Gene told you that story, did he? Wasn't the best time in our lives, but it all worked out in the end. We don't have to worry about supplies now. We can have them brought in on the *Uchuck*. She's the supply boat for all the folks around here." She added eggs to the now empty frying pan. "Gene's gone down to get Jens. He wanted to spend the night down at his own place, but I don't think he got much sleep. The light was on all night and I saw him moving around a couple of times."

Dan nodded. "Has to be tough. Any word from the cops?"

She shook her head. "No. Nothing."

Dan hesitated for a few seconds. Should he tell her about the footprints? It would explain why he was leaving the cove when there

49

was bad weather coming in, but it would raise hopes that maybe shouldn't be raised. Probably better to keep his mouth shut.

As Mary handed him a plate, they heard the sound of voices approaching the house. "Here. Might as well get started."

▶ "Going to be a pretty hard trip." Gene nodded toward the barometer. "Doesn't look like it will blow too long, but it's already strong enough to slow you down. Sea's building too."

Both men glanced out the window at the spray being hurled off the rocks below.

"Should be better on the inside," Dan answered. "I'll head for Tahsis if it's rough, but I'd really like to get to Louie Bay. Make it an easy trip up to Kyuquot once it clears." He had used his rendezvous with Claire as his excuse for leaving.

"Sounds like a special lady." Gene smiled across the table at his wife. "You'll have to bring her down here. Like to meet her."

"I'll do that," Dan said as he stood up. "Thanks for breakfast, Mary. It was great." He turned to go, then remembered Walker's parting words. "Ahh, you'll let me know if anything happens here?"

Mary glanced at Jens. He was sitting at the table, his food untouched in front of him. "Of course," she said. "We're going to go back out and check the cove again as soon as we've eaten. Walk the beaches . . ."

There was a screech of wood as Jens shoved his chair back, and without saying a word, he stumbled past them and disappeared outside. Gene glanced helplessly at Mary and stood up to follow him, but she put a hand on his arm. "Let him go. I think he needs to be alone for a while. I'll go get him when we're done here."

She looked back at Dan. "You take care. I'm sure you know what you're doing, but it's going to get nasty out there. You certain you have to go?"

He smiled, warmed by her concern. "Yeah. I think I do. But I'll be fine. Walker's coming along for the ride. Going to meet up with some of his friends in Esperanza."

He turned to Gene and found the man looking at him oddly.

"Walker's going with you?" he asked.

"Yeah," Dan answered. "That a problem?"

"No," Gene answered. "No, it's not. Just seems an odd thing for him to do. He always comes and goes in his canoe. Won't even use the *Uchuck*, although they take canoes and kayaks all the time." He shook his head and then asked, "I don't suppose this has anything to do with Margrethe, does it?"

Dan looked at him and sighed. He couldn't lie to these people. Margrethe was part of their community, almost family, and they deserved to know what was going on even if nothing came of it. Besides, Jens was no longer there to hear the story. He had gone back to his house.

"Maybe," he answered. "Walker found some footprints. Two people. We figure they headed out on the trail."

Mary turned to stare at him, the food forgotten. "My God! Do you think it was her? Margrethe?"

Dan shook his head. "I don't know. If Walker's right—and it's a big *if*—then I guess it could have been."

"Did you tell the police? Did they check it out? I didn't see them—"

Dan interrupted the rush of questions. "Yes, I told the police, but by the time they got here, the grass was dry and standing up again. There was nothing for them to see. And the trail only led down to the outside beach anyway. The tide had washed anything else away. Walker figures they might have gone onto the trail—the one that leads up to Louie Lagoon—so we're going to go up there and keep an eye on things at that end."

He watched as all the same doubts and questions he had asked himself played across their faces, until Mary broke the silence.

"We should tell Jens. He—"

"No," Dan said. "I don't think that's a good idea. He would probably take off on the trail himself, and he's in no shape to do that." He looked from one to the other. "Look, we don't know for sure that it was her—and even if it was, she might be with someone who's armed. Someone who could be dangerous." He looked pointedly at Gene. "Remember the blood we found?"

51

Gene nodded. "Yeah, you're right. But damn, it seems crazy to think of Margrethe out there on that trail. A lot of it's along the beach or crossing rivers. If it's her, she sure as hell didn't go voluntarily." He turned to Mary. "We'd better keep this to ourselves."

She nodded, a troubled look on her face. "I guess you're right."

Dan smiled at her. "Just keep an eye on the cove. If you see anything odd—anyone that looks out of place—call me." He paused and looked around the room. "You do have full phone service here, don't you?"

Gene nodded. "We do now. The coast guard in Tofino added some bandwidth to the microwave tower a few years back."

"Great," said Dan. "I've got VHF, SSB, and satellite on board. The works. I'll turn them all on. You shouldn't have any trouble reaching me."

He turned to go. As he stepped out of the doorway, a shrill ring tore through the air.

Gene laughed. "And speaking of phones," he said, "I'd better go and answer that one. You take care of yourself. And keep in touch."

"Will do." Dan nodded to the two of them and headed out to the walkway. He was almost halfway across when he heard Mary calling him.

"Dan! It's for you."

He turned and stared at her. "For me?"

She nodded and held out a receiver.

Who on earth would be calling him at the lighthouse? Who even knew he was there? An image of Claire flashed into his mind. She was the only person who knew where he was. If she was in trouble . . . He ran back and snatched the receiver from Mary's outstretched hand.

"This is Dan. Are you okay?"

There was a pause on the other end, and then a very male voice drawled, "I'm fine, but thanks for asking."

Dan felt relief mingled with shock. It was his old boss, Mike Bryant, now promoted from head of the anti-terrorist squad to commander of the South Island Division.

"Mike? How the hell did you know where to find me?"

"I didn't. At least, not until a half hour or so ago when I got a call from the marine squad. Tried calling you on the boat but didn't get an answer, so figured I'd try the light."

Dan shook his head. "The marine squad? How would they know where I am? And why would they care? What's going on?"

"That's what they want to know. They got a call from North Island Division asking them to check the beaches for a missing woman. Seems they're stretched pretty thin, so when they were told you were in the vicinity, they asked me to get hold of you. I didn't know if you'd still be there, but . . ."

"Well, I'm glad you're not telling me the Nootka lighthouse was just a lucky guess. I was beginning to think you had found a psychic!"

"Nope—no psychic, although the fact you're still there may very well be lucky for us. I just got off the phone with my boss. I'm putting you back on the job."

This time Dan jerked the receiver away from his face and stared at it as if it had turned into a venomous snake. It was several seconds before he brought it back to his mouth. "You're what?"

"Listen. You had an incident there, right? Some woman went missing?"

"Yeah. Her name's Margrethe. She's the wife of the assistant light-keeper here. Why? Has she been found?" Dan looked over at Gene and Mary. They stood transfixed, their eyes glued to his face.

"No. But there has been a body found. A couple of fishermen found it. It was in the water up at Aktis Island. That's just off Kyuquot, which I understand is pretty close to where you are?"

"Yeah. Not too far. I'm heading up there in a few days to meet Claire. But if it's not Margrethe, then what has this got to do with me? Or you, for that matter? That would be North Island."

Mike ignored the jibe. "It's got nothing to do with Margrethe—at least as far as I know. The body is some Native kid. Just a youngster. Maybe thirteen or fourteen. The guys from the detachment at Tahsis went out to pick him up, and one of them asked a couple of the folks he knew in the village there if they recognized him. They did. Seems the kid might have been from Gold River."

"Huh." Dan noticed Mary and Gene still staring at him and moved away. Hearing about a dead kid was not something they needed to experience right now. "Well, that's a bitch, and I'm really sorry to hear it. It's sure going to be tough for his folks and all that, but I still don't see why you needed to track me down. There's nothing I can do about it, and I know there's a detachment in Gold River. Two of them were over here yesterday: their names were George and Parker, as I recall. I met them."

"Yeah, well, that's part of the problem. Just let me finish, okay?" Mike's voice had lost its jovial tone and become completely serious.

"Sure." Dan felt a familiar current of excitement shimmer through his body like a low-voltage electric shock as old circuits and neurons responded to the first scent of a new case. But it was tempered by something else. Something new. Reticence? Fear? Caution?

Mike continued. "Okay," he said. "Seems the kid—if it is the same kid—wasn't quite right. His mother's an alcoholic, and they figure he had Fetal Alcohol Syndrome. Lived with his grandfather, but kept running away. Hated school. Wouldn't wear shoes. Wanted to live in his traditional territory like his ancestors lived. Hunt and fish and all that. They caught him stowing away on the freight boat, the *Uchuck*, a couple of times, but mostly he hitched a ride with fishermen or tourists. Couple of times he stole a boat. Always ended up in the same place. Want to guess where that was?"

Dan sucked in a deep breath and let it out slowly before he answered. "Nootka Island." He made it a statement rather than a question.

"Yep. Right first time. But not just Nootka Island. Friendly Cove. I think the proper name is Yuquot?" Mike didn't wait for confirmation. "And that's where you are, right?"

"Right."

"Good. So here's the thing. First, the timing is right. Seems the body hadn't been in the water long—that's why it's in such good shape—but the coroner figures it was just about the right amount of time for some kind of current that runs along the coast there to carry it up from the lighthouse at Nootka. She says it couldn't have come all the way from Gold River. Would have taken too long, plus the water is warmer in the inlet that leads out of there—Muchalat Inlet it's called—so there would have been more deterioration. Same thing for Tahsis or Zeballos.

"So anyway, the Tahsis guys called Gold River and asked them to check to see if the kid is missing. Turns out he is. And Gold River told them about that missing woman and some blood they found on some driftwood over there in the cove—I think you know about that too? So they put a rush on the DNA analysis. They don't have all the results back yet, but it looks like the blood type is a match. So the kid was probably stabbed to death—did I tell you he had stab wounds?—and put in the water right there in Friendly Cove."

"Jesus!" Dan's mind had kicked into high gear. "So now we've got a mutilated totem, a murdered kid, and a missing woman? This whole thing gets weirder by the minute!"

There was a slight pause on the other end of the line, and then Mike came back again. "Glad it's got your attention, because it's your case now."

Dan straightened. "What? Are you nuts? I'm retired, remember? I haven't been on the force for two years!"

"Year and a half, actually. If it was two years, I couldn't reinstate you."

"Reinstate me? You're crazy! Check your records. I retired in April, after . . ." Dan didn't—couldn't—finish the sentence. He remembered not only the day, but also the hour and the minute.

Mike ignored the hesitation. "April is when you handed in your papers, yes, but you had a whole bunch of accrued leave and overtime, so it didn't take effect until late December. So—a year and a half."

"Mike, listen: this is crazy. You can't do this. It won't work. I've forgotten most of the stuff I knew. I don't have the resources. Don't have the contacts. Shit, I've been pulling a pension every month. No one is going to buy it!"

"Already done—and I'll e-mail you a list of all our assets on the island." Mike paused for a minute. "And if I recall correctly, you did pretty damn good last year without any of those resources and contacts."

"That was different and you know it."

There was silence on the line, and Dan could hear the sound of his own breathing.

"Dan, listen to me. We're spread very thin on the west coast. You know that. And you're already there, on the ground. The Gold River guys who went out there said you already had some ideas—"

"Which they totally dismissed," Dan interrupted.

"Whatever. You're there. You know the people there. You know what's happening. All I'm doing is giving you the authority to call in whatever assistance you need to get the job done—and my guess, knowing you, is you're already working on it anyway."

Dan blew out a deep breath he hadn't known he was holding. It seemed Mike knew him all too well.

"Shit. So if I agree to this—and I'm not saying I do—who would I report to?"

He could almost hear Mike grinning on the other end of the connection.

"His name's Gary Markleson. He's the commander for the North Island Division, based in Port Hardy. He's got all the details."

Mike gave Dan the phone number and then added, "He's even got a name for you to check out. Seems you might have one of our nastier customers up there in your neck of the woods."

► NINE ◄

► "Please!"

He didn't know which was worse, trying to make progress on this piece-of-shit trail or listening to that whiny voice squeaking at him. Every time he heard it—and he heard it often—it set his teeth on edge.

It had all gone wrong. He should've known better than to join up with Pat again, especially now that Pat was with Carl. Sure, Pat was smart. Hell, the whole thing had been his idea in the first place. But ideas were nothing. Everybody had them. "Let's do this" or "Let's do that" or "Hey, how about . . ."

Ideas were great and wonderful and all that, but it was the planning that counted, and those two couldn't plan their way to the outhouse. They were bad luck, both of them. He should've just done the job on his own. He was familiar with the city of Victoria, knew the gallery—knew all the galleries, for that matter. And he'd had a good head start, too. He'd been released over a month before Carl, and nearly three months before Pat. Plenty of time to set it up. And he could have done it, no problem. It wasn't like he was some low-life street punk holding up liquor stores and snatching purses for a living. He was a pro. He'd been doing the high-end stuff for years: galleries and professional offices and the rich-bitch mansions with their fancy security systems. He could do it all. Would have still been doing it if he hadn't taken on Marty as a partner. That had been a mistake. He'd let himself be talked into it by the slick son of a bitch, and Marty had landed both of them in the slammer. Well, at least that wouldn't happen again. Marty wouldn't be talking anyone into anything anymore. He had made sure of that.

Now look where he was. Scrambling along some godforsaken trail that wasn't really a trail at all, just . . . west coast: rough, wet, slippery, and at times so overgrown with salal it was damn near impassable. Jerry cursed as one of the tough, gnarled stems caught his foot. Salal was a pestilence, put on this useless bloody island for no good reason he could think of. Its leaves were like leather, and the tangled stems formed an almost impenetrable barrier that filled every open space. You couldn't break it or step over it or even push your way through it. No, you had to thread yourself through, one step at a time, untangling each branch, placing each foot carefully so you didn't twist an ankle—or worse—as you tried to pull it free. It even encroached on the trail in places, and he had been forced to stumble and dodge through the goddamn stuff, dragging the stupid bitch behind him, until he finally found his way down to some rock-strewn beach, and then the fucking tide had come in and he had been forced to scramble back up again.

And then there were the creeks. He'd crossed two already, wading halfway up to his ass in freezing water and dragging the whiner behind him. The whole thing had been cursed from the start. What were the chances that in a place as remote and empty as Yuquot there would be some fucking Indian kid asleep in the grass? Or that some goddamn woman would happen to be up at four o'clock in the morning, looking out the window of one of the only three houses there? It was crazy. He should have finished her off down there on the beach. Left her with the kid. He didn't know why he hadn't. But she had come out of nowhere, like a goddamn ghost with her long, pale hair hanging down around her face and that white jacket with some friggin' Indian picture of a thunderbird and a snake painted on it. He'd thought at first she was an apparition, some kind of spirit the kid had conjured up, and he'd panicked. Nothing surprising there. He had seen pictures that looked like her before, when he was a little kid, at some of the gatherings his mother had dragged him to, and he'd heard the stories

58

about *Bukwas*, the king of the ghosts, who only became visible at night, and *Dzunukwa*, the cannibal woman, who could speak to you with your grandmother's voice and lure you to your death. The Indians in the joint had told the same ones. He hadn't really believed them, of course. He knew better. He knew they were just stupid Indian stories, but out there on the beach, it was like they had suddenly come true. It wasn't until the whiner had tried to run from him, and he'd grabbed her arm without thinking, that he realized she was real. A real, live woman—and he'd never killed a woman.

At least the air was warming up a bit now that the sun was getting higher, but his wet clothes were sticking to his skin, leaching the heat out of his body and making every step a torture. His feet were so cold in his soggy runners he could barely feel them. Between all that, and the goddamn salal, and having to drag the stupid, bleating cow along with him, it was damn near impossible to stay upright.

He glanced up through the trees at a small patch of blue sky that was slowly being pushed south by a mass of dark clouds. They didn't seem to be moving fast, but they were moving, and they were headed this way. Another goddamn problem.

"Please!"

That voice squeaked again, and he gave a vicious tug on the rope he had tied around her skinny wrists.

"Shut the fuck up!" he snarled, wishing for perhaps the twentieth time that he had killed both of the assholes right there when they had interrupted his search. Why the hell hadn't he? So she was a woman. So what? He hadn't been thinking right, that's what. He had been upset by finding the totem empty, and he was already wired by doing the kid. He had known he didn't have a lot of time to look around—dawn came early at this time of the year—and if he didn't find the stuff, Pat and Carl would be back to get it, and then he'd be a goddamn laughingstock.

He had stumbled up to the old cemetery, tripping on roots and rocks and shit. He hadn't really looked at the old graves the other times he had been there, hadn't cared a damn about them then and didn't now, but he did remember that there had been all kinds of stuff left there with them—carved poles, old sewing machines, dolls, even a pair of shoes. If Pat and Carl hadn't been able to use the old totem, any of those would have worked to hide the stuff. And he'd been right. He'd found it. It was right there under one of the fallen poles. He'd seen the signs of disturbance in the exposed earth, which gleamed in the moonlight where the old wood had been moved. He had actually had the stuff in his hand, had been about to open the bag to take a look, when some instinct had made him turn around to make sure he was alone, and he'd seen her. She'd been standing down there on the beach beside the kid, looking like an apparition or a ghost or something with her weird white hair and white coat glowing almost silver. He'd been so spooked by her appearance he had almost dropped the stuff, but he'd had enough smarts to hide it again. Someplace different, of course, where Pat and Carl couldn't find it.

Hell, she'd come out of nowhere like some kind of fucking night spirit that would disappear with the dawn or would give him some protection or something. Protection? Shit. Truth was, she was just a nuisance. A problem he needed to take care of.

He could feel the knife pressing against his hip, and he let his fingers run along its contours. He could always do it now—her body probably wouldn't be found for months in this thick tangle of vegetation. Maybe never. But the truth was he didn't really know if he had the stomach for it. He wasn't a stone-cold murderer. He had never killed anyone who didn't deserve it. Not on purpose anyway. Wouldn't have done it this time if the two of them hadn't surprised him like that. First the kid, lying there in the grass, and then the woman appearing out of the gloom. They had scared the shit out of him. Killing the kid was just a gut reaction, over before he knew what was happening. Not really his fault—although the cops wouldn't see it that way. They'd throw the whole fucking book at him. Lock him away for life. Assholes.

He glanced back at the skinny form stumbling along behind him. She was really slowing him down. Maybe he should just do it. In for one, in for the other. What difference would it make? It would sure make it easier if he didn't have to keep dragging her along. There were still close to eighteen miles to go, if his figuring was correct, and all of them would be tough. And then there was food. Jesus! He hadn't thought of that. He could find enough for himself, but it would be harder feeding two—impossible, because how would he get it if he had to keep hold of her? She'd take off the second he took his eyes off her—although he could always tie her to a tree.

But what would he do with her when they got to the lagoon? He couldn't flag down a boat or a seaplane if he had her with him. And what would he do with her after that? Shit! What the hell was he doing? He had to pull himself together. She had seen him kill the kid. She was a witness, for God's sake. He should never have dragged her out here. He had to get rid of her. Now!

His hand found the knife again, and he slid it out of its sheath, letting his fingers test the edge on the blade. His eyes rested on the woman's bedraggled figure for a moment, taking in the pleading eyes staring back at him, pale lashes spiky and wet with tears. He could tell just by looking at her that she was on the brink of yet another whine. Hell, it would only take a second. One quick jab and it would be over. He wouldn't even have to move the body; he could just push it down into the thick mounds of salal. Easy.

He had leaned in toward her, his hand reaching out for her arm as he prepared to pull her in tight against him, when he heard a noise. Voices. They were faint, but they were there, and in some strange way they sounded close. What the hell? Was nothing going to go right?

He relaxed the rope as he took a step toward the clifftop he thought the voices were coming from. It sounded like there were four people, maybe two men and two women. They were close enough that he could make out the odd word, but they were distorted, with a strange, almost hollow quality. Sort of like an echo. Of course! He wasn't the only one who knew about this trail, even though it was remote and rough. There were always assholes wanting to prove how tough they were. These had to be hikers, and they were down below on the beach. They had to have come in from the other end, from the lagoon. It would take them a while to make it up the cliff. They might even spend a little time on the beach before they started up, but sooner or later they would make the climb. They had to. The tide would force them up. And then what?

He couldn't let them see him. The only option was to go back—but that was impossible. They would have found the kid's body by now and there would be cops all over the place. He had to keep going. He looked into the bush. Maybe he could make his own trail. Stay close to the trees where the salal was thinnest until he found one of the logging roads that wandered across the island.

He turned back to the woman. She hadn't moved, probably hadn't even heard the voices. She was still standing exactly where he had left her, her feet stuck deep in the salal and her eyes wide, looking like a deer caught in a hunting lamp. Stupid bitch. He would be doing the world a favor getting rid of her. He started back toward her, and as he moved, his foot caught on a root, catapulting him forward into the undergrowth. He put his hands out to break his fall and felt both the rope and the knife slip from his fingers even as he heard the crash of footsteps. The woman had come to life, startled out of her stupor by his fall. Shit!

He struggled to push himself up, his fingers scrabbling through the salal for the knife. Goddamn it to hell. If she made it to the top of the cliff where the hikers could see her, it would be all over—although maybe he could come up behind her and give her a push. Yeah. If he did it right, they'd never see him. Make it look like she had fallen.

He jabbed his hands through the tangled branches, feeling them tear his skin and rip his fingernails. He had to find the damn knife. He would never be able to make it without it—he needed it for food as well as taking care of business. He pushed a little to the right, and then to the left, forcing his hands back in through the tough foliage. Finally his searching fingers felt the smooth wood of the handle. Yes! Maybe his luck was changing. There was no way they could pin the kid on him if they didn't even know he was on the island, and if he could get rid of the woman, maybe make it look like an accident, he'd be free and clear.

He had to move quickly, though, before whoever was down below realized he was there. He stood up and looked back toward the ocean, sure the whiny bitch would have headed for the voices, but he saw only open sky along the edge of the cliff. Where the hell had she gone?

Why wasn't she screaming? Calling out to the people below? Had she jumped? Fallen?

The sound of feet crashing through the bush intruded again, a little quieter now. Farther away. Shit! She had gone the other way. Into the bush instead of toward the beach. She had to be crazy—or maybe just stupid. But it didn't matter. Might even work out better. He could catch up with her, easy. Just have to drag her a bit farther through the bush. Although maybe he could just follow her—that would be even easier—and when they were well away from the coast, he could simply leave her. Walk away by himself. There was no way someone so useless could find her own way out. She would die in there, and his problem would be solved.

▶ TEN ◀

▶ Dan passed the phone back to Gene, his mind still reeling from the conversation he had just had with Mike. He was back on the force. Margrethe's disappearance was now his case. And he had a murder to investigate. He couldn't take it all in. He glanced down at the piece of paper he held in his hand. He needed to call this guy—the commander of the North Island Division—and find out just what the hell was going on.

He looked up to find Gene and Mary staring at him.

"So you're a cop again?" Gene asked.

Dan smiled and shook his head. "That's what the man said, but I'm not sure he can really do that."

"Sounded pretty certain to me."

Dan snorted. "Yeah, Mike always sounds certain. Figures it's his job to sound certain. Thinks that way everyone will believe him. But I've known him to pull more than a few con jobs when he wants to get his own way." He waved the piece of paper. "I'll call this guy from the boat and see what he has to say."

"Does this mean you can follow up on that trail Walker saw?" Mary asked.

He looked at her. "Maybe. But I really won't know till I've talked to . . ." He looked down at the paper again. "Gary Markleson. He's in charge of the north island for the RCMP. Do you guys know him?"

They both shook their heads, and just then a gust of wind swept off the ocean and raced through the gap below the walkway, setting up a discordant hum in the metal that immediately drew their attention to the oncoming storm. Dan looked out the window. There were small streaks of white on the water.

"I'd better get going. The sooner I leave the better—and Walker will be wondering where I am. Keep in touch, okay?"

▶ Walker was sitting in his canoe at the end of the float, apparently talking to someone on the cabin cruiser they had seen come in earlier. As soon as he saw Dan approaching, he ended the conversation with a brief wave and pushed off. The little powerboat let go its lines and headed back the way it had come as Walker paddled toward *Dreamspeaker*'s stern.

"Must have been a good breakfast," he said as Dan let his dinghy drift in beside Walker's canoe. "Me and old Jackson could smell the bacon all the way down here."

Dan nodded absently, his mind still churning as he watched the old powerboat head back out of the cove. "He that friend of Sanford's you were talking about?"

"Yeah," Walker answered. "He's looking for his grandson. The kid keeps running away. Usually comes here. Ray and Sanford keep an eye out for him."

A surge of adrenalin brought every nerve in Dan's body to full alert, and his gaze riveted on Walker. "Say again? His grandson? How old is this kid?"

Walker looked at him. "What? You know something about him? He up at the light or something?"

Dan stared back at him, unable to answer, his mind racing. This had to be the kid Mike was talking about. The kid whose body had been found in Kyuquot. The kid whose blood was on the driftwood. And that was his grandfather who had just motored past only moments ago. A man Dan needed to talk to—at least, if he really was back on the force and working the case.

He shook his head. It was all happening too fast. He needed time to get himself together. To get back into his old persona. But even as that thought coalesced, another one formed: did he really want to?

Walker was still looking at him, waiting for an answer.

"No," Dan said. "He's not up at the light. Just Gene and Mary and Jens. And Margrethe is still missing." He climbed onto the grid and started to hook the dinghy up to the davits. *Dreamspeaker* was bucking at the end of her rope, the water in the cove already restless. "But I did hear from Mike, and he gave me a bunch of new information." He tightened the straps, then reached down to pull the canoe up onto the grid. "Can you lift that end? We can tie it on the grid. It'll be too rough to tow it. We'll get everything squared away and get under way and then I'll bring you up to date."

They got both of the small vessels secured, and Dan went forward to the wheelhouse, leaving Walker to follow. By the time Dan had the engine warmed up and the course entered into the computer, Walker had joined him, easing himself into the chair at the navigation station. Neither man spoke as Dan nudged the ship up on the anchor, hauling in the heavy chain until the last link was snugged to the winch.

"You get hold of those guys you were talking about?" Dan asked as *Dreamspeaker* nosed out into the open water of the sound.

"Yeah. They'll be waiting for us at Esperanza."

"Huh," said Dan. "So is this another 'learning to be Indian' camp?" He hadn't forgotten Walker's description of the camp they had received assistance from the previous year.

Walker laughed. "Yeah," he said. "You could call it that."

"You got a lot of these camps?" Dan asked.

"Not as many as we should have," Walker answered, his voice suddenly serious. "We already lost four generations to the white man's schools. Can't afford to lose another one to bright lights and booze."

There was a note of bitterness that Dan hadn't heard before, and it surprised him. It wasn't that he thought Walker had nothing to be bitter about. Dan knew better than most just how much the man sitting beside him had given up to those same siren calls, but it seemed out of character. Even all those years ago, when Walker had been in the hospital, mostly confined to a wheelchair and struggling through months of painful physiotherapy as he came to terms with a lifetime of physical limitation, he had taken full responsibility for his own actions, always meeting his problems head-on with both acceptance and good humor.

"Something bothering you?" The current was running against the wind, building up a steep chop that made steering difficult, and as Dan fought to hold the ship on course, he couldn't spare a glance at Walker, even though the man was sitting just across from him on the other side of the wheelhouse.

There was silence for a while, and then Walker gave a short bark of laughter.

"Yeah, guess you could say that. We lost two kids from my band last month. Both fifteen years old. Both runaways. Nice kids just looking for some fun. Couldn't find it on the reserve, so they hitched down to the big city and met up with the usual crowd, who fed them some bad dope. End of story."

More silence, then another harsh laugh. "Sound familiar?"

Dan nodded, his eyes still focused ahead. "Yeah, it does. Saw a lot of that in my time."

The seas calmed a little as Dan steered into Cook Channel and the protection of Saavedra Island. "The Gold River band has lost a kid too," he said, finally able to take his eyes away from the windshield long enough to glance at Walker. "Probably that boy you were talking about."

"What? Jackson's grandson?"

Dan could feel Walker's eyes boring into the back of his head. "Jackson's the name of that man you were talking to on the float, right? The guy on that old boat?"

"Yeah. He was looking for Darrel. His grandson."

Dan nodded. "Couple of fishermen found a floater—a body—in the water just outside Kyuquot. It was a kid, maybe thirteen or fourteen years old. The coroner said he hadn't been in the water long. Guess the guys up there knew about the blood we found, put two and two together, and asked her—the coroner—whether he could have drifted up from Nootka Island, and she said that would be about right." Dan glanced at Walker again. "They checked the blood. It was a match."

"Ah, goddamn it." Walker sighed. "Gonna break Jackson's heart. He really loved that kid."

Dreamspeaker forged ahead, her big diesels rumbling steadily below.

"Mike tell you how he died?"

"Yes," Dan answered. "He was stabbed."

From the corner of his eye, Dan saw Walker turn to stare out the window.

"Jesus, you're just full of good news, aren't you?"

It was Dan's turn to give a short bark of laughter.

"Oh, it gets better. He gave the case to me."

Walker's head snapped back.

"He put you back on the force? He can do that?"

Dan shrugged. "He says he can. I'm not so sure. I'm gonna call the guy in charge of the north island. See what he says."

"Better call him pretty quick then. The kids at the camp aren't going to want to go out with a bunch of cops."

Dan swung the wheel to turn the boat into Tahsis Inlet. Both the wind and the sea were quieter in the narrow channel.

"There's not going to be a bunch of cops, no matter what happens. That's why they want me back—they don't have anyone else. Only difference would be that I could call in for advice, maybe ask for air surveillance, stuff like that." He paused and then added, "And I could wear a weapon. That might be a good thing. Mike said we might have a 'nasty customer' up here."

"No surprise there," Walker said. "The guy's already killed a kid and kidnapped a woman."

"Yeah," Dan agreed. "Which means asking any kids to get involved is a seriously bad idea, so maybe we should skip Esperanza."

Walker shook his head. "You going to go out there on the trail by yourself?"

Dan looked at him. "I don't know. I guess I have to. It should be okay. I'm pretty fit and I've got good rain gear."

"Yeah," Walker replied. "I guess you might be fine. You might even find the trail, although Sanford said it's pretty tough to find from the Louie Lagoon end. But you might not. And even if you do, you might get lost farther down. Or you might get caught by the tide on one of the beaches. Or get swept out by one of the rivers. One thing for sure is you'll be slow. These kids live here. It's their island. They know where the trail is. They've been on it fifty times, maybe a hundred. They know where to find food. They know the beaches and the tides. They know where to cross the rivers. And they can move fast. They won't try to catch the guy. They're not stupid. They'll just find out where he is. And they'll be just another group of hikers as far as he's concerned."

It was the longest speech Dan had ever heard Walker make, and in many ways it made perfect sense. But like most of the ideas Walker came up with, it put Dan in a very bad position. Even as a civilian, it didn't feel right to involve a bunch of kids in something as dangerous as this could be. And if he really was back on the force, there was no way in hell he could sanction it. On the other hand, it was a public trail, and if Walker and his friends wanted to pursue it, there was nothing Dan could do to stop them. He had learned that lesson last year as well. It was Walker who had taught it to him.

"So how old are these kids?"

Walker shrugged. "Old enough."

"Gee, thanks," Dan replied. "That really helps."

"You going to make that call anytime soon?" Walker asked. "We're making pretty good time. Be in Esperanza in half an hour."

► E L E V E N ◄

► The wind dropped as *Dreamspeaker* entered Tahsis Inlet and moved into the lee of Nootka Island, but the waves were still steep and high. Dan waited until the sea had calmed a bit before he called Gary Markleson. The commander of the north island answered on the first ring.

"Been expecting to hear from you," he said as soon as Dan introduced himself. "Where are you?"

"I'm in Tahsis Inlet, heading for Louie Bay. Might not make it if the weather kicks up in Esperanza Inlet, but I'll give it a try."

"You going to go on the trail?" Markleson asked.

"I'm not sure," Dan answered. "I guess I need to know where I stand with you before I make that decision."

"My information is that you've been remounted. You're back on the force. Same rank as before. I can't tell you all the details because I haven't received them yet, but I do know you're officially on loan to me from Victoria. I've got both a fax and an e-mail confirming that. Signature at the bottom of the e-mail is Mike Bryant, CO down at the south end—I think you know him? And the fax is from the desk of the big man himself. The deputy commissioner."

Dan shook his head and stared out through the windshield as Tsowwin River slid past. He felt disoriented, off-balance, a part of him steering up a narrow, rain-streaked inlet on the western edge of Canada, and a part of him back down with his old squad in Victoria.

Nothing felt real; not the lighthouse with its missing woman, not the body up near Kyuquot, and certainly not this conversation.

"You still there?"

Markleson's voice brought him back to the present.

"Yeah. So what's with this body?"

Dan listened as Markleson gave him the details. The kid's name was—or had been—Darrel Mack, fourteen years old, from Gold River. Dan heard Walker swear as he heard the confirmation he had been dreading. The boy had been stabbed and put in the water somewhere around the Nootka light. The Gold River detachment was contacting the family, but there was already a confirmed identification.

"You got a coroner's report yet?" Dan asked.

"Got a prelim. I can e-mail it to you. The final won't be ready till the end of the week."

"Okay. So what's the word on this 'nasty customer' Mike mentioned to me? You know anything about that?"

"Oh yes," Markleson replied. "In fact, it may be more than one."

"Jesus! You running a bad-guy convention up here or something?"

"Certainly seems like we're pretty popular with the wrong crowd right now," Markleson said. "If you like, I can send you all the background details plus some photos."

"Sounds good," Dan said. "But maybe just give me a quick rundown now, so I know what I'm looking at. I'll be turning into Esperanza Inlet pretty quick here and I'll need to get off the line."

"Sure." Dan heard the rustle of paper as Markleson looked for whatever he needed. "Yesterday the Tahsis detachment picked up two guys who were released from the federal pen down at William Head a month or so ago. Victoria put out an APB for them after some high-end gallery was broken into, a guard was knocked unconscious, and a bunch of jewelry was taken—pretty fancy stuff worth a lot of money. Seems these guys had made a career out of that kind of thing, so they were the obvious suspects."

"Okay," said Dan. A conviction on a robbery charge could certainly earn a stay in William Head, but it wasn't anything of concern to him, and it didn't necessarily account for the "nasty customer" label. "Anything else?"

"Oh yes, there's more. Seems like at least one of them has a real taste for beating up anyone who happens to be around at the time. Very handy with a length of pipe, among other things. He's put several people in hospital and bruised up quite a few others. No record of using a knife, and no one died of their injuries—at least, no one that we know of—but it sounds like that might have been mostly luck."

"Huh. What time did our guys pick them up?"

"Early. They were at the gas station outside of town, on the Gold River road. There are a couple of rooms there that the truckers sometimes use. Not exactly five-star accommodation, but I guess it's a bed."

"Do the guys in Tahsis still have them there?" Dan asked.

"Yes, but not for long. Victoria sent a couple of guys up to question them, but there's really nothing to hold them on. No sign of the missing stuff, no tools, no weapons. Nothing. And they're saying they're up here looking for work. It's a long way to come to look for a job, and there's not much going around here, so that seems pretty unlikely, but one of them, Carl Rainer—he's the one who likes to do the beating—does have a family connection in the area, so I guess it's possible. Anyway, they've served their time, so there's not much we can do. They'll be out on the street again by tomorrow morning, maybe even later tonight. I've asked Tahsis to keep an eye on them but that's it. Rainer has an uncle that lives in Kyuquot so the work thing might be real."

"Okay, send me their stuff," Dan said. "I'll have a look at it and get back to you."

He ended the call and glanced at Walker. "You okay?"

"Yeah. I'll call Sanford from the camp. Let him know about Darrel."

Dan nodded. "Couldn't have been those guys that did that. No way they could have gotten over to Tahsis fast enough—and even if they did, no way they would want to hang around."

"Yeah."

The two men fell silent and the cabin filled with the sibilant discord of rushing wind and restless water. A Thayer's gull soared across the channel ahead of the boat, black wing tips outstretched, caught in a fast-moving current of air. Dan let his eyes follow its passage as it sailed above the dark cedars lining the shores and disappeared from sight. The tops of the trees were tossing in the wind, the branches moving in a frenzied dance. He checked the chart again. The weather would allow them to reach Esperanza, but they weren't going to get any farther. As soon as they passed Zeballos Inlet, they would be exposed to the full fury of the wind.

"No way we're going to be able to reach Louie Bay until this eases off," he yelled to Walker, nodding toward the trees. "The wind will be dead ahead once we make the turn out of Esperanza. Might have to hole up there and wait until it blows over." A rumble of thunder and a vivid flash of lightning gave emphasis to his words.

Walker grunted an acknowledgment. "Kw-Uhnx-Wa is angry," he said.

"What?" asked Dan. "Who the hell is Kwu . . . whatever?"

"Thunderbird," Walker replied. "Lightning Snake is his friend. You should listen to him."

It was Dan's turn to grunt.

▶ A narrow ribbon of water opened up to port, its northern shore dotted with the decaying remains of buildings. There had once been a thriving village with a cannery and a fish-reduction plant located there, but it had long ago disappeared, its name replaced on the chart by the symbol for "ruins." Dan had seen that same word printed on many of his west-coast charts, and it never failed to move him, in a way he couldn't fully understand. Nostalgia, maybe. Some forgotten memory passed down to him years ago. "Ruins" usually pointed to the fading relics of a lifestyle he had barely glimpsed on the few fishing trips he had been able to share with his father, but it had engendered a passion and fervor in the man that still resonated with his son. Dan swung the wheel and turned *Dreamspeaker* into Esperanza Inlet, feeling the boat heel to starboard as the wind picked up.

"They're not going to be able to work in this," he said.

"You talking about your crowd or mine?" Walker asked.

"Mine," Dan answered. "They usually bring in dogs and a helicopter for something like this, but there won't be any scent left for the dogs,

73

and the helicopter wouldn't be able to get off the ground. Even the search and rescue boys won't be able to go out until this is over."

"Huh," said Walker. "Guess it's a good thing us Indians are such savages. We don't mind getting wet."

Dan glanced across at him. "You're not still thinking about asking these kids to head out there, are you? They'd have to be crazy! It's impossible."

"Might be for your lot. Mine might be thinking differently."

Dan didn't bother answering. There was nothing he could say, and he didn't think it would be an issue anyway. There was no way anyone was going to get across to the other side of the inlet, let alone hike through the bush to the trail.

▶ Half an hour later, Walker leaned forward and pointed through the window to where the square shapes of buildings were starting to emerge from the gloom. "Pull in to that second wharf. The small one," he shouted, fighting to make himself heard over the sounds of the storm.

Both men had been silent as Dan fought to make headway against the wind and the waves, and Walker's voice seemed to reverberate through the wheelhouse.

The tiny community of Esperanza slowly appeared through the sweeping curtains of rain. It was an odd collection of both very new and very old houses, scattered haphazardly across a flat outcropping of land that protruded from the base of a massive rock face. A large lodge with a glass front sat right on the water near the head of a high wharf, but farther away, on the other side of the point, Dan could glimpse smaller houses and another, lower wharf jutting out into the water. That was where Walker was pointing.

"Might not have enough depth over there," Dan shouted. "I'm going to have to go past and drift down on it. No way I can come in from this side."

"What does she draw?" Walker asked, nodding down toward the deck.

"Fifteen feet," Dan answered. "And the tide's falling."

"Might be a problem," Walker agreed. "Better use this first one then. I know the water's deep there. The guys will be watching for us anyway. They'll figure it out."

They were both quiet as Dan battled the weather in order to make a wide circle upwind of the wharf. *Dreamspeaker* heeled and wallowed as he turned her broadside to the wind, but then the motion eased as he nosed her behind the point, coming dangerously close to the shore before swinging her bow back out. If he had to leave for any reason, he wanted to make it as easy as possible. He briefly put her into reverse to stop her forward motion, and then the wind caught her again and pushed her sideways onto the wharf. Dan shrugged into his rain gear, went out on deck, led out some extra lines both fore and aft, and then started to climb over the railing. A voice stopped him.

"Need a hand?"

Three men were standing below him. He hadn't seen any of them approach. Two were Native, and the third, who stood a little apart, was white—almost as white as Jens, his pale hair just visible above his pale face, which was framed by the hood of his rain jacket. It was one of the Native men who had spoken.

"Thanks," Dan answered. "Maybe tie those lines straight across. I'm going to set up some springs to keep her off."

The man nodded and wrapped the forward line around a cleat, gesturing for his partner to do the same with the stern line. "You got a passenger with you?" he asked.

Dan nodded. "That would be Walker. You want to come on board? He's up in the wheelhouse."

Dan walked back to the stern and opened the gate, standing aside as the two men climbed the ladder onto the deck.

"Sam." The older of the two held out his hand in greeting. "This is Jared."

"Welcome aboard. Why don't you go on forward while I get the spring lines rigged. I think Walker's waiting for you."

Sam nodded, and the two men started across the deck while Dan climbed down onto the wharf.

"Welcome to Esperanza." It was the white guy's turn.

"Thanks," said Dan, extending his hand as he introduced himself.

"Reverend Steven," the man replied. "Are you a friend of Sam's?"

"Never met him before. Why?"

"Oh, nothing. It's just that he doesn't often come over here. Certainly not to greet people."

"He doesn't live here?"

"Not really. He and Jared have a camp somewhere back in the woods. We see them occasionally, of course—they sometimes use the wharf—but they keep pretty much to themselves."

"Huh," said Dan. "So these houses here are all private?"

"They all belong to Esperanza Ministries. We use them in the service of the Lord."

"Ministries?" Dan asked. "For some reason I thought this was a hospital."

Reverend Steven smiled, although it was more like a grimace as his thin lips stretched back across his gaunt face. "There used to be a hospital. The Esperanza Mission Hospital. Dr. McLean started it back in 1937, but it closed many years ago. Now we offer counseling and crisis intervention, and in summer we run youth camps." The information was given in a curiously singsong tone, as if it was something learned by rote. There was a pause, and then the man turned away and gestured toward the jumbled community. "It's a place where people can learn about the Creator."

"And you're the director?" Dan asked. There was something about the reverend that bothered him. The man seemed too uptight and formal to be the director of a remote mission that offered counseling and youth camps.

"No, not at all. I'm only here in a temporary capacity. The director—you'll meet him if you stay for a few days—was called away on a medical emergency."

Dan nodded. That made sense. "So Sam and Jared run one of the camps?"

"Oh no. No. They're not associated with us in any way." The answer came almost too fast, and Dan thought there was a definite note of disapproval there.

Reverend Steven quickly changed the subject. "Are you planning on staying long?"

"I'm not sure," Dan answered. "Am I okay here for a couple of days?"

"Of course. We always welcome visitors. Will any of Jared's people be joining you?"

Again Dan thought he caught a hint of—was it disapproval or just concern?

"Maybe, although probably not—or at least not for long."

"I see. Well then, I will leave you to your guests. You're welcome to come up to the lodge later on. We gather there after our evening meal. We have some musicians among us who like to share their gifts in celebration of the Lord."

"Thanks," Dan said. "I appreciate the offer."

▶ Walker had moved to the cabin, and he and his friends were sitting around the table. All of them turned to look at Dan as he stepped inside and took off his rain gear.

"The Reverend Steven stay ashore?" Sam asked. His gray hair was pulled back and tied with a wide leather thong, and he wore a buckskin vest over a heavy denim shirt and faded blue jeans. Dan guessed he was in his late sixties, but he could have been older. He spoke with a soft voice and the slurred, glottal sounds that suggested he was more at home speaking his traditional language.

"Yeah," Dan answered. "He invited me up to the lodge after dinner to celebrate the Lord and praise the Creator. I'm sure you would be welcome too."

"The Reverend Steven and I have different Creators," Sam answered, smiling to take the sting out of his words. "We honor them in different ways."

"Odd kind of guy for a missionary," Dan said. "Seemed to be wound pretty tight."

"He only likes tame Indians." Jared spoke for the first time, and there was no mistaking the hostility. "Gotta worship at the white man's shrine."

Dan looked at him, taking in the scars on both his neck and hands, and the tattooed knuckles. He didn't think Jared was much older than Walker, but he looked like he had spent some hard time in a hard place.

"Sounds like you don't like the man very much."

Jared shrugged. "I guess he's doing his job. Be better when the other guys get back."

Sam and Walker both nodded in agreement.

"Yeah. Sanford told me Earl and his people do some great work here," Walker said. He looked at Dan. "Earl's the guy that runs this place." He smiled. "You tell the Reverend Steven you're a cop?"

Dan shrugged. "Nope. Didn't think he needed to know—and I don't know that I can really say I'm back on the force anyway. Don't have a badge. Don't have anything but a phone number I can call. Why?"

"Sam here was telling me that ol' Steven heard the call of his Creator while he was serving time for beating up a couple of kids. Native kids, as it happens. Guess the parole board liked the fact that he had seen the light and let him out early."

Dan looked at the three faces across from him. Three pairs of black eyes looked back at him, expressionless, waiting to see what his reaction would be. He looked out at the wharf, empty and rain swept. What Walker had told him fit with his impression of the man he had just met. He had felt there was something not quite right with the Reverend Steven. "Do they have kids here?" he asked.

"Not at this time of year. They will later, when the camps start up," Sam said.

"Earl know about this?"

"No way. Earl wouldn't have let him off the boat if he'd known his history. Earl had to leave in a hurry, so he just took whomever the home office sent to him. We'll have a chat with him when he gets back. Ask him to phone and check the reverend out."

Dan nodded. "When did he get here?"

"Four days ago," Sam answered. "They sent the mission boat down to Gold River to pick him up."

"Huh." Dan glanced across at Walker. The timing meant the reverend couldn't have been at Friendly Cove, but that didn't mean he couldn't have been involved in some way.

"I just might phone and check him out myself. There seems to be way too many bad guys up here right now." He stood up. "And I need to make a few calls anyway. I'll be up in the wheelhouse if you need me. Help yourselves to coffee, and I think there's still some juice in the fridge."

TWELVE

▶ The staff sergeant who answered the phone said Gary Markleson was out. Dan left a message to say he had called and would call back later. Next on his list was Mike, who for once was in.

"So exactly how official am I?" Dan asked him. "Do I have a badge number, or is this just you trying to get me to work for free?"

Mike laughed. "Well, I would have if I could have, but I know you too well to try that. No, this is official. You have the same badge number as before. It's just been reactivated. They're gonna courier it up to Markleson—he might already have it by now—and he'll send it out to you with one of his guys."

"Hmm. So who would I call to find out more about the robbery they were looking at those two guys for? The two they picked up in Tahsis."

"That would be downtown Victoria. Guy named Hathaway. You thinking they might be good for the kid?"

"Nope. I'm thinking about the totem."

"The totem?" Mike's voice conveyed both surprise and confusion. "What totem?"

"The old totem at Yuquot. Someone hacked it to pieces the same night the woman went missing and the kid was killed. I've been trying to figure out how it's connected."

"Hell, maybe it isn't connected," Mike replied. "Might just have been some tourist with a hard-on."

"Don't think so. And there weren't any tourists. Place was empty except for the people on the lighthouse."

"Huh. Well, give Hathaway a call. He'll be able to fill you in."

"I'll do that," Dan replied. "And you can check out the Reverend Steven for me."

"Who the hell is the Reverend Steven?" Mike asked. "And how do you find these people? Who was it last year? Annie and Toothless Tom were their names, as I recall."

Dan laughed. "Yeah. Good folks those—at least, Annie is. Tom's crazy as a loon, but he's harmless. I'm not sure I can say the same about the Reverend Steven though."

"Okay, I'll check him out for you and let you know as soon as I find out anything," Mike said, then ended the call.

Dan's third call was to Claire. He listened to the phone ringing and was about to hang up when she finally answered.

"Dan! You almost missed me. I'm just heading off to yet another meeting. I think this must be about the tenth one with the same department! Just different people. Where are you?"

Dan leaned back in his chair, enjoying the sound of her voice as he looked at the rivulets of rain coursing down the windshield. "Esperanza," he answered.

"Esperanza? Is there anything there? I thought the old hospital closed down."

"It did," he replied. "It's some kind of mission now. They give counseling sessions and put on youth camps and stuff."

Claire laughed. "Are you in need of a counseling session? I'll be up there in a few days, and I'm pretty good at pillow talk."

Dan smiled, feeling a surge of warmth run through his veins. "Yes, you are, and you're very good at a lot of other things too—although a few more days is a long time to wait. I may need more than just pillow talk to calm me down."

He could hear the smile in her voice. "Ummm. I think I know of something that might help."

"Really? I wonder what that could be."

They discussed some therapeutic possibilities and variations for a while and then got back to Claire's arrival in Kyuquot.

"Your meetings going okay?" Dan asked.

"Yes. Better than I expected, even though there are an awful lot of them. But that's government bureaucracy, and I should be used to it by now. There's no way around it. And I've got the seaworthiness approval on the boat. I'll be picking up the certificate. the day after tomorrow. After that it's just the sign-off and I'll be on the road."

"So no holdups?"

"Can't see any, unless it's the weather. I heard there's a storm out there. Is it really bad?" she asked. "Are you safe in Esperanza?"

"Sure. I'm actually just sitting here at the wharf with Walker, waiting it out."

"Walker? Our Walker? He's there?"

"Yep. Our Walker, and yes, he's here. He's out in the salon talking with two of his friends."

"That's unbelievable! Where on earth did you meet up with him?"

Dan explained, but he didn't fill her in on why Walker had come up to Esperanza with him. That could wait for later. He also didn't tell her about the murdered kid or the fact that he was—at least temporarily—back with the RCMP. He wanted to tell her all of that face-to-face, not over a telephone line. It was going to be an interesting conversation, and it was not one he was looking forward to. He had no idea how she would react.

▶ Dan checked his watch. He knew he should call Hathaway, but he figured it was time to join the conversation in the salon. He got there just in time. Sam and Jared looked like they were about ready to leave.

"Sorry I took so long," Dan said as he sat down across from them. "Walker fill you in?"

There were nods all around.

"Darrel was a good kid," Sam said. "His granddad brought him over to a couple of the summer camps here, but Darrel didn't like them. Kept coming over to us. Wanted to learn how to track, how to find food. He was learning about plants: which ones were good to eat and which ones to leave alone. Even tried chewing up some cedar bark so he could weave his own hat."

Jared gave a harsh bark of laughter. "Almost broke his leg clumping around on those damn hunks of bark he tied to his feet that time. Said they were his Indian sandals. Looked more like a pair of old snowshoes."

Sam nodded again, a quiet smile on his face as he let the memories linger, then looked at Dan, his gaze suddenly flat and hard.

"So you think this guy on the trail is the one who killed Darrel?" he asked.

Dan shook his head. "We don't know for sure there is a guy on the trail. All we know is that a woman is missing from the lighthouse and that Darrel was probably killed down on the beach at the cove. Walker and I saw a trail of footprints through the grass . . . he must have told you all this already?"

"Yeah, he did. Seems like when you put it all together, whoever killed the kid must have taken the woman and dragged her onto the trail."

"It's certainly a possibility. But we have the folks up at the light keeping an eye out for anybody coming off the trail at that end, and I'm planning on heading over to Louie Lagoon as soon as this storm eases up, so I'll be able to see anybody coming off at this end." Dan looked out the window and frowned. It was so dark outside it looked like the middle of the night rather than late afternoon. "The police are already looking for the woman. They'll send up a chopper as soon as this storm quits, and maybe put a boat out to check the beaches. And I'm going to talk to the guys in Tahsis and Gold River as well. Tell them to check anyone calling for a water taxi or floatplane. If they're on the trail, we'll find them."

He let his gaze linger on each man in turn, trying to read their faces and hoping he had been convincing enough to prevent anyone from trying to tackle the trail himself. They all remained quiet, their faces expressionless.

Sam broke the silence first. "Sounds good," he said as he rose to his feet. He looked at Walker. "You gonna be staying with Dan here for a while?"

Walker nodded and glanced over at Dan. "Yeah. Unless he throws me out."

Dan looked at him and smiled before he turned back to Sam and Jared. "Walker's always welcome to stay. You guys are too, if you want to. It's pretty nasty out there."

Sam nodded. "Appreciate the offer, but we need to be going. Might see you tomorrow if you're still here."

Dan watched as the two men put on black rain jackets and disappeared into the dark curtain of rain, and then he turned to Walker. "They're not going to try going on the trail in this, are they?" he asked.

"Don't know," Walker answered. "Guess they'll go back and talk about it. Make their own decision."

Dan looked out across the deck. "No way to get over there anyway," he said, speaking more to himself than Walker.

▶ The gloom outside showed no sign of lifting and the rain continued to beat its incessant percussion on the cabin roof. Dan got himself a beer, left Walker poking through his CD collection, and was heading back to the wheelhouse when the radio came to life. It was Mary at the lighthouse.

"Hey, Mary, what's up?"

"Two things. We had a group of people come off the trail. Two couples. They're cold and wet and tired, but they're in pretty good shape. They're up here waiting for a water taxi to pick them up."

"They see anyone heading the other way?"

"No. They said they didn't see another soul the whole time they were out there."

"Huh. Okay. What's the second thing?"

"The Gold River police called. There was a boat stolen from there a few days ago. The owner doesn't know exactly when, because he hadn't checked it for a few days, but it probably fits with Margrethe's disappearance. Anyway, they found it washed up on Bligh Island, across from Resolution Cove. That's right across the sound from here. They said the fuel was turned off and the tank was more than half full, so it looks like maybe it drifted there on its own."

They chatted for a few more minutes and then said goodbye. Dan clicked the microphone off and tried to sort the new pieces into the puzzle, but he still couldn't make them fit. The stolen boat might explain how Margrethe's abductor arrived, but the footprints said they didn't leave that way. Maybe that had been the original plan, but with her fear of boats and water she would have resisted, and controlling her as well as starting and steering a boat would have been difficult, if not impossible. So that might account for the footprints leading toward the trail, and if the boat had simply been left on the beach, it could have floated away on the rising tide, which would account for the fuel being turned off and the half-full tank. But where did the Native kid—Darrel—fit in? And the desecrated totem? He shook his head. He was still missing something, and he needed to find out what it was before more bodies washed up around Kyuquot. Maybe the guys down in Victoria could help.

Hathaway was out of his office, but it didn't take long to track him down.

"You put out an APB on a couple of guys you thought might be good for a robbery," Dan said once he had him on the phone. "They were found up in Tahsis yesterday, and you sent someone up to question them."

"Yeah," Hathaway answered. "We got nothing. We're going to have to kick them loose—and that really pisses me off—but there's nothing to hold them on. Seemed like their kind of job, but maybe I was wrong. Why? You find something?"

"Nope. I'm working on something else. Just thought maybe there was a link," Dan said. "Seems odd they headed up this way. There's nothing up here. Nowhere to get rid of anything but junk, and I was told it was pretty high-end stuff that was missing."

"You could say that," Hathaway drawled. "Ever hear of Bill Reid?"

"That the artist? The Haida guy who did that big sculpture over at Vancouver International Airport?"

"Yeah. It's called *The Jade Canoe*. He did that and a lot more."

"So someone stole some sculptures? Those would be pretty hard to move," Dan said. "Can't see them leaving the city."

"It wasn't the big stuff," Hathaway said. "Reid was into a lot of things: sculpture, carving, painting, but mostly jewelry. Gold and silver bracelets and rings and stuff like that. That's what was taken. A bunch of jewelry. Could have fit it all into a small bag."

"Huh. So anything show up yet?"

"Nope. Not a sign—and it's been over a week. Got all our ears out and there's a pretty big reward, but it's like it disappeared into a black hole."

"You think it was a special-order job?" Dan asked. If it had been, then not only was the stuff gone, but there would be no possible link to Nootka. No one on the island would have the desire or the means to buy a collection of high-end jewelry.

"Could have been, I guess," Hathaway answered. "But it would have been a hell of a lot easier to just buy it from the gallery."

"True," said Dan. "So these guys you were looking at. They always work together?"

"Pretty well, at least in the last few years. Patrick Kevin Sleeman and Carl Jakob Rainer are their names. Sleeman's the brains. Rainer's the muscle. Sleeman used to work with another guy, Jerry Coffman, but that was a long time ago. Jerry was a nasty little bastard. Mean as a rattlesnake but not as smart. Guess there was a falling-out and Jerry struck out on his own. We picked him up on a manslaughter charge a few years ago and sent him off to William Head for a spell."

"William Head?" Dan asked. "Isn't that where the other two were? Sleeman and Rainer?"

"Yeah," answered Hathaway. "Now that I think of it, it was. Just give me a minute and I'll see if our friend Jerry is back out on the street. You thinking they might have joined up again?"

"I don't know," Dan said as he listened to the tapping of a keyboard. "I'm just trying to put a whole bunch of pieces into the pot and shake 'em up. See if anything falls out."

The tapping stopped. "Well, look at this. I guess it's possible. Says here Jerry's been out almost four months."

The two men fell silent as they thought about the possibilities. It was Dan who spoke first.

"So how much was it worth?" he asked.

"The jewelry? Glad you asked," Hathaway said, and Dan heard the sound of paper rustling as the detective searched for the figures. "Here we go. One gold killer whale pin, eighty-five thou. One gold bracelet, sixty-five thou. One set of silver cuff links, eighteen thou. One brooch, silver, fourteen thou. Two gold rings . . . you want it all?"

"Jesus!" Dan said. "Just give me the total."

"About half a million," Hathaway replied. "Give or take."

► THIRTEEN ◄

► Dan asked Hathaway to send him a copy of the file on Jerry Coffman and then called Gary Markleson again. This time he was in.

"You still got those two guys there? Sleeman and Rainer?" Dan asked.

"Yeah, but we're just about to kick them loose. Why?"

"Any chance you could get one of your guys to ask them a question? Nothing to do with the robbery. It's about another guy Sleeman worked with a few years ago. I just want to know if they've seen him recently or know where he might be."

"We can try. No guarantee they'll talk to us though. Who's the guy?"

Dan gave him the name. He wasn't too hopeful it would result in anything, but he had to find some thread somewhere that he could pick loose.

"I'll call you back if we get lucky," Markleson said and hung up.

Dan wandered back through the cabin. The door to the aft deck was open and he could see Walker sitting under the overhang. He went out and joined him, and the two men sat together in companionable silence, peering out into the rain. Out here, it didn't look like the solid sheet of gray it had appeared to be from the wheelhouse. Darker streaks undulated through the saturated air, and the sound of raindrops hitting the water ebbed and swelled above the slap of the waves. The rhythmic percussion it created was almost hypnotic, and Dan felt himself relax as he let himself drift along with it. He could actually smell the rain, he realized. Not the sharp ozone scent that came when it first started, and not the rich loamy smell of wet earth that came later. This was different. It was the smell of rain itself: clean, fresh, laced with an elemental tang that was oddly invigorating.

A strange snuffling intruded into his consciousness, loud enough to be heard above the rain and the waves, and he turned his head to see a river otter appear on the wharf beside the boat. It was quickly followed by another.

"Might have to build an ark if this keeps up," Dan said.

Walker shook his head. "Nah. I'll just tie my canoe to a mountaintop. Worked for my ancestors in the great flood."

Dan laughed. "There's not much room for animals in a canoe."

"Don't need room," Walker answered, a quiet smile on his face. "Kanekaluk will take care of them."

"Kanekaluk?" asked Dan. "Is he another one of your spirits?"

"Yep. The Transformer. Comes from the Upper World. Gigame' Kana'l, the Creator, sent him to warn the people about the great flood. He's the one who gave Raven and Otter and Gull and all the rest of them the ability to take off their masks."

"Was Lightning Snake one of them?" Dan asked.

"Nope. Lightning Snake is Thunderbird's friend. Thunderbird carries him around under his wings. Uses him to catch whales—and people, if they piss him off enough."

Dan shook his head. "Hell. I'll never be able to remember all that stuff."

Walker looked at him. "Doesn't matter. You don't have to. They're not your ancestors or your stories." He chuckled. "But you might want to keep an open mind."

Dan nodded. He had learned that lesson last year when he spent some time with Walker. It was one he hoped he would never forget. He turned away to watch the rain again. "Yeah. You're right. I'll do that."

▶ They sat for a while longer, until hunger drove Dan back inside. He took some frozen ravioli out of the freezer, put it in a pot of water, and set it on the stove. Walker made his way inside just as Dan was heating up a can of tomato sauce to go with it.

"You always eat frozen stuff like that?" he asked as he watched Dan pour the sauce over the squares of pasta.

"What? You don't like ravioli?" Dan asked.

"Ravioli's fine. It just seems odd to eat frozen food when there's fresh all around you."

"Fresh? What're you talking about? There's no store within miles. Not even a town. And I don't see any orchards or market gardens anywhere out there."

Walker eased himself down onto the settee and gestured at the porthole. "Salmon. Halibut. Rockfish. Sea cucumber. Oysters. Mussels. Clams. Kelp. Herring. Herring roe. Ferns. Horsetail shoots. Camas root. Berries." He sucked in a long breath of air. "It's a restaurant out there. Best food in the world and it's all free."

"That's easy for you to say. I don't know how to even recognize most of those things, let alone find them and cook them."

"So what happens if your freezer quits?"

"I open a can." Dan brought over the two plates and slid them onto the table. "That's where this sauce comes from."

Walker shook his head. "Hope you never run out of cans."

"Jesus!" Dan stared across the table at his guest. "You said I talked too much? Shut up and eat."

Walker laughed and complied. The two men were almost finished their meal when the radio came to life again.

▶ "So we asked Sleeman and Rainer about Jerry Coffman like you wanted," Markleson said as soon as Dan answered. "Seems our two princes not only know the man, but claim they saw him recently. They were very willing to tell us about it, too. Let me read you what they said. I've got a copy of the notes our guys took."

Dan heard some papers rustling.

"Here we go," said Markleson. "This is from Sleeman. 'Sure I know Jerry. He was in William Head same time as me, but he got out before I did. Carl and I ran into him a few days ago in Gold River. Couldn't believe it, but there he was, large as life. He was having a coffee in this coffee place we went into. Said he was heading over to Moutcha Bay to take some stuff over to some friends.'"

"Moutcha Bay?" Dan asked. "Where's that?"

"Just east of Nootka Island," Markleson answered. "There's a fishing lodge there. You can drive in to it from Gold River."

"You think this guy Jerry is likely to have friends over at a fishing resort?"

"Nope. Not if he's a friend of these two. Moutcha Bay's a pretty nice place. It's almost new. Only been there a couple of years, and I know the guy that built it. Nice guy. He runs a very tight ship and he's very picky with his staff. He would have done any new hiring over the winter and checked them out very, very well." He was quiet for a minute, then added, "Plus this is the start of the high season, and he would have been booked solid for months now. No way our friend Jerry would know anyone over there. He's only been out of William Head for four months; I checked. Sleeman was telling the truth about that. Jerry got out ahead of both him and Rainer. The guy I talked to at the detachment down in Victoria said Jerry Coffman's got a file three inches thick: robbery, assault, manslaughter, you name it. Apparently, he's very quick with a knife. They think he might be good for at least a couple of murders, but they could never prove it so the most he got was manslaughter."

"Yeah. That's what they told me too," Dan said. "Those guys you've got there said they saw Jerry in Gold River?"

"Yeah. Seems kind of odd they'd all be in Gold River, doesn't it? I can ask the guys over there to check and see if there's any record of them at one of the hotels—although Sleeman and Rainer would've had to pass through there to get to Tahsis, so they may have just stopped for a coffee on the way."

"They got any millionaires hanging out in Gold River? Anyone who might be interested in half a million dollars' worth of fancy jewelry?"

Markleson laughed. "Not likely. The town almost died when the pulp mill closed a few years back. Still got some logging, and they get a good few tourists for that supply boat that's based there, but there's a hell of a lot of empty houses and very few jobs."

"Huh," said Dan. "Seems like something must have brought those three over to this side of the island. Any chance you can get someone to send some mugshots over to Gold River and Moutcha Bay and show them around? See if anybody has seen these guys hanging around?"

"Sure. You thinking they're working together?"

"Be a pretty big coincidence if they just happened to head out here at the same time, and we already know they all have a fondness for artwork. The Bill Reid jewelry would certainly count as their kind of stuff, and if there was no trace of it when you picked up Sleeman and Rainer, then maybe we should be looking at Coffman—and I think he might be the guy we're looking for over on Nootka Island too. The one who killed the kid, and maybe took the woman."

As he said the words, Dan felt a familiar spark of electricity ripple across the synapses in his brain. The excitement of the hunt was starting to build. For the first time since he had arrived at Nootka and learned of Margrethe's disappearance, the pieces of the puzzle were starting to come together. They didn't all fit yet, but he could feel the pattern forming.

"You might want to tell your people in Tahsis to watch out for him too, although I have no idea why he would split from his buddies unless he was delivering the jewelry, and he certainly wouldn't be doing that over in Friendly Cove." Another thought struck him. "Unless he had set up a meet with a buyer there, although it doesn't seem likely. Not at that hour of the night. But you might want to check with the guy who runs Moutcha Bay. See if any of his customers took a late-night run or had any visitors."

"Will do," Markleson said. "I probably won't be able to catch him until around eight o'clock. He's usually down on the docks around now. Likes to welcome the guests back in and BS with them, and he always eats in the dining room. Says it helps repeat business if he gets to know his customers. But he goes back to his office after that. I'll catch him there. It'll be quicker than trying to send anyone over."

Dan thanked him and hung up. It was only six at night. He had two hours to wait. He went back into the cabin and sat back down. Walker was sprawled on the settee.

"You got any way to contact Sam or Jared?" Dan asked.

Walker shrugged. "Don't need to," he said.

"Yes, you do. They need to know who it is on the trail so they don't try and go out there."

"You figure you know who it is?"

"Yeah, and he could be dangerous."

"We already knew that. He killed Darrel."

"Walker, if I'm right, this guy has just been released from prison, and he's probably killed a few times before. We need to keep people off the trail till we get this sorted out. Once this weather clears, I'll get the dogs in there. Go in from both ends."

"Kids will have found him by then. You won't need the dogs."

"You're not listening. We have to make sure the kids don't go in."

Walker grinned. "Too late. They went in hours ago. Probably over near the head of the lagoon by now."

Dan stared at him. "That's not possible. They couldn't get across there in this weather."

"Why not? It's just rain and wind. They get a lot of that here. They're used to it." He reached into his jacket and pulled out a small two-way radio. "Sam called me right after they left."

▶ FOURTEEN ◀

▶ Leif Nielson drained the last few drops of beer from his glass and signaled the waiter for his bill. He had no desire to return to Kyuquot, but he couldn't delay it any longer. He'd been staying with an old friend, Pete McLintock, for the last couple of days, but to stay any longer would be to seriously overstay his welcome. Leif knew that Pete had been happy enough to see him when he had arrived in Tahsis two days ago, still cringing from that gruesome discovery over at Aktis Island. The man had greeted him warmly, listened to his story, fed him a meal of halibut and crab, and offered him the use of his couch for a couple of nights, but Pete was at heart a loner. He lived by himself in a small cabin set back in the bush on the outskirts of town, and that was the way he liked it. This morning he had started hinting that two nights were enough, and Leif knew better than to push him. It wouldn't be fair to Pete, and it would be the end of an old friendship. Besides, it wouldn't get him anywhere anyhow. It wasn't only that Pete needed his space. Leif needed to get back home. The fishing resort in Kyuquot would be counting on him to return to work. They would be short-staffed without him, and he couldn't—wouldn't—leave them stranded with the busiest time of the year just starting up.

He had hoped getting away for a few days would help him forget the image of those small, bleached, bloodless hands, and the undulating strands of black hair spread out on the water like some strange seaweed, but it was still with him. It intruded into his days and haunted his nights, vivid dreams of pale limbs and medusa-like heads waking him every time he drifted into a restless sleep. He was not sure he would ever be able to get it out of his memory.

He paid the waiter and left the restaurant. He figured he must be getting soft in his old age. He had seen death before. You couldn't live to his age without having it come to visit someone close to you, and you couldn't live on this coast without losing friends or even family to the sea: fishermen whose boats were swamped by rogue waves or driven ashore by the wind, others who were caught up in the nets or the machinery or who simply fell overboard, some who slipped from the rocks or lost their way. It happened. You simply went to the funeral, drank a few beers with those left behind, and got on with life. This should have been no different—except that it had been a kid, and that made all the difference in the world. He had known it was going to haunt him the second he realized what he was seeing in the water out there at Aktis. Knew it long before the police had brought the body ashore and asked him to look at it to see if he knew who it was—or who it had been, because there was no trace of life left in that empty face lying on the cold steel stretcher.

He made his way down to the float where he had left his boat. The worst of the storm had passed and the clouds were starting to lift, although the rain, which had eased to a steady drizzle, still obscured the inlet in a gray mist. He nodded to the two men who stood at the bottom of the ramp, clambered into the cockpit, and started to unsnap the cover. He would have to get fuel for the trip back, but with luck he would be at the Kyuquot dock by midafternoon.

"You heading over to Nootka Island?" The voice caught him by surprise. He had been too caught up with his memories to hear anyone coming.

"Nope," he replied, turning to see the two men he had passed just minutes before. "Kyuquot."

"Any chance you could drop us off? We'll pay you for your trouble."

Leif looked at them. They were an odd-looking pair, one dark-haired and slightly built, with sharp features and alert blue eyes, the other much taller, wide and solid, with a dull, unblinking stare. He had never seen either one of them before, and he didn't think they looked like locals. Pretty well everyone in the area worked in logging or fishing or mining. Outside work. Hard physical labor. These guys were in pretty good shape, but their hands and faces were pale and smooth and spoke of a lot of time spent indoors. Government workers, maybe. Or bankers. Sat at desks all day and worked out in a gym.

"Nootka's a pretty big island," Leif answered. "Where do you want to go?"

"Flynn's Cove," answered the shorter of the two. "We're going to one of the cottages there for a few days. I don't think it would be far out of your way. Wouldn't take you long."

Leif nodded. "Yeah, that's true. It's not far. Almost on my way, really, so I guess I could get you there all right, but it's going to be a pretty rough trip. Wind's dropping, but the water's still pretty rough. You got any rain gear? And how about luggage? How long's it going to take you to get that?"

The man shook his head. "It's all over there at the cottage already. We were supposed to meet up with some friends, but we got here late and missed our ride. They've already taken everything over on the water taxi."

"Okay," said Leif. "But you're either going to be mighty uncomfortable or very wet and cold. Maybe both. I've been working on the boat. Got the cabin all stripped out, so there's no good place to sit except on the floor or out in the cockpit."

"We'll be fine," the man answered. "You leaving right away?"

"Yeah, pretty well," Leif replied. "Just got to get some fuel. You may as well come aboard now and we'll head over to the fuel dock."

"Thanks," the man said as he stepped aboard. "I'm Pat. This is my partner, Carl."

Leif nodded and shook the outstretched hand. "Leif," he said. "Make yourselves comfortable while I get sorted out."

▶ The old Campion made good time in the protected water of Tahsis Inlet, Leif letting the 150-horsepower stern-drive Volvo reach almost twenty knots as he steered down the narrow waterway. He slowed as he turned into Esperanza Inlet and moved into more open water. The wind had dropped and veered, but there were still gusts, and the waves, while not high, were steep and close together, making for an uncomfortable ride. His guests had chosen to stay in the cabin, which suited Leif just fine. He didn't mind making a few extra bucks, but he was in no mood to entertain two strangers.

The wharves at Esperanza were empty, and he quickly left them behind as he curved around the jutting finger of land across from Zeballos Inlet. The mist that had blanketed everything throughout the morning was almost gone, burned away by a pallid sun, and the air was full of birds eager to find whatever edible gifts the storm had left them. Gulls and terns circled overhead, soaring on wind currents as they uttered their harsh calls. Bald eagles perched along the shoreline or scavenged the beach. A patch of water off to his left boiled with sudden activity, glittering with light and stippled with the flash of tiny scales as a school of herring wheeled and darted in a futile attempt to avoid some unseen predator. He wondered if they had been driven in from the open ocean, just a few miles ahead. Maybe they had noticed that small body as it drifted up the coast, perhaps accompanied it on part of its journey . . .

He was thankful to have his reverie cut short when the two men emerged from the cabin.

"Where are we?" It was the man who had introduced himself as Pat, the same one who had done all the talking back on the dock in Tahsis. His friend still hadn't uttered a word. For all Leif knew, he might be deaf and mute.

"Just passed Zeballos Inlet," Leif answered. "Should be at Flynn's Cove in about half an hour. Maybe a little more."

"Not much traffic out here," the man said as he looked around. "Looks pretty well deserted."

"Not many people live around here," Leif answered. "Those that do usually use the inside passage. It's safer and easier—unless you live in Kyuquot, and then you don't have a choice."

"That where you live?" the man asked.

"Yeah. Lived there all my life," Leif answered.

"Huh. Well, I hope we haven't delayed you too much. Wouldn't want whoever's waiting for you to get worried."

"No one there to worry about me," Leif replied. "My wife died a few years back. Now it's just me."

"Sorry to hear that," the man said as he turned to his companion, who was sitting behind him in the cockpit. "We were just talking about heading up to Kyuquot to catch ourselves a nice salmon, right, Carl?" He reached down and picked up an old baseball bat that Leif kept in the cockpit to kill the fish he caught. "Must be some pretty big ones up there if you need this. What do you think, Carl?"

Leif felt the boat rock as the bigger man stood up. He caught a hint of sudden movement and heard a faint rushing sound. And then he heard and felt nothing at all.

▶ "You done?" Pat asked Carl. He had taken over the helm when Carl hit the old man on the head, and had slowed the boat to little more than an idle. Just enough to keep it moving ahead.

"Give me a minute," Carl answered. "It ain't easy with the damn boat rockin' like this. Can't you turn it or something?"

"Just do it!" Pat raised his voice to shout above the noise of the waves. "Someone could come along at any time. Can't see more than a few hundred yards. Maybe not even that."

"I'm trying." Carl sounded short of breath. "The old bastard's heavier than he looked."

The boat heeled sharply as Carl lifted Leif's inert form up onto the gunnel, and then it swung back upright as the body slid off and tumbled into the sea. Pat barely heard the splash.

"So what do we do now?" Carl carefully wiped a smear of blood off the baseball bat and put it back into the rack before moving forward to stand beside Pat at the companionway hatch. "How the hell do we figure out where to go when we can't see nothing?"

"We'll be okay," Pat replied. "This mist is starting to clear, and we've got radar and GPS." He tapped the hooded screen in front of him. "And there's no rush. Remember what the cops asked us?"

Carl just stared at him and didn't answer.

"They asked us where we were on Saturday night," Pat said. "Remember that?"

"Yeah. That's right. They asked us about the cove—if we'd been there. And they asked about Jerry too. If he was with us or if we'd seen him." Carl paused for a minute as he tried to recall the conversation they had had with the cops the previous evening. "And they asked us if we knew anything about the old totem too."

"That's right. They did. So let's think about all that." Pat slid a quick glance at his partner. "Saturday was the day we left Gold River and went to the cove. We left Jerry in that house and told him we'd be back for him."

Carl nodded. "Yeah."

"But before we left the house, you and I were talking about where we could hide the stuff. You remember that part? We were in the living room."

"Yeah." Carl's voice took on a note of excitement. "You said we could take it over to the cove and hide it in the old totem." He paused, a look of confusion twisting his mouth as he looked at Pat. "But that didn't work out. We couldn't do it because that kid was there."

"That's right." Pat nodded. "But Jerry didn't know that. That little asshole must have heard us talking and figured he'd rip us off. I'll bet he tried to follow us. Maybe stole a boat or got a ride, like we did. Went straight to the totem. Probably hacked it to pieces or something. That would be like Jerry. And that's why the cops were asking us about it."

Carl didn't answer right away, and Pat could almost feel him struggling as he tried to figure out what had happened that night at the cove. Finally, he turned and looked at Pat, confusion still obvious in his face.

"So how come we have to go look for Jerry? The stuff wasn't there. We never put it in the totem, so there was nothing for him to find."

"That's true," Pat answered. "But Jerry's not stupid. He'd figure we must have changed the plan. He'd keep looking. And he knows the island. Not too hard to figure out where we'd go next. Not too hard to find the stuff if you know what you're looking for."

"Shit! You figure he's got it?"

"Yeah, I'd say there's a pretty good chance. And I figure he might have used that knife of his to get rid of any witnesses."

Carl stared at him. "That's crazy! Why would he do that? It'd be easy to just wait until they were gone. Nobody stays there long anyway."

Pat gave a snort of derision. "Jerry doesn't believe in waiting. Got the patience of a grasshopper. And that kid we saw didn't look like he was going anywhere."

Carl shook his head. "Doesn't make sense. You don't know that."

Pat swung the wheel to avoid a piece of driftwood, then turned to look at Carl. "So why do you think the police are looking for our friend Jerry?"

▶ FIFTEEN ◀

▶ Five o'clock in the morning in Louie Bay, a deep curve on the south side of Nuchatlitz Inlet, itself a wide, twisting vee that bit deep into the northwest shore of Nootka Island. In the east, the first soft fronds of dawn were sending pale tendrils into the night sky and pulling up a gray mist from the damp earth. The dense cedars that stood sentinel along the shore slowly disappeared into the sinuous ribbons of fog, and the entire bay was wrapped in silence. The wind had dropped and veered, and the birds had yet to venture out. Even the fish were staying deep, maybe feeding on schools of herring or on the plankton stirred up by the storm.

It was a time Dan cherished, when the silence and the solitude allowed the building energy of the new day to spark an echo deep within him. He poured himself a cup of coffee and took it out onto the deck. The fog was getting thicker, and he leaned against the railing as the bay closed in around him, watching his world gradually shrink and slow until it seemed he was the only living thing for miles, perhaps the only living thing in existence, isolated on this puny boat floating on its little patch of sea.

He couldn't describe the feeling it gave him, couldn't put it into words, but both peace and exhilaration were part of it. It was as if he was contracting into himself and yet expanding out into the universe at the same time, his consciousness opening wide even as his physical surroundings diminished. He had never been more than ten miles from shore, but he thought it would be like this if he ever crossed the ocean: a vastness with nothing in sight, empty from horizon to horizon, with only the sound of the waves or the steady drone of the engine to keep him company.

He took a sip of his coffee and pulled his wandering mind back to the present. He had lain awake the night before, trying to fit all the pieces together, and for the first time he felt a picture beginning to emerge that made sense. The major crimes unit down in Victoria figured Sleeman and Rainer might be good for the theft, and Jerry Coffman had once worked with Sleeman and had been in William Head with him. They might well have talked about what they would do when they got out. Probably had. So there was a good chance Coffman had joined up with Sleeman and Rainer once they were released. Or maybe he had simply shadowed them, figuring he could hone in on the action somehow. That might make more sense. But one way or another, the three men had come together. There had been no call for Sleeman and Rainer to lie about seeing Coffman—although he thought they had lied about where he was going, probably in an effort to shift attention away from themselves—and it was simply too much of a coincidence that all three would end up in this isolated and empty part of the world unless they had a common reason. Dan figured that reason could very likely involve the Bill Reid jewelry. Why they would go to Gold River he had no idea, but there were several possibilities. Rainer had relatives in the area. Perhaps they had helped him to arrange a contact. Or maybe a buyer was going to meet them there—or perhaps at Moutcha Bay or even Tahsis. Any of those places would work very well for someone with a boat or access to a seaplane. They were quiet and out of the way, but accessible enough that strangers would not stand out, especially at this time of year, when hiking, boating, and fishing were all in full swing. But why had they split up? And where did Friendly Cove fit into the picture?

The salon door opened behind him and he heard Walker make his way across the deck.

"You find the coffee?" Dan asked as Walker leaned on the rail beside him.

"Yeah. Thanks. Can you give me a hand with the canoe?"

"Yeah, sure. But if you want to wait a few minutes, I'll get you some breakfast first."

"Don't need any. I'll get my own later."

Dan looked at him, then shook his head. "Your call. So what's the plan?"

"Don't have one. Just go out and look. See what I can see."

Dan pulled the paddle out of the locker while Walker clambered down to the grid, and then the two of them untied the canoe and lowered it into the water.

"You got a radio?" Dan asked as Walker slid down into the canoe.

"Nope," Walker answered. "Not a VHF anyway. Just the two-way Sam left with me."

"Hang on a minute and I'll get you one," Dan said.

He went back to the wheelhouse, took a handheld VHF from its charger, and carried it back to the stern.

"Here. It's fully charged, so it should last a few days. Call me if you see anything."

Walker looked at the radio. "This the same one you gave me last year?"

"Yeah," Dan answered. "I've got another one in case I need to head out in the dinghy, although they're mostly line-of-sight, so the range might be a bit iffy."

Walker just nodded and kept looking at the radio.

"What? You have a problem with it?" Dan asked.

"Nope. Not as long as you don't try to call me," Walker replied.

"Why can't I call you?" Dan worked at keeping his impatience in check.

"Pretty hard to sneak up on someone if there's a radio blaring."

"Walker, how the hell are you going to sneak up on someone? You'll be out on the water in your canoe, and the guy you want to find will probably be around the outside, on the beach."

Walker grinned. "Lots of little creeks and rivers on this island. I can get around a lot quicker and easier than someone trying to walk through the salal."

"Fine," Dan said. "Turn the damn thing off if you want to. Just keep it with you in case you need it—and be careful. This guy is dangerous."

"Okay." Walker flipped the switch and stuck the radio in his pocket. "You going out on the trail?"

"No. You were right. I'd be too slow. I'm going to call Markleson and see if they're putting a helicopter up, and then I'll maybe take the dinghy around to check some of the beaches myself. The wind veered last night, so the sea should be pretty calm."

Walker nodded and let go of the rope. He dug his paddle into the water and the small boat surged forward. As he disappeared into the fog, he lifted his hand in farewell.

Dan went back inside, called Markleson, left a message about the helicopter, and then changed into weatherproof pants and jacket. He grabbed a couple of snack bars and stuffed them into his pocket on his way back out, smiling as he thought of what Walker might say about prepackaged chocolate-covered raisin and nut bars for breakfast, and then he swung the dinghy down and climbed in. Walker had headed northeast, past the opening to Louie Lagoon, toward the mouth of a small river. He would follow him as far as the entrance to the lagoon and then head down into the lagoon itself, where there was supposed to be a rough path that connected to the trail. Once he had taken a look at that, he would head back out toward the point and into Nuchatlitz Inlet. He could cruise west along the shoreline and see how it looked on the outside. The short-term forecast had been good, although there was another low forming somewhere out on the Pacific and it could bring in another system in a day or so.

▶ Six young men followed Jared as he paddled across Esperanza Inlet to the northern shore of Nootka Island. All of them bore the scars of lives lived on the hard streets of a city far to the south, and all had returned home to embrace the culture they had thought left behind. They took no food, no supplies of any kind, and carried no clothes other than those they were wearing. They carried their canoes up into the trees, well above the high-tide line, and then made their way inland through the forest. Over the years, logging companies had cleared large areas of the island. Many of those areas had regrown, and the fallers were now working on second-growth trees high up on a mountain above Kendrick Arm, on the east side of the island, but the rough roads they had bulldozed through the valleys still remained. Deciduous trees—alder and maple—were already starting to encroach along the verges, their leaves bright against the darker hemlock and cedar, and wild roses grew between the thick tangles of salal. Where the land dipped, patches of fern were re-establishing their dominion over the wounded land, but there were still pathways through it all if you knew where to look. Jared and his team were familiar with all of them.

They split up as soon as they reached the point where the roads diverged, four taking the northwest branch, and the remaining three heading south. Both roads led through deep valleys and up into the mountains, but side roads would take them almost as far as the trail itself. The island was over two hundred square miles in size, but they had traveled every inch of it, and using the old roads to cut across from their landing place made their journey easier than many they had taken previously. They would travel until it became too dark to see, and then they would rest till first light edged into the sky. With luck, they would reach the trail by nightfall the next day.

▶ In Victoria, the wharves and floats that lined the harbor were crowded with yachts of every shape and size, and a clear sky heralded the start of the annual Swiftsure International Yacht race.

Claire Ryan would normally be one of the thousands of spectators lining the seawall, but this year she was too caught up in planning her departure for Kyuquot to worry about it. She had hauled her twenty-eight-foot Boston Whaler out of the water after it had passed its official inspection and loaded it onto its trailer. The boat and trailer were sitting in the driveway of the house she was staying in, waiting for her to hitch it up to her truck and start the journey up to Fair Harbour. She hoped that would happen on Wednesday.

She ran her hand through her short blond hair before shuffling through the stack of papers in front of her for perhaps the fifth time, checking them against a master list she had clipped to the inside cover of a plastic file folder. Every item on the list had a checkmark, except for two, and every checked item had the required dates, and the required stamps, and the required signatures at the bottom. The back pocket of the folder held two copies of every one of them. Tomorrow was Tuesday, the day she had been told she would receive the official certificate of seaworthiness for the boat, based on the tests it had been subjected to over the last few days. She would make the requisite two copies of that and add them to the file folder. Add another checkmark to the master list. That would leave one. In order to check that one off, she would have to present the whole lot of documents to the Pacific Maritime Research Institute and obtain its formal letter of acceptance. She expected to get that the following day, Wednesday, when she drove through Nanaimo on her way north.

It was time to go. Claire hadn't worked out on the water since the previous year, when the boat she had inherited from her father, *Island Girl*, had been sunk by a bunch of thugs up near Hakai Pass. She missed the boat and the memories it had held of shared time with her father. She missed the challenge and the excitement that her various research projects brought. She missed being out on the ocean every day, watching life unfurl around her as the tides rose and fell and the water advanced and receded. She missed the sounds and smells and movement the ocean provided. And she missed Dan Connor, the man who had helped Walker rescue her.

The realization made her smile. They were such different people. He was a man she would never have expected to like. She had spent all of her adult life, except for a brief and disastrous marriage to a bureaucrat, among fishermen and scientists. Dan was a cop—or at least he had been until a few months before she met him. He had even served in the anti-terrorist squad, surely one of the most dangerous and violent areas of a dangerous and violent profession. His friends were cops. She had met a few of them when they had been at the marina: big, serious guys who were quick to laugh but slow to relax. Men who hummed with a fine tension, drawn taut like a thin guitar string waiting to be plucked. Watchful men. Hard men. If anyone had asked her before last summer, she would have said that Dan was the last person she would have thought of going out with.

But she had gone out with him. Had even moved in with him on his boat, *Dreamspeaker*, where they had spent six very pleasant months together. And now she missed him. Missed his easy smile and easy conversation and the dark shadows that haunted his eyes every now and then when he thought she wasn't looking. She even missed Walker, and Walker was already out there with Dan, where she wanted to be. Three more days and she would be out there with them.

► SIXTEEN ◄

► The mist formed again as Dan approached the entrance to Louie Lagoon, opaque ribbons caressing the rocky tidal shelves and twining wraithlike through the silent ranks of old-growth trees. The harsh sound of the motor echoed off the rocks, violating the stillness of the morning, and Dan reached back and turned it off, letting the tiny boat drift as he retrieved a pair of oars from their holders. The sudden return of quiet was greeted by the appearance of a mink foraging on the shore, and a bald eagle settled onto the top of a dead cedar tree. It peered down at Dan from its perch, watching with unblinking yellow eyes for several minutes before turning its head in a haughty gesture that appeared to bestow approval. A year ago Dan might never have seen it, but the short period of time he had spent on the water with Walker when they joined forces to find Claire had taught him much. More than that, it had awakened senses that had been dormant most of his life. Now he recognized the pale green scent of new leaves, and the soft murmur of feeding fish. He could feel the silken touch of air left by a passing bird or a swaying branch. He could hear the changing whisper of the sea as the tide pushed it into and over the shore. Those perceptions had opened up a new world, vastly different from the physical focus of his previous life as a police officer. He might never gain the knowledge or the sensory awareness that Walker possessed, but he had learned enough to see things through a very different lens.

Dan rowed slowly into the deepest part of the lagoon, gliding over the shallow bottom, with its clusters of orange and purple sea stars, and letting his senses absorb the movements and sounds and contours of this remote and secluded waterway. He knew there was no chance of finding Margrethe and her abductor here. They wouldn't have had time to make it this far even if Margrethe was a willing participant, which he figured was pretty well impossible. What he wanted to do was familiarize himself with the shoreline and get to know the area well enough that when he returned, he would be able to recognize things that were out of place. What he needed to do was find the entrance to the trail.

He found it at the very end of the lagoon. There was an opening in the trees where a glimpse of pale sky formed a line through the dark canopy. It was partially hidden behind a jumbled mound of driftwood. Anyone exiting the trail would have to scramble over the piled logs first and then wade out into the lagoon through a patch of weeds and grasses to a waiting boat or floatplane. It wouldn't be easy, and it certainly wouldn't be fast, which meant that a water-taxi operator or a floatplane pilot would have plenty of time to call in a description to the Tahsis detachment.

Dan scribbled a note to himself to check that both Tahsis and Gold River had contacted all the floatplane and water-taxi companies, and then he turned the motor on and headed out of the lagoon. There was another entrance to the trail at the bottom of Louie Bay, where it narrowed into a tidal channel barely wide enough for the dinghy to pass through, leading out almost to the open ocean.

The second entrance was easier to find than the first, but it would be harder for anyone using it. The rocks were jagged and wet, swept with sea spray, and huge logs thrown up by past storms were wedged into the crevices. Low tide might make it a little more accessible, but it would still be an awkward passage, and it too would be slow. Good. Time to get back to *Dreamspeaker* and call Markleson.

▶ The call to Markleson took less than five minutes. The coast guard was out checking the beaches, and both Tahsis and Gold River detachments were on the alert. They, in turn, had called all the local floatplane and water-taxi operators. They had also talked to the people who ran the *Uchuck*, the supply ship for all the remote communities in the area, and to a couple of crew-boat operators based in Zeballos. No one had reported a request for a pickup, and the coast guard hadn't reported a sighting.

Dan put the microphone in its bracket and went back out on deck. It was not yet noon, the mist had completely cleared, and there was a small patch of blue sky off to the west. There was nothing more he could do except wait. He knew Walker would call him if he found anything—or if Jared and his group came across anyone.

He looked north, back toward the outer entrance to Esperanza Inlet and the northwest tip of Nootka Island, a point of land that formed Nuchatlitz Marine Park, where Claire would be spending much of her time once she arrived. She had told him it was one of the most important habitats for the sea otter population she was studying, and the islets and reefs surrounding it were home to numerous tide pools where she could observe intertidal life. They had talked about it over a glass of wine the evening before he left, and Dan had found himself catching her excitement, although his was directed more toward the archaeological sites that were a feature of the park. The Nuu-chah-nulth people had lived in the area for over four thousand years, and their story was written in the buried remains of their ancient villages and in the middens that surrounded them. A desire to understand their history was yet another thing Walker had awoken in him.

It was a quick trip across the open entrance of Nuchatlitz Inlet to the park, and the shallow draft of the inflatable let Dan navigate through the reefs easily. He didn't have a lot of time to spend here, but an hour couldn't hurt. As he dodged jagged pinnacles of rock skirted with seafoam, and wove through groups of tiny wave-washed islets, he suddenly realized he was following almost the same path Darrel's small body would have taken on its journey to Aktis Island. The thought sobered him, and he looked out across the water, seeking some sign of the current that had carried it. His brain conjured an image of a wide river surging north through the ocean, its surface smooth and dark, but in fact there was nothing except the oblivious march of the waves on their relentless passage from Japan.

He pushed the image from his mind. It was time to get back to *Dreamspeaker* and to reality. He needed to check in with the locals and find out what was happening. He steered the inflatable back in, closer to shore, and turned it south. A flash of light off to his left caught his attention, but he was too far away to see what had caused it. Probably a piece of glass on the beach. Nuchatlitz was getting to be a popular destination for kayakers and campers, and the beaches were no longer pristine.

The flash came again. And then again. Curiosity made him slow the motor and turn toward it. He thought the three flashes had been regular and fairly close together. Maybe something metallic or glass floating in the water, catching the light as it rose and fell on the waves. A fishing ball, perhaps, or a piece of flotsam from the tsunami in Japan rolling in the shallows.

Dan nosed the dinghy into a cluster of small islets that stood off the shore, and as he emerged on the other side, three more flashes winked out at him. These were regular too, but farther apart. He reached for the binoculars he always carried in his pack, but before he could lift them out, yet another three flashes winked in quick succession, and a surge of adrenalin coursed through his bloodstream, replacing curiosity with a sense of urgency. SOS. The universal call for help. Someone was in trouble.

The beach he had glimpsed was tiny, set deep into a cleft in the shore. It was also empty. Dan steered as close as he dared and scanned the rocks that surrounded it. The wave surge and the spray made it difficult to see anything, and the wet black basalt reflected the light and hid the rocks' contours. He was close enough to feel the undertow as the water surged, rebounded, then surged again, and he worked the engine to hold the boat as steady as he could. There had been no more flashes, but perhaps that was because his angle of view had changed.

The shoreline curved sharply east in a deep indentation, and the beach disappeared from sight. There was no way the signal could have originated from this side—the rocky cape would have hidden it completely. Dan reversed his course and motored back. He couldn't go any slower, and he couldn't get any closer. He would just have to hope that the change in angle allowed him to see whoever had sent that call for help.

He crept past the rocks, fighting the waves and the water, letting his eyes roam across the jumbled mass of rock as he searched for a sign of something alien: a shape, a flash of color, a movement. Anything. He was almost back to the beach when he saw it, and even then he wasn't sure. There was a hint of yellow. A narrow line of bright color that disappeared from view almost the same second he saw it. It hadn't looked natural.

He turned the dinghy again, focused on the area where he had seen it. There! Now that he knew where to look, it was a little easier to locate, but it was still impossible to identify. Was it where the signal had originated? Why were there no further flashes?

He tried to nose the little boat in closer, but the wave surge threw him back. There was no way he was going to be able to check it out from this side. He would have to go back to the beach and scramble out over the rocks. It would be dangerous, but not as dangerous as trying to go in by sea, and at least there was a chance of succeeding.

Once again he reversed direction, but this time he headed straight for the beach, increasing his speed until the dinghy was bouncing off the tops of the waves. The sound of the propeller dropped to a low growl as it dug into the water and rose to an ear-piercing whine as it spun uselessly in the air. He couldn't judge the dangers. If he came down in a trough and hit a rock, it would be all over, but he needed the speed. He could think of only one reason why the flashes would have stopped.

The beach was smooth, the crushed shell so white it was almost silver. Dan pulled up the prop just before it hit the bottom and allowed the shallow vee of the rigid hull to drive up and settle into the sand. He grabbed the emergency medical kit and a length of rope he kept on hand, and then stumbled over to the rocks. Thank God he had worn gloves. They protected his hands as he clawed his way up onto the outcropping and started across. He didn't dare stand up. If he slipped, or a rogue wave caught him, he wouldn't stand a chance. He crawled crab-like across the surface, his fingers searching for crevices to hang on to, his toes slipping as he pushed himself forward. He was soaked to the skin in seconds.

Five minutes became ten. Ten became fifteen. He felt as if he'd run a marathon, yet he was only sixty yards from where he had started. But he was close to where he needed to be. Just beyond his fingertips, the rock curved down toward the water. To his right there was a dark shadow, duller than the surrounding rock, which might indicate a narrow cleft. If he was correct, that was where he had seen the flash of color.

He edged closer, his eyes narrowed against the salt spray, and peered over the edge. The sunlight only reached a few feet down, and sea foam filled the darkness below that, but there was something there. It wasn't yellow, but it was something.

A wave broke against the base of the rocks, sending a column of water shooting up into the cleft. Dan saw movement and realized he was seeing the flap of a jacket lifting. There was a quick flash of yellow—maybe a life vest or a sweater, and then a pale hand reached out and pushed against the rock.

"Hey!" Dan yelled, all discomfort forgotten. "Up here!"

The water sucked back down, and the darkness returned. It made a perfect backdrop for the white face that slowly twisted around to look up at him.

▶ There was no way Dan could get down to whomever it was, and no way the man could get up, so the rope was the only possibility. Dan inched back a few feet to get away from the worst of the spray and then sat up and slid the braided nylon off his shoulder. His fingers were so cold they kept fumbling the rope as he tried to form a slipknot, but finally it was done. He lay down again and crawled back to the cleft.

"You still there?" he shouted.

The pale face appeared again.

"I'm going to drop a rope down. There's a loop in the end of it. See if you can get it under your arms."

The hand that reached up moved in slow motion, and Dan knew there wasn't much time. He watched as the rope was pulled down, inch by agonizing inch, and fought the urge to scream in frustration at being a bystander unable to do more than watch. He knew that anything else he did now would only make it worse. Distract rather than enable.

With his free hand he reached into a pocket and removed his VHF radio. He needed to get help fast. Even if he succeeded in pulling this guy out of the crevice, he couldn't get him over the rocks and into the dinghy by himself.

Dan saw the rope slip under one arm, and he carefully moved the end he was holding in an effort to help the process. The other arm was going to be harder. The crevice was not perpendicular, and the angle meant that the man's body weight was pressed to one side.

Moving the rope to his left hand, Dan checked that the radio was set to Channel 16 and pressed the talk button.

"Mayday. Mayday. Mayday. This is Dan Connor."

He kept the radio close to his mouth and his eyes on the man struggling below.

"Mayday. Mayday. Mayday," he repeated.

VHF radio was line-of-sight. All he could see here was open ocean. Would anyone hear him?

"Dan Connor. This is the *Uchuck*." The voice that boomed back at him was so clear Dan found himself looking around for the ship itself.

"*Uchuck*. This is Dan Connor."

"What is the nature of your emergency?"

Dan explained the situation and described his location as well as he could. He didn't have GPS on the dinghy, but he knew this would all be familiar territory to the crew of the supply boat. They plied these waters seven days a week.

"We have notified the coast guard and will have someone out to you in about ten minutes." The response was calm and confident.

Less than ten minutes later Dan heard the roar of an outboard, and an inflatable with three men aboard appeared around the point. He called the *Uchuck* again, and between them, they guided the dinghy in to the beach.

The *Uchuck* crew members knew what they were doing. One of them snapped on a harness, and the other two quickly lowered him into the crevice. In less than ten minutes they had lifted the unknown man out onto the rocks, wrapped him in a blanket, and were tending to his most obvious wound, a gash on the side of his head.

"The captain called the coast guard. They're sending out a chopper to medevac him to Campbell River." The leader of the rescue team clicked off his radio.

"Think he's going to make it?" Dan asked.

"I don't have enough medical training to make a guess. He has to be pretty tough to have made it this long. I guess if he can beat the hypothermia, he should be okay."

Dan nodded. "Be good to know how he got here."

"Couldn't have come far. Water's too cold to survive for very long. Might have come overland from one of the coves or inlets. The whole park is riddled with them."

"Any of you check his pockets for ID?"

"No. And we can't do it now either. That blanket's probably all that's keeping him alive. It's got a couple of heat packs in it. You lose the heat, you're going to lose him."

▶ The *Uchuck* crew left as soon as the coast guard helicopter arrived, and Dan left soon after. He would call Markleson as soon as he got back to *Dreamspeaker* to have him check for any reports of missing people and to ask him to put out a request for the public to keep a lookout for an abandoned boat. He also wanted to follow up with the hospital at Campbell River. He needed to find out who the man was and what had happened to him. It could have been just an accident, but there was something about that head wound that suggested otherwise. And the timing was suspicious too. Maybe it was just a coincidence—but Dan didn't believe in coincidence.

▶ SEVENTEEN ◀

▶ Deep in the old cedars, the only sounds were the rushing of the wind through the branches and the occasional scurrying of animals. The salal that had scratched and gouged her skin as she pushed her way through it had been replaced by sword ferns, most of them taller than Margrethe herself, and the ground where she crouched was soft and wet. She was exhausted, so tired she had actually fallen asleep standing up the previous night, her arms wrapped around a tree, but she hadn't slept long. The noises of the forest had woken her, and she had pressed herself closer to the damp bark, trying to become invisible, trying to disappear, willing herself to be anywhere but where she was.

It hadn't worked, of course. This was the third day of her nightmare. Three nights earlier she had returned to her room after taking a cup of tea down to the workshop, where Jens—dear, gentle Jens—was working on the repair of a piece of machinery. It had been late and she was tired, looking forward to bed, but there had been a bright moon pouring a river of light across the water, and she had stopped to look out the window. It was a view she loved, at least in the moonlight. The cove became almost magical at night when the moon silvered the water and darkened the trees, and she could forget that it was this same ocean that terrified her in the light of day. Forget the fear that grabbed her by the throat and knotted her stomach every time she went near it. Looking back, she remembered smiling as she looked out at it. Remembered the feelings of contentment and pleasure that had washed over her. And then, just before she turned away, a flash of light had caught her eye and drawn her back. There was someone on the bank, just above the beach. She could see movement, two figures, one bigger than the other, the smaller one wrapped in something patterned, light and dark, and the other all black except for a glimpse of pale face and hands. She thought for a minute they were hugging, or even dancing, but then the flash of light came again. And again. Always at the end of an arm lifted high into the moonlight and then swung down in a glittering arc. She stared at the scene in fascination for a few seconds, unsure what she was seeing, and then the smaller figure slumped to the ground. She gasped in shock as the realization hit. The glint of light had to have come from a weapon of some kind. Probably a knife. She had seen someone being stabbed. Horrified, Margrethe watched in disbelief as the larger figure moved away and up the hill, toward the path leading to the church and the cemetery, leaving the other lying inert.

Blind instinct had driven her to the door. She couldn't just turn away and go to bed. She had to check on that small, motionless form. Without stopping to think, she pushed her feet into a pair of boots and threw a jacket around her shoulders. She was almost at the middle of the walkway when she realized she hadn't told Jens what was happening, but it would take too much time to go back now, and she wouldn't be away long. If she wasn't too late to help, she would do whatever she could—use her clothing, her jacket, whatever was needed—to make that small figure comfortable, and then go back. She did pause to look for any sign of whoever had headed toward the path, but she saw none, and she knew that once she was down on the beach, she wouldn't be visible to anyone unless they were looking out from her bedroom window.

She was too late. She knew that the moment she turned the small body over. The ashen face was a face she knew, and as she leaned over it, her tears washed away the blood that smeared the smooth cheek. Her eyes stung even now as she remembered it.

She had checked for a pulse, but there was none. He was gone. Past any help she could give him. Her hands touched the slashed tatters of the red and white blanket he had worn draped across his shoulders, and she carefully folded them back around him, unconsciously patting them into place, knowing it was useless but needing to do it anyway. His name was Darrel. He had visited her a couple of times, watched her weave, helped her pick grasses and early wildflowers. He had reminded her of a young deer, curious but wild, always poised for flight. She was so immersed in her sorrow and her memories that she hadn't been aware of the man returning. Hadn't sensed his presence until his hard fingers closed on her shoulder.

A disturbance intruded into her reverie, and she crouched lower under the ferns. She hadn't seen the man since yesterday, but he could still be close by. Walking through the sword ferns was easier than stumbling through the salal, and while their dense fronds made concealment easier, that would be true for him as well.

She huddled against the wet earth, the smell of humus and leaf litter filling her nostrils, feeling her heart thudding in her chest, sure that the sound of it could be heard for miles around. The minutes ticked by, and she willed herself to stillness, letting her fingers rest on the earth to sense any vibration, straining her weak ears to pick up any sound. A bird fluttered down and landed close by, pecking for insects along the arching stems, and she let herself relax a little, but not for long. A shiver of movement in the fronds made her tense again. She knew what it meant. She had watched it happen around her as she pushed through the ferns, each arching frond pushing against its neighbor and setting up a diminishing shimmer of movement like the patterning of raindrops on water. But this was weaker. Barely there.

It came again, and then again, several more times in quick succession. The movement seemed more pronounced in one direction, but she had no way of telling where the source was, or how close. Maybe the man knew she was here somewhere and was taking care to move quietly, but that didn't make sense. Why would he stay in the same place yet move enough to create a disturbance? She scanned the plants around her, turning her head to try to pinpoint the source, but the fronds were still again. Had she imagined it? She reached out a hand and used the tip of her index finger to gently part the giant fronds just enough to allow her to peer out, but there was nothing to see except more ferns and, above them, the soaring cedar trees. If her tormentor was there, he must be crouched down as she was, perhaps planning to wait her out.

Margrethe stayed huddled under the ferns until her cramped muscles forced her to move. Her body was shivering with cold and with fear—although the blind panic she had felt in the first day of her captivity had somehow disappeared. There had been no further disturbance, and she had to move, even if it meant creating noise herself. She pushed herself up slowly, wincing with pain as blood flowed back to her torn skin and cringing with fear at the tiniest whisper from the fronds. The bird gave a sharp call of alarm, loud enough for her to hear, and flew off into the forest gloom. There was no other movement.

She took a cautious step forward. Then another. She felt a twig crack under her foot and she froze again, imagining a sound like the clap of thunder in the stillness of the forest. The ferns shuddered, and then there was a sudden blur of movement, and she caught a glimpse of swift gray forms flickering through the shadows. Wolves. She had often heard them from the lighthouse at night. She almost laughed as she let herself breathe again. Compared to the man she was running from, they were a welcome sight—although only a few days ago, they would have terrified her. Maybe, if she survived this, she would be able to tackle that ridiculous fear of the ocean she had had since childhood, and then she and Jens could go out fishing, and beachcombing, as she knew he would love to do. In any case, the wolves disappeared so quickly that she couldn't really be sure she had seen them. It was hard to believe they had been more frightened of her than she was of them, but that must have been so. She had heard there had been hunters on the island. Perhaps the wolves had thought she was one of them. Not that it mattered. They were gone, and she needed to move as well.

▶ Walker pushed aside a low branch and turned his canoe into a narrow channel. On his previous visits to the island, he had explored many of the rivers and creeks that carried the rain from the top of the mountains down to the ocean, but not all of them, although that was unimportant. The twisting waterways were the lifeblood of the earth, and he was at home on all of them.

He had been born into the Raven clan, but his family crest, his *'na 'mima*, was the Salmon. It was Salmon who had emerged from the sea long before the great flood, taken off his mask, and transformed himself into the human ancestor of Walker's family. It was Salmon who had given his people their vast knowledge of the ocean, and the tides, and the rivers. And it was Salmon who had taught them their stories and their dances, and given them the masks they used to honor him, generation after generation, in the ceremonies of the Hamatsa and the potlatch.

The rivers and creeks Walker traveled were where the salmon came to spawn and die, giving life to the bear and the wolf and the eagle, and nourishing the earth even as they laid the eggs that would become the next generation. They were where the deer drank and the otter swam. They were where the oceans began, and where they ended, having transformed into the rain that completed the endless circle of life. He was part of that circle, and it embraced him wherever he went.

He had seen many of the island residents since he started out that morning: a family of otters that slid down the bank to play beside him; a pair of raccoons who watched his progress with bright, curious eyes; mink darting among the trees. But he hadn't seen any sign of Jared and his group, or of Margrethe and her captor.

The channel widened and Walker steered closer to the bank, keeping to the shadows of the trees. The silence of the forest and the gentle flow of the water on its journey down to the ocean gave him time to think. He had been caught off guard by Dan's announcement that he had rejoined the police force, and Walker's initial reaction had been to distance himself from the man who, in spite of their troubled history, had become a friend. The reaction hadn't surprised him. There was nothing surprising about wanting to distance himself from anything to do with the police. Every memory, every experience he had ever had that involved the police, was heavily seeded with pain and regret and loss. The police—and Dan himself—had played a major role in a part of Walker's life that had resulted in both a prison sentence and months on a rehabilitation ward. He still carried the scars, both visible and invisible. Some of them, like the damage to his legs, would never disappear.

What had both surprised and pleased him was how fast he had gotten over it. Since his release from prison more than nine years ago, he had spent most of his time alone. Other than the time spent with his family in their small village farther up the coast, and with Percy at his "learning to be Indian again" camp, as he had once described it to Dan, Walker had become almost a recluse. His home was a simple shack he had built from driftwood washed ashore in a small hidden cove on one of the many islands that dotted the shore near Hakai Pass. When he wasn't there, he was out on the water in his canoe, catching the fish and harvesting the sea life that sustained him. It was a simple life, but it was the life he had chosen, and it satisfied him. Two or three times each year, when he felt the need for human companionship, he paddled south to his village and spent some time with family and friends. Less often, he would travel over to Gold River to visit his sister and her husband, which is where he had met Sanford and discovered the waterways of Nootka Island. When Walker had run into Dan the previous year, it was the first time he had talked with a white man since leaving the city. And asking Dan for help was the first time he had ever reached out to anyone.

He smiled as he thought about the incongruity of their friendship—and it *was* a friendship. The reality was that Walker liked Dan. Liked the man regardless of the color of his skin or his cultural background or even his job. Liked his straightforward, open approach to the world around him. There was no arrogance, no subterfuge, no prejudice—and Dan was probably the only cop Walker had ever dealt with who lacked the last item on that list. Sam and Jared had seen it too. Walker had expected them to close up, even leave, as soon as they heard Dan was back in the RCMP. Instead, they had seemed relaxed in Dan's company, had trusted him with their knowledge of the Reverend Steven. Walker had never seen Jared trust a white man before. That alone spoke volumes.

He reached out and grasped a tree root that protruded into the water, holding himself steady as he listened to the murmur of life around him. Above the sound of the water, he could hear bird chatter, and the soft patter of small feet on the leaf litter as some denizen of the stream bank searched for food. A quiet snuffling as something larger, perhaps a black bear, scented the air. A faint rustle of leaves as an animal moved through the brush.

He let go of the root and pushed the canoe back out into the channel. The sounds he heard were the everyday sounds of life on the littoral, and they told him he was the only human close by. If there had been anyone else, there would have been only silence.

EIGHTEEN

Dan made it back to Louie Bay in less than an hour, the inflatable bouncing and flying off the tops of the waves. *Dreamspeaker* still swung lazily on her anchor just as he had left her, enclosed in the quiet embrace of the bay. It was a peaceful scene that was completely at odds with the one he had just left.

He tied the inflatable to *Dreamspeaker*'s stern, scrambled on board, and headed straight for the wheelhouse. He needed to call the hospital in Campbell River to see if anyone had come up with identification on the man he had helped rescue.

The woman who answered the phone at the Campbell River Hospital put him through to Admitting, who in turn passed him on to a detective called Johnson. It seemed Johnson had arrived just minutes before and was asking the same questions.

"You guys should really learn to talk to each other," the woman said with more than a hint of asperity. "It would save everyone a lot of time."

Dan gave Johnson his badge number and explained how he had found the guy.

"Oh yeah," Johnson said. "The coast guard guys told me about you. Said you thought it might not be an accident?"

"Hell, I don't know," Dan answered. "I'm no medic, and I barely got a look at him. He was wedged down a crack in the rocks when I found him, and the guys from the *Uchuck* wrapped him up in a blanket as soon as they pulled him out. I'm working on another case—actually, two cases—and it just seems to me there are an awful lot of people getting hurt in an area where there aren't that many people to start off with."

"Know what you mean," Johnson answered. "Coincidence only stretches so far. Problem is the guy's still out of action. The rescue team said he was unconscious the whole time they had him, and now he's up in the intensive care unit. The people here say he'll be there for a while. They'll call me when—or if—he wakes up."

"They tell you what his chances are?" Dan asked.

"Not really. They never do. But reading between the lines, I'd say better than fifty-fifty."

"Huh. Tough old bastard. If he came off a boat, that water was damned cold. You got an ID yet?"

"Nope, but the folks in Admitting here at the hospital should have it pretty soon—unless he wasn't carrying any, which is a possibility if he was just out there fishing. Anyway, they'll let me know one way or the other, and I'll give you a call as soon as I know. You think he might be involved in one of those cases you're working on?"

"Not really," Dan said. "I've got a missing woman and a murdered kid. But there's also a couple of bad guys floating around, and some weird things keep happening, so you never know."

"I heard about the kid," Johnson replied. "Nasty business. You got any leads?"

"Maybe," Dan answered. "We think the guy who did it may be on the trail that runs up the west coast of Nootka Island. We're putting a helicopter up, and people are watching at either end, so if he's there, we should be able to get him. May know more then."

"Good luck," Johnson said. "I'll check with the hospital again and get back to you."

Dan gave him his contact information, thanked him, and clicked off the microphone. Now what? He had told Johnson they should be able to get the guy who was on the trail, but it had been three days now and they hadn't even caught a glimpse of him. What if they were wrong? What if he and Margrethe were miles away, not only off Nootka Island, but off Vancouver Island as well? It was only a two-hour ferry ride from Vancouver Island to the mainland, and only a twenty-minute floatplane trip to either downtown Vancouver or the airport. They could be anywhere by now.

And what about Walker? How long would he paddle up and down the creeks and rivers that crisscrossed the island, in search of a man who might not be there? Or a man who might be there and could be very dangerous? And then there was Jared and his group. They were out there too. And he couldn't get hold of any of them. Couldn't do anything to help them. Shit! It was like last year with the black ship happening all over again—except this time it was Margrethe, not Claire, who was being threatened. And, like last year, he was stuck here doing nothing. Damn it. There had to be something he could do.

He picked up the microphone again. Maybe Markleson had some new information. At least he could confirm whether the helicopter was up or not. Dan was about to press the switch when a voice came over the speaker.

"Dan Connor?"

"Yeah?" Dan answered. "Who's this?"

"Johnson, from Campbell River. We were just talking a few minutes ago."

"Yeah. Thanks for calling back. You got something for me?"

"Yep. The hospital has an ID on that guy you found. He had a fishing licence in his pocket. Turns out he's a fisherman. Comes from Kyuquot. His name's Leif Nielson."

"Huh. He have his own fishing boat?"

"No idea, but you should be able to check him out pretty easily. Kyuquot's a real small place. Too small for us to have anyone posted there permanently, but I think the guys in the Tahsis detachment go out there every week or so to check things out. They'll probably know him."

"Yeah. Thanks again."

▶ Dan called Markleson as soon as his conversation with Johnson was finished.

"Leif Nielson?" Markleson said, surprise in his voice.

"Yeah. You know him?" Dan asked.

"Not personally, but I know the name. He's the guy who found that kid."

"Darrel Mack? The kid who was stabbed to death down in Friendly Cove?" This was getting stranger by the minute.

"That's the one. I've got the file right here in front of me. It says Nielson and a friend were out at Aktis Island collecting oysters when they saw the body floating in a kelp bed. They hightailed it back to Kyuquot and called our guys in Tahsis. Tahsis said both men were pretty upset."

"Nielson is a fisherman. So were they out there in a commercial fishboat collecting oysters?" As far as Dan knew, the only oysters collected commercially were grown on oyster farms in the calmer waters on the eastern side of the island.

"Nope. They were in a small boat that Nielson owns. He works as a fishing guide for the resort up there, but I guess he was in his own boat. Most of the folks up there have their own boat. His friend—the only name I have here is Archie—lives over in Houpsitas, on the reserve. That's on the other side of Walter's Cove, just across the water from Kyuquot. They said they went over to Aktis to get the oysters for their dinner. The guys checked them out and everything seems legit. They've both lived in Kyuquot all their lives. Everybody over there knows them."

"Huh. Is there anyone there in Kyuquot I can talk to?" Dan asked. "Someone who might know what Nielson was doing out there in Nuchatlitz?"

"Well, you can ask Tahsis. They might know of someone. They go over there to Kyuquot every couple of weeks."

"Okay, I'll do that," Dan said. "Did we get a helicopter up?"

"Yes. It made several passes over the trail. Came up empty. Didn't see anybody or anything."

"Okay, I'll give Tahsis a call. Thanks for your help."

▶ Before he called Tahsis, Dan sorted through the stack of paper charts in his chart drawer. He had never used them—the computerized navigation system he had installed on *Dreamspeaker* used digital charts—but they had come with the boat when he bought her, and he had kept them as a backup in case of a computer failure and because they reminded him of those long-ago fishing trips with his father. The chart he pulled out was labeled CHS 3604, NOOTKA SOUND TO QUATSINO SOUND. He laid it out on the chart table and studied it for a while, tracing the coastline with his finger. Then he took out a blue pencil and used it to mark the locations that kept cropping up: Gold River, Friendly Cove, Tahsis, and Kyuquot. Another dot marked the end of the trail in Louie Lagoon, and he added yet another for Moutcha Bay. The dots formed a tight cluster toward the bottom section of the chart. He switched to a red pencil to mark where Darrel Mack had been killed, then added a second red dot to indicate where he had found Leif Nielson in Nuchatlitz Marine Park. After a couple of minutes, he added a third to indicate where Rainer and Sleeman were picked up. It joined the blue dot he had already made next to Tahsis. The red dots formed an even tighter cluster. If he ignored both Gold River and Kyuquot, assuming them to be simply convenient departure points and, in the case of Darrel Mack, an unplanned arrival point, all the dots circled Nootka Island. He wasn't wrong in concentrating on the trail. The chances that all of these people were here accidentally were almost nil.

Dan kept the chart in front of him as he called the Tahsis detachment.

"Got a couple more questions for you," he said. "I heard you're keeping an eye on those two guys you were questioning for Victoria? The guys you kicked loose?"

"Rainer and Sleeman? Yeah. We were. But they're gone." The voice on the other end of the connection sounded tired.

"Gone? Do you know where they went?"

"Nope. Constable Horvath tracked them to a restaurant, but he had to leave them there to take another call. When he checked back, they had left. Couldn't find anyone who had seen them go, but we haven't seen them anywhere since then, and that was early this morning. This is a small town. We would know it if they were still here."

"Think they've holed up with someone?"

"Why would they? They know we're looking at them. More likely to get the hell out of here."

"Yeah. But where would they go?"

"Probably heading back to the city and got a ride over to Gold River. Lot of traffic heading over there. Lot of boats, too, now the storm is over."

"I guess you're right," Dan said. "And speaking of boats, you know anyone I can talk to in Kyuquot who would be familiar with one of the residents there?"

"Well, almost everyone there knows almost everyone else. It's a real small community. Most of our guys know everyone too. Who are you interested in?"

"Guy called Leif Nielson. I found him more dead than alive on the rocks over in Nuchatlitz Park. He's in Campbell River Hospital, in the intensive-care ward. I was hoping I could talk to someone and find out how he got there."

"Leif Nielson?"

It was the second time Dan had heard someone repeat that name with a tone of incredulity in his voice, and he heard himself make the same response as he had the first time.

"Yeah. You know him?" The same question, but this time he got a different answer.

"Sure. He's a good old guy. We all know him. You say he's in the hospital?"

"Yes. He's suffering from hypothermia and he has a nasty head wound, but he was still alive an hour or so ago."

"Jesus! You sure it's him? He was just here. Jack—he's one of our guys—said he saw him down in the restaurant this morning."

Dan let his eyes drift back to the chart with its cluster of dots. "That the same restaurant Sleeman and Rainer were in?"

"Yeah. The Westview. It's down at the marina. Jack was keeping an eye on them, but he got called out on a domestic-violence report. Turned out to be nothing, but when he got back, they were gone."

"Was Nielson still there?"

"Damned if I know, but you can ask Jack yourself. He just walked into the office. Hold on, and I'll get him."

Above the hiss of empty air, Dan heard the sound of a brief conversation, and then a new voice boomed from the speaker.

"Dan? This is Jack Horvath. You were asking about Leif?"

"Yeah. I understand he was in the Westview restaurant this morning. Was he alone?"

"Yep. He was sitting in a booth right by the window. Asked me how I was doing."

"Sleeman and Rainer were there too?"

"Sure were. But they were way over the other side."

"So when you got back from that domestic-violence call, Sleeman and Rainer had gone?"

"Yep. I asked the waitress where they went, but she said she was too busy to notice. Said as long as they paid the bill, she didn't pay them any attention."

Dan grunted. "Sounds like business as usual. How about Nielson? Was he still there?"

"Leif?" There was a pause as Jack checked his memory. "Nope. He was gone too. Not that surprising. I was gone for over half an hour."

"Huh. Do you happen to know how he got to Tahsis in the first place?"

"Well, I can't say for sure, because I didn't see him arrive, but he's had the same boat for years—a little cabin cruiser with an inboard/outboard. He keeps it in real good shape. Does all the work on it himself. You might want to check with Pete Reilly down at the marina. He runs the wharf. Not much goes on down there that he doesn't know about."

Another phone call. Dan figured he was becoming more of a telephone operator than a detective. This new job was turning out to be all about sitting on his ass and making phone calls. Even Walker, with legs so badly damaged he could barely walk, was out there doing more than he was. Dan had always liked to be where the action was, liked to be involved. It was the reason he had joined the RCMP. And the RCMP had given him all the action he could handle. But that had been on the anti-terrorist squad. There the rules had been different. They had worked as a team, never alone, and they had drilled into his brain that you did not involve civilians. Yet here he was, back in the saddle again, doing exactly that.

He sighed as he picked up the microphone and put in a call to Westview Marina. Minutes later, Pete Reilly confirmed that Leif had arrived in his own boat three days earlier. He also told Dan that the boat was no longer there. It had left early, with three people aboard. Pete had recognized Leif, but he didn't know who the other two were.

▶ NINETEEN ◀

▶ Pat Sleeman turned the boat they had taken from Leif Nielson back toward Esperanza. The water was smoother now that they had the wind behind them, and they could make good time.

"We going back to Tahsis?" Carl asked.

"No, we're not going back to Tahsis," Pat replied, working to keep his impatience under control. Carl had already proven his usefulness several times over, but it certainly hadn't been in the brains department. In fact, if Pat was honest about it, Jerry was a whole lot smarter, and his quickness with a knife was just as useful as Carl's strength, maybe more so, but Jerry was too volatile, too unpredictable, and the son of a bitch couldn't be trusted for one second.

"So where we going?"

Not smart, but certainly persistent.

"We're going to Friendly Cove."

Carl's eyes lit up and excitement tinged his voice. "We going to get the stuff?"

Pat sighed. "No, we're not going to get the stuff. Not with the cops out there watching us. We're just going to take a look and see if it's still there. Make sure our friend Jerry didn't help himself to it."

"Shit! You think he took it? What are we going to do if it's gone?"

Pat looked at his partner. "Then, my friend, you and I are going to find Jerry and get it back."

"How we going to do that? We don't know where he is."

Pat smiled. It wasn't a pleasant smile. "Actually, I think I just might."

"Huh. You think you can find him quick? That guy you said would take it can't wait around forever."

"He won't have to. Jerry's still close. Those cops told us that."

"They did?" Carl's heavy face looked puzzled, but he didn't say anything more, and Pat didn't bother trying to explain.

They retraced the route Leif had taken just a short time ago, passing the entrance to Zeballos and the two wharves at Esperanza once again, but this time, when they reached Tahsis Inlet, Pat steered south around Nootka Island instead of north toward the town of Tahsis. Boat traffic was picking up with the advent of better weather. They passed a big seiner heading out to the open ocean, and the channel was full of small power boats, but no one paid them any attention. Out here they were just fellow travelers going about their ordinary business.

As they emerged into Nootka Sound, Pat slowed the boat, needing to steer by the unfamiliar GPS chart in order to find his way. He wanted to avoid being seen by someone who knew Leif and his boat and who might have the urge to chat. The season was heating up at the tiny fishing-resort community of Nootka, just east of Friendly Cove, and seasonal residents were joining the tourists there. Some of them might have been coming there often enough to know Leif.

Pat took the long route around the south side of Saavedra Island to stay well clear of the resort, then steered in close to the headland between Boca del Infierno Bay and Friendly Cove. That allowed him to enter the cove as far away as possible from both the lighthouse and that one lone house that sat in the middle of the cove.

He slowed the revs before they entered the cove to keep the noise down and then cut the engine early, letting the boat drift gently in to nose up onto the shallow beach, well away from where any other visitors might be gathered. He and Carl stepped out, then tied the bow line to a log lying well above the high-water line. They needed to get to the cemetery, but the two of them would take their time, make themselves look like regular tourists.

"Let's walk along the beach for a ways. Check the old totem out," he said to Carl.

"What for?" Carl replied. "We never hid the stuff there."

"Because it's what every visitor does, and we want to look like regular visitors, don't we?" Pat said. "And besides, we need to see what those cops in Tahsis were so interested in."

"Might be a bunch of people there," Carl said as they scrambled up the bank.

"Doesn't matter. Even if we meet up with somebody, it won't be a problem. Nobody here's going to know who we are. The boat's the only thing we need to be careful about. People might recognize it and start asking about the owner."

They saw the yellow crime-scene tape as soon as they arrived at the top of the bank. It was draped around a section of driftwood on the beach. A second loop encircled the old totem, which had been moved from its resting place in the seagrass to a small clearing lower down.

"Shit," Carl whispered as he saw the tape. "We should get out of here. Something must have happened. There'll be cops all over the place."

"Jerry happened," said Pat. "That's what. And the cops have gone. There's no police boat at the wharf." He pointed to the long red structure that jutted from the shore beneath the lighthouse; a large rigid-hulled inflatable with a red stripe was tied alongside. "That's a coast guard boat."

"I dunno, man. It don't feel right. We should go." Carl had stopped walking and was looking nervously around.

"Just act normal, for Christ's sake. Either that or stay down at the boat and I'll go take a look."

Pat turned and started toward the totem, and after a moment's hesitation, Carl joined him.

"Holy shit. Look at that!" Carl stared at the mutilated totem, where bright new wood shone out in a blazing testament to the wounded shapes of the bear and snake. "That's weird, man."

"That's Jerry, that's what that is. I told you. He was looking for the stuff." Pat's face was hard and he had lost his smile. "That son of a bitch followed us here."

A rustle in the grass caught his attention, and he turned to see someone approaching from the direction of the house.

"Hi." The man was Native and looked to be in his late fifties. He was carrying a bucket and a shovel, and Pat figured he must be the owner of the house. "Sorry, but this area's closed."

"Yes." Pat's smile was back in place. "I can understand why. What the heck happened here?"

The man shook his head. "Wish we knew. Happened a few nights ago. Had a young boy murdered too." He pointed down to the beach with its own circle of crime-scene tape. "Right there on the beach."

"Wow. Murdered? That's nasty." Pat shot a quick glance at Carl to make sure he was not about to interrupt with one of his inane comments, but Carl was staring down at the beach. "The police have any ideas?"

"Not really, but they've closed the trail, so maybe they figure the guy went out there. Took Margrethe with him."

"Margrethe?" asked Pat, suddenly confused.

"Yeah. She's one of the lighthouse people. Good lady. She disappeared the same night."

"Huh. Well, I sure hope they catch him soon. Thanks for letting us know." Pat started to move away before the conversation got too involved, then stopped. "Are the church and the cemetery still okay to visit? We'd sure like to see something while we're here."

"Sure. No problem there. It's just this area and the trail that are closed. If you take the path over there by my house, it'll lead you over to a boardwalk. Just follow it up. There's a Welcome Pole up there too."

"What's a Welcome Pole?" Pat asked.

The man smiled. "It's a tradition of my people. We carved a special pole to welcome people to our village. You will understand when you see it."

"Thanks." Pat reached out his hand. "Appreciate it."

▶ "I knew it," Pat said as soon as they were alone. "That little asshole."

"I don't get it," Carl said. "It don't make sense. Why would Jerry kill a kid? And take a woman? He don't do that kind of shit."

"Jerry does exactly that kind of shit. Takes out anything and everyone in his way without even a minute of thought. I don't know what the woman is about—you're right: that doesn't make sense—but it's Jerry. All of it. I know it is." Pat shook his head. "Jesus Christ, we gotta deal with this. I'm not going to go down for murdering a kid and kidnapping some woman."

Carl looked at him. "We did the old guy on the boat." Carl was slow, but occasionally his comments hit the mark.

"That's different," Pat snapped. "They're not going to find him—and even if they do, it'll look like an accident. The old bastard fell overboard. Hit his head. Happens all the time. Jerry would have used his knife. Pretty hard to make that look like an accident."

Carl slowly nodded his agreement.

▶ They sat in the church for exactly fifteen minutes. Pat timed them on his watch. Carl spent the time staring at the carved figures that stared silently back at him. Pat fumed. And schemed. The police had the trail blocked off. They would be checking everyone coming off it. If Jerry was on it, they would get him. But Jerry knew the island. Hell, his grandmother had been a member of the band that had lived here. He was the one who had brought Pat and Carl here to show them the cove in the first place. He knew the paths and the rivers and the creeks. And he knew the logging roads. He had talked about them, pointed out the log dumps and the camp at Kendrick Arm. He would know the police were looking for him. No way would he stay on the trail and make it easy for them.

The alarm on his watch pinged, and Pat turned it off and stood up. "Let's go," he said.

The men left the church and followed the gravel path up the hill. The cemetery lay at the edge of the forest, above the open bowl of the cove where only the whisper of the wind kept it company. It was small, with only a few graves, but each had an engraved headstone. Some of them had been eroded by time, but all were still legible, and each told its own silent story had the men cared to read them. They didn't. Instead, they moved straight to one of the oldest graves. It

135

was surrounded by an iron fence, which over the years had taken on a patina of age that blended with its surroundings, and the ground around it was covered with grass and ferns. A small pole had been carved to give testament and honor to the occupant, but time and weather had done their work and it had fallen many years ago. When Pat and Carl had last seen it, just days earlier, it had rested on its side, with the carved figures looking out over the forlorn green mounds. Now it lay on its back, the crumbling beak of a thunderbird broken off, and the earth around it gouged and raw. They knew they would have left some signs of disturbance when they slid the bag under the pole, but nothing like this. This was a message.

Pat wheeled away and stared out toward the ocean, his mind racing. Behind him, he could hear Carl's rage start to build.

"Shit!" Carl accompanied each word with a smack of his hand on the fence. "Goddamn it! It's gone."

"I told you," Pat answered. "Jerry's got it."

"Shit," Carl said again. "I'm gonna kill that little bastard."

"Yes," Pat said. "But first we have to find him. Let's get back to the boat."

"The boat?" Carl asked. "What the hell good's the boat? You said he was on the trail."

"He probably started on the trail," Pat said, working through the probable scenario as he spoke. "But he wouldn't stay on it. He knows the logging roads. The cops won't be watching them."

"Logging roads? What the fuck good are logging roads? We can't find him on those. They're all over the goddamn island."

Pat looked at him, an unpleasant smile twisting his mouth into a sneer. "Yes, they are. But, as Jerry told us, they all end up in the same place."

▶ TWENTY ◀

▶ Dan checked his watch. Almost six o'clock. Still a few hours of daylight left, but not enough to do a proper search, and Leif's boat could be anywhere by now. Even if he convinced Markleson to contact every marina and resort in the area, it could still take days—or even weeks—to find it. There were just too few people and too many inlets, and too many deserted coves and bays, but he had to try. He shook his head as he reached for the microphone yet again.

"Run that past me again," Markleson said after Dan had made his request. "You figure this wasn't an accident?"

"It could have been, but unless Nielson can tell us what happened, we're not going to know. Either way, we need to find the boat. We know where he ended up, and we know he wasn't in the water long, so if it was an accident, we should be able to figure out where the boat would have drifted. I'll work on that tonight. I've got all the tide and current tables loaded into my computer, and I can talk to the coast guard people at Comox. But if it wasn't an accident, it's even more important that we locate the boat. We need to find out what happened as fast as possible."

There was a brief silence on the other end, and then Dan heard Markleson sigh.

"Okay, I'll have someone get to work on this right away—assuming they're not already working on one of your other requests."

The sarcasm was clear, but Dan thought it was more in jest than in anger.

"Thanks," he said. "I appreciate it. Sorry to dump all this on your plate."

Markleson laughed. "No need to apologize. That's the nature of the job up here. I'll let you know if we get anything."

He clicked off, then came back on. "Hey, you still there?"

"Yeah," answered Dan. "Why?"

"Just wanted you to know we're still working on one of those requests. You asked my opposite number down at the south end—who, I believe, is a friend of yours—to check up on the Reverend Steven? Well, he called us when he couldn't reach you and asked us to let you know he's working on it. He had to contact the head office of the mission to get the guy's full name. Said he had to give them a bullshit story about checking the records of everyone involved in youth camps so they didn't try to stall him. He got a response a couple of hours ago, but he hasn't had a chance to run it yet. He said he'll let you know when he gets anything."

"Uh, thanks. That's great."

Dan grimaced as he replaced the microphone. Between finding Leif Nielson and learning of Sleeman's and Rainer's disappearance, he had completely forgotten about his request to check out Reverend Steven. Not that it mattered. The reverend was another issue entirely, and Dan already had enough on his plate to worry about: Jared and his group were wandering around Nootka Island somewhere, and Walker was out there paddling up some godforsaken creek. He couldn't contact any of them, and he didn't know if or when they would contact him. He gave a snort of derision. Two days back on the force, with two major crimes on his docket, and all he had done was send civilians into danger and make phone calls. Reverend Steven could wait.

Hunger pangs drew Dan down to the galley. He hadn't eaten lunch, and breakfast—a cup of coffee and a handful of granola—had been a long time ago. He would have liked nothing better than to sit down to a full meal, but he didn't have the time or will to raid the freezer. A peanut butter sandwich would have to do. In a couple of days he and Claire could cook up a real dinner and sit down together in the salon with glasses of wine. Her hair would gleam in the light from the old brass lantern he had salvaged from his father's boat, and which hung from the cabin ceiling above the table, and she would smile across at him—unless, of course, he hadn't found Margrethe and the guy by then and had to spend all his time looking for them. And unless Claire decided she couldn't cope with the idea of him being a cop. Why the hell hadn't he told her? Because he was an idiot, that's why, and he would have to explain to her why he had delayed.

He threw the jar of peanut butter back into the cupboard and slammed the door. The latest volume of the tide and current tables was on the bookshelf, and he grabbed it and took it with him to the wheelhouse. It might not be much, but at least he could do something to get this case moving.

It was late when Dan finished his research. He had checked every parameter he could think of, going back and forth from the chart to the current tables, adding in the wind directions and velocities he had received from the coast guard weather station, checking them against the probable time Nielson had gone into the water and figuring in the height of the tides that could either allow passage or block it completely. He leaned back in his chair and stretched his shoulders. His eyes stung and his head hurt—probably from low blood sugar as much as fatigue—but the maze of pencil lines he had created converged into a satisfyingly small circle. He had been lucky. The tide was rising when Nielson left the marina in Tahsis and the current would have been running east, flooding north into the inlets. If the engine on the boat had been switched off or in neutral when Nielson went overboard, the boat would have been pushed back in, rather than out toward the open ocean where it could be impossible to find. Even if he had fallen off with the engine still running, the current would have caught the bow of the boat and pushed it north and east. Either way, the boat would end up somewhere around Graveyard Bay or Espinosa Inlet. If Dan grabbed a few hours of sleep and left early, as soon as it was light, he had a good chance of finding it. Unless, as he suspected, Nielson's injury had been no accident. Then he would have to search in an entirely different area, and that could take all day.

He set the alarm for 4:30 AM and climbed into his bunk, his mind full of lines and angles, circles and contours, which spun and merged as they dissolved into sleep, but it was only three hours later, and still full dark, when he was woken by a loud noise. Struggling up through the layers of sleep, he thought first that *Dreamspeaker* had dragged her anchor and was on the rocks.

"Shit," he yelled as he fought his way free of sheets and blankets to fumble for the light switch. "Shit! Shit! Shit!"

He hadn't checked the anchor when he'd gotten back on board yesterday. Hadn't thought he needed to. He should have known better. It was always the things left undone that came back to haunt you. Hadn't his father taught him that? And hadn't his years in the RCMP reinforced it? If he lost *Dreamspeaker* through his own negligence . . .

His hand was reaching for the electrical panel, fingers searching for the switch that would turn on the spotlights up on the mast, when the noise came again, and he froze. That wasn't the scrape of rocks. That sounded more like something—or somebody—knocking on the hull. Surely it couldn't be happening again. If that was Walker, arriving again in the middle of the night . . .

Dan grabbed a pair of jeans as he passed his cabin and took the time to put them on. The sweater he had been wearing when he went to bed was lying on the chair, and he pulled that on too. Whoever it was, Walker or Jared or some other nocturnal visitor, they could damn well wait till he got dressed.

It was Walker, of course. He was sitting in his canoe, one hand on the swim grid, the other shielding his eyes as he stared up into the beam of the flashlight Dan was holding on him.

"You want to turn that off before it ruins my night vision entirely?"

"Night vision, hell," Dan answered. "You've got to stop doing this. Can't you just paddle around in the daytime and sleep at night like the rest of us?"

Walker shrugged. "Doesn't work that way for me. I sleep when I can, where I can. Sometimes I can't."

Dan sighed, and his anger evaporated as he reached down to take the rope Walker had held out to him. "Fine, but do you think you could at least let the rest of us get some sleep? I work better when I've had at least a few hours in the sack."

Walker's only answer was the infuriating grin that Dan had come to recognize as the end of any further conversation.

"I guess I'll go and put on some coffee," Dan said, resignation in his voice, as he started back to the cabin. "No way I'm going to get any more downtime tonight."

▶ The coffee was brewing by the time Walker made his way to the salon. He stopped in the doorway to take off his jacket, then sat down on one of the settees and slid along it till he reached the table. Dan poured two cups and then joined him.

"You find anything, or are you just here for a social visit?" Dan asked as he pushed one of the cups across the table to Walker, his smile taking the sting out of his words.

"A little of both, I guess," Walker answered. "I was kind of hoping I could get one of those fine frozen meals you make so well." He grinned at Dan, waiting to see if he would take the bait, but Dan let it go, simply staring at Walker over the rim of his coffee cup.

Walker shrugged. "I've got some news," he continued. "I didn't find anything, but a couple of Jared's people found me. They said they hadn't seen anyone on the trail itself, but the other group—Jared split them into two teams of three—has found a track. Seems someone came off the trail and headed east through the forest."

Dan stared at him. "Only one person?"

"That's what they said."

"I guess there's no way of knowing who it was—or where he or she is headed?"

"Not yet, but whoever it is might not be heading anywhere. Might just be lost. On the other hand, if he—and the boys said 'he,' not 'she'—knows the island, he might be trying to find one of the logging roads. Guess there's a lot of them. That's how Jared and the boys get around—they follow the old roads. Either way, it shouldn't be too long till Jared figures it out. I'm going to go back over there and wait. One of them will come and tell me when they've caught up with him."

"One person." Dan was talking to himself as much as to Walker. "So maybe we're wrong thinking Margrethe and the killer are together. Maybe she went on the trail by herself, and whoever killed the kid came and left by boat."

"Maybe." Walker looked doubtful. "Or maybe he's killed her and it's him on the trail. Sounded like a pretty tough trail for a woman who's scared of the water. Sanford says a lot of it is along the beach."

Dan nodded. "Yeah. That's what it says on the computer too. But maybe that's why she left it. She's scared of the ocean, so she figured the bush would be better."

The alarm sounded and Dan went to turn it off.

"Going somewhere?" Walker asked when Dan returned to the cabin.

"Yeah," Dan answered. "But I might have to leave a little later than I'd planned."

He hated the idea of getting back on the phone instead of going out and doing something concrete, but he needed to talk to Markleson again and ask him to have someone contact the logging companies, tell them to be on the lookout for anyone on one of the roads. He also needed to check with Gold River to see if they had come up with a definite ID on the boat that had been found on Bligh Island and to find out whether they had found any fingerprints on it. If it had been Darrel who stole it, it didn't tell him any more than he already knew, but if they could put Jerry Coffman on board, Dan would at least know for sure that Coffman had been—and probably was still—on Nootka Island.

"You planning on coming back? I don't want to spend hours paddling around waiting to give you Jared's information if you're not going to be here."

"What?" Walker's question had interrupted Dan's train of thought. "Oh, sorry. I'm going to take the inflatable and go out and look for Leif Nielson's boat. Shouldn't take too long."

"Who the hell is Leif Nielson?" Walker asked.

Dan laughed. He was usually the one asking Walker questions. Now it was the other way around. "Hang on. I'll go get us another cup of coffee and then I'll fill you in. It's been a pretty busy day."

▶ "So Nielson is the guy who identified Darrel?" Walker asked when Dan had finished bringing him up to date.

"Yeah. He's a fisherman, or at least he used to be. Now he works as a fishing guide. Guess he's lived in Kyuquot all his life. Seems like everybody knows him."

"You think he's going to make it?"

Dan shrugged and mentally added yet another call to his growing list.

"Claire still going up there?"

"Claire?" Dan asked, confused by the sudden change of topic.

"Yeah, you know. Blond. Cute. Lost her boat last year to those guys in the black ship. I think she spent some time with you for a few months over this past winter."

"Very funny, Walker. I know who you're talking about. I just wondered where you were going with your question."

Walker smiled. "Kyuquot's a pretty small place. Remote. Seems like there's a lot of bad stuff going on, and with you busy down here, she'll be on her own. She okay with that?"

Dan let the question hang in the air between them as he thought about it. What were the chances he'd be finished down here in time to go and meet her? Right now he didn't even know who he was looking for, let alone where to find him—or her—or them.

"You haven't told her, have you?"

Dan's eyes met Walker's across the table and he shook his head. "No."

"Not even about you being back on the force?"

"No."

It was Walker's turn to shake his head. "For a guy who talks so much, you're sure a lousy communicator."

TWENTY-ONE

► Walker left as soon as the first faint glimmer of light seeped into the dark sky. He promised to return as soon as he heard or saw anything. Dan gave him a key and made him promise to call on the radio if there was any news.

It was too early to contact either Markleson or Gold River. Both detachments were too small to be open twenty-four hours a day, and staff would take turns being on call at night. This wasn't an emergency, and the information Dan needed would be in the office anyway. That left him with almost four hours to spare. Not enough to catch up on sleep—assuming he could even get to sleep again, which was doubtful with Walker's comment reverberating through his brain—but plenty of time to make himself a good breakfast. And he could do with one. He hadn't had a decent meal for a couple of days—since his breakfast with Gene and Mary before he left Yuquot, now that he thought about it. No wonder he was hungry. He opened the freezer and pulled out hash browns and bacon, then dug in the storage locker below the floorboards to find the eggs that one of Claire's friends had given him. Unwashed and straight from the farm, they would stay fresh for weeks.

Claire. Her image flooded his brain. He could see her out on the farm, the sun lighting her hair and warming her shoulders as they walked across the field, the smell of newly mown grass rising around them. He could almost hear her voice, soft and slightly husky with sleep, calling from the stateroom to ask him if the coffee was on yet. She would be curled under the down duvet, her hair tousled on the pillow . . . Dan grimaced as he hacked off a thick slice of bacon and dropped it into the pan. He knew why he hadn't called her. It was a mixture of cowardice and fear—with maybe a little guilt thrown in. He had to tell her he was back with the RCMP—it wasn't fair not to—and he had no idea how she would react to that. Nor did he know how she would react when she found out he was looking for another missing woman. Certainly it would bring back memories of what had happened to her last year, of the men who had sunk her boat and hunted her. No way that wouldn't be painful. And, to make it worse, there was now the very real possibility that he wouldn't get up to Kyuquot in time to meet her when she arrived. Shit!

He carried his breakfast out on deck and balanced his plate on the wide mahogany cap rail at the stern. As he ate, he watched the sun slowly paint in the details of the forest: dark cedars, green firs, the graceful drooping branches of the hemlocks, the bright flash of new leaves on the maples. The shore emerged from night, barnacle-encrusted rocks slowly taking form, and the first minks and otters appeared and started to scavenge for food. Overhead, two gulls flew by, screaming a welcome to the dawn, and somewhere close by he heard the sharp tapping of an oystercatcher as it broke open its first catch of the day. Life out here was simple, immediate and straightforward. It was only humans who made it so damn complicated. Or was it just him?

Sighing, he scraped the last remnants of his meal into the water for the fish and gulls to fight over, and headed back inside. Like him, Claire was an early riser. She would be up by now, getting ready for the road. It was time to call her. She answered on the third ring.

"Hey," he said, relishing the sound of her voice even as worry tightened his throat. "Good morning."

"Dan! Where are you?"

"Louie Bay. Where are you?"

"Campbell River," she answered. "I should be able to launch the boat this afternoon; then I'll stay in Fair Harbour tonight and head for Kyuquot in the morning. We can have lunch at that little place on the wharf—if it's still there."

Her voice was eager, excited. It made it even harder for him to say the words he needed to say.

"Dan?"

"Yeah."

"Is something wrong?"

He took a deep breath, found both his courage and his voice, and told her. He told her about the totem, the blood, Margrethe, the boy's body, Mike's phone call, the guy he thought was on the trail. The only thing he didn't tell her was his fear that she might not want him if he was back on the force. The silence that filled the air after he had finished echoed in his head as he stared blindly out the window, waiting, hoping, praying, for her to say something. Anything.

"So when did all this happen?"

At the sound of her voice, Dan felt himself start to breathe again. He wasn't out of the woods yet, but perhaps there was a glimmer of hope. At least she was still talking to him.

"It started four days ago when I arrived in Friendly Cove. I wasn't sure about the cop part until the night before last—and it's still hard to believe."

The silence deepened. It writhed and stretched between them, twisting every nerve until he heard it scream inside his head. When she finally spoke again, it was in a monotone.

"Wow. I . . . I don't know what to say. Four days. And you're back on the job? I guess—there's a lot to think about."

"Hey, it's still me. I haven't changed, but I can't just walk away from this."

"No. You can't. I understand that. I just . . . It's a lot to take in." She paused. "Look. I have to go. I have to get the boat organized."

"Wait!" Dan struggled to hold back the panic rising in his chest. "Why don't you call me tonight. Or in the morning if you like. Or maybe it would be better if I call you." He knew he was rambling, but he couldn't help himself. "I might still be able to get there, but if I can't—if I'm still here in Louie Bay—you could come down and join me. Check out the otters at Nuchatlitz."

He cringed at the pleading tone he could hear in his voice, but he couldn't help that either. He had to make her understand. He couldn't lose her. Not now. But there was no answer.

"Claire?"

"Yes." Her voice was flat. "I'll—I need to think about it. I'll talk to you tomorrow." There was a click and suddenly all he could hear was emptiness.

Dan stared out the windshield, his fingers white where they clutched the microphone. If he had lost her, it was his own damn fault. How could he have been so stupid? He had to go up there and talk to her, face-to-face. Explain what had happened and why he hadn't told her right away. But how could he, with Margrethe still missing, maybe out on the trail with Jerry Coffman?

The day seemed to grow darker after that. Perhaps some clouds had moved in and shadowed the sun, but he didn't want to go outside and see. What the hell was it about him that kept attracting this kind of shit? Normal people didn't get called on to find missing women everywhere they went, or find blood on some piece of driftwood when they were walking along a beach. Hell, if he'd left the marina just a few days later, the whole thing would have been solved and he would be just another Nootka Island lighthouse visitor. Maybe Walker was right. Maybe that lightning snake he talked about had chosen Dan to fix whatever was happening. It was crazy, but it made as much sense as anything else. And it didn't matter anyway. Coincidence or lightning snake, the reality was that it was all on his plate now, and if he didn't get it sorted out quickly, more people could die. With or without Claire, this was one he couldn't screw up.

▶   His eyes scanned the scattering of dots on the chart while he called Gold River and listened as they told him the boat they had found on Bligh Island had been identified. It was the one that had disappeared from the Gold River marina, and the forensic guys had lifted some fingerprints from both the dashboard and one of the oars. None of them belonged to Darrel, whose prints were on file from his previous escapades, but at least some of them belonged to Jerry Coffman. Dan nodded as he heard the news. It was the confirmation he had been hoping for. A corner was starting to come loose.

The call to Markleson was next and took only a couple of minutes, as did the one to the hospital in Campbell River. Markleson would ask the logging companies to watch out for and report anyone they saw on the logging roads, and the hospital said that Nielson was still unconscious. It was time for Dan to get out on the water and look for Nielson's boat.

He pointed the inflatable just west of north and headed straight up to Catala Island Marine Park, north of Nuchatlitz and well past the cove where he had found Nielson. He planned to start his search to the east of Yellow Bluff and follow the shoreline in to Port Eliza. If he found nothing there, he would continue on to Espinosa Inlet and the area around Graveyard Bay. If he still hadn't located the boat, he would keep going as far as Zeballos Inlet. After that, it was unlikely that any abandoned boat was going to be found anywhere, and his search would change to trying to locate two suspects in a stolen vessel. He had just reached the entrance to Zeballos Inlet when his VHF came to life. It was Walker. He was back aboard *Dreamspeaker*.

"You find anything?" Dan asked.

"Not me, but Jared says it's a guy."

"He sure?" Dan shook his head even as he spoke the words. It was a stupid question. Of course Jared would be sure.

In any case, Walker didn't bother to answer, and Dan hurried to fill the silence.

"Did he see him? Was there a description?" he asked.

"Nope, and nope. But he says the guy knows where he's going—and he might be Indian."

"What? How the hell can he know that if he hasn't seen him?"

There was a pause, and Dan could picture the trademark grin and shrug.

"Jared heap smart Indian." The taunting words were softened by the teasing tone of voice.

"Very funny," Dan said. "I'm serious here, Walker. If it's the guy I think it might be, we need to pick him up."

Walker's voice turned as serious as Dan's. "Whoever he is, he's still in the bush, but Jared says this guy knows the trails, and he's following them. Knows what to eat too. Jared says it looks like he might be heading for one of the logging roads. If he does that, he'll end up at Plumper Harbour in Kendrick Arm. All those roads end up at the same place. That's where the logging companies are based."

Kendrick Arm. It was the name Dan had seen on the chart when he was checking for places someone might take a stolen boat. One of the very few places there was access to the interior of Nootka Island. Maybe he should change his plans and look there first.

"You planning on heading out again?" Dan asked.

"Yeah. Guess I'll go back and see if Jared turns up anything else."

"How about you come with me down to Kendrick Arm? I need to see if Nielson's boat is there."

"That's the guy from Kyuquot, right? The one who found Darrel?"

"Yeah. I found him on the rocks. He's still unconscious over in the hospital at Campbell River."

"I thought he fell off his boat?"

"Maybe. Or maybe he was pushed."

"Jesus! This gets weirder by the minute," Walker said. "Why do you want me along?"

Dan grinned. "I miss the pleasure of your company?"

Walker's snort of derision was loud and clear. "Yeah, right."

"Okay, the truth is, I need a second pair of eyes, and yours are good. These guys might have tried to hide the boat. Besides, two men in an inflatable might seem less out of place than just one guy."

"Especially if one of them is Indian," Walker drawled.

"Yeah. That too."

► It was almost three by the time Dan had retraced his journey back to *Dreamspeaker*, collected Walker, and made the run down to Plumper Harbour, at the south end of Kendrick Arm. The sun was starting to dip behind the trees lining the summit of the island, casting the shore into shadow.

"You know what color the hull is?" Walker asked.

"It's blue. Why?"

"Be easier to see if it was white. It's pretty dark under those trees. We're going to have to go in close."

"Not a problem. This thing only needs a few inches of water."

"I wasn't thinking of the draft. We're going to look pretty obvious poking along and checking everywhere."

Dan shrugged. "Can't be helped. If that boat's here, we need to find it. Maybe we could pretend we're looking for oysters or something."

Walker raised his eyebrows. "I'm impressed. You know oysters live in the ocean."

"Yeah, yeah. Just keep your eyes open."

They moved in close to the shore and crept northward, toward the log-sort operations that crowded the water at the upper end of the arm. Every now and then there was a gap between the trees and they could glimpse the rough surface of a logging road, but there was no sign of a boat.

"Maybe I was wrong," Dan said after they had worked their way through the floating rafts of logs. "Either that or they've already left. Guess we should head back and I'll try again tomorrow."

"Might want to keep going a bit farther," Walker said.

"We can't go any farther," Dan answered. "This is the end of the arm."

Walker looked at him and shook his head. "Not for a small boat," he said. "Just keep going straight ahead."

"There's nothing there. You can see where it ends up ahead."

Walker smiled and said nothing.

Dan sighed and shook his head. "Fine, but if we're late getting back, you can cook dinner."

The inflatable moved slowly up the narrowing channel and closer and closer to the northern shore. Dan was about to cut the engine when a gap barely wide enough to fit through opened up on his starboard side. He glanced at Walker as he nosed his way through it.

"This didn't show on the chart," he said as the channel widened a little. "Where the hell are we?"

"Still in Kendrick. There's another opening to the inlet up ahead about a mile. It's also too small to show on that fancy chart you got."

"Huh. Well, if no one knows about it, they're not going to be here—and the roads all lead from the logging camp, and that's back there at the . . ."

He fell silent as Walker raised his hand and pointed ahead to a clump of hemlock whose branches overhung the low bank and drooped down to the water. Through the dark needles, a patch of blue paint glimmered.

TWENTY-TWO

► It was taking too long. He should have found the fucking road by now—although it wouldn't really be a road anymore, just a trail. The logging companies hadn't used it for years and it would be mostly overgrown. So what else was new? Everything on this goddamn island grew like a weed: salal, ferns, cedars, hemlocks. All of it. And it was all the same: wet and useless. Even if the logging road had been new, it would have been rough. Those logging assholes didn't build fancy roads just to haul trees out. They sent in bulldozers and hacked out a passage barely wide enough for the trucks to follow. Hell, they didn't even put gravel on most of it, so when it rained—which was most of the time—it turned into mud. It had been six or so years since he had been here, so by now the road would have almost disappeared, covered up by encroaching vegetation.

Back when he was a kid, and his grandmother had dragged him out here to pick berries and dig roots and shit, he had hated the rain. He'd hated everything about the forest: the damp green smell of the undergrowth, the fetid brown odor of the swamps, the incessant drone of insects, even the endless chirping of birds as they moved through the trees. He still hated it, but now it served his purpose. In fact, it was just perfect for his needs. There would still be a bit of a path under the young trees, where the topsoil had been scraped away by the bulldozers and the trees' roots found less nourishment to sustain them. Once he found it, he could follow it all the way down to Kendrick

Arm. The trees would make him invisible to anyone in a helicopter, like the one that had flown over him a couple of times that second day, and they would hide him from the logging trucks he knew were still working on other roads: he had heard them grinding their gears as they maneuvered their heavy loads down the mountain. He would be able to move unseen by anyone or anything, like a ghost.

The thought of a ghost made him think of the woman, and he caught himself glancing nervously into the forest. Jesus! What the hell was the matter with him? There were no ghosts. That was all some fairy-tale shit from when he was a kid. The woman sure hadn't been any fucking ghost, even if she had looked like one. The goddamn ugly bitch would be dead by now, and good riddance. Dead and rotting deep in the salal where they'd never find her. She must have been some freak of nature with that weird white skin and that long white hair. He shuddered as he thought of the wet strands clinging to the sunken cheeks, straggling down over the pale forehead. And those eyes. They had been sort of like ice. Or beach pebbles. Kinda shiny and gray. Yeah, that was it. Like those shiny gray stones on the beach that the mask carvers had sometimes used. She had looked like a fucking mask. That was what had freaked him out back at the cove. She had looked like the Dzunukwa mask his grandmother had on her wall, except in white. A ghost of a ghost. Shit, no wonder he had been spooked.

He shook his head to clear the memory. He had to make up some time, and the only way he could do that was to find the goddamn road. He knew he was behind schedule. Pat and Carl had said the buyer had "a limited window of opportunity." Yeah, that was it: "a limited window of opportunity to make the purchase." Phony assholes. What they really meant was that they had to move fast before the cops figured out what was going on. They had set up a meeting for Thursday, just before noon, which gave them a few days after hiding the stuff to make sure the cops weren't on their tail. At first Jerry had figured that was an odd time to meet, but then he realized it was late enough in the day that Pat and Carl could make sure they got there first. That way they could watch to see if the buyer came alone. Of course, this had been back when Jerry thought he was part of the team, before they had tried to set him up with the cops. Well, he was going to show them what "set up" really meant, so he had to be there for that meeting, and if he had kept track of the passing days correctly, that meeting was going to happen tomorrow.

He paused to check the position of the sun. It was filtering through the trees just behind his right shoulder, dappling the ground around him with light, and it told him that he was headed in the right direction. So where the hell was the road? Maybe he needed to move east for a while. As he recalled, the road swerved north before turning back west and then turning again at an outcropping of rock just before it hit the coast. If he could find it before it made that northward curve, he could save a bunch of time.

He looked for an opening in the forest that would allow him to move in an easterly direction, and as soon as he saw one, he pressed his way into it, pushing aside the sword ferns and dodging the occasional low branch. It was slow going, but he thought the trees were thinner up ahead, and maybe there was a flicker of pale green in the gaps, caused by the early leaves on the wild rose and salmonberry shrubs that were growing up in the space created by the old road. If he was right, he might be able to make Kendrick Arm by dark, certainly by the morning, and if he was really lucky, the buyer would have the same idea those assholes Pat and Carl had and would arrive even earlier than they did. That's sure what he would do anyway, so if the buyer was as smart as he was, then he, Jerry William Coffman, could beat out Pat and Carl altogether. He could show the guy his sample—the ring he had taken from the bag before he slid it under that old sewing machine—and then take him to the cove for the rest of the stuff. Hell, Pat and Carl would never even have a clue as to what had happened. He patted the ring, sitting deep in his pocket, letting his fingers run over the raised shapes on its surface. He could just picture their faces when they realized the buyer wasn't going to show. Too bad he wouldn't be there to see it, but he and the buyer would be long gone, the deal already completed. He grinned at the thought but then forced his mind back on track. He couldn't count on that. Maybe the buyer wasn't that smart. Maybe he would arrive right on time, and Pat and Carl would already be there. Whatever. It still didn't matter, because Pat and Carl would have to take the guy back to Yuquot with them to get the stuff—and it wouldn't be there. Jerry giggled in delight as he thought of it. So who was the stupid one now?

▶ Pat watched through the trees as an inflatable moved up the channel with two men aboard, following it until it passed out of sight and the sound of the motor faded. Nothing to worry about. Looked like a couple of local guys—he thought one of them might be Native. Probably out crabbing, or maybe they had some business with the logging outfits. Either way, they weren't going to affect him.

He moved back up through the trees to where he had left Carl.

"You stay here and watch that road. I'm going to go down to the office at the log dump. See if they've had any visitors."

"You figure Jerry's just gonna walk here along that road?" Carl asked. "That's a long way, man. How's he gonna get here all the way from Friendly Cove? That's all the way on the other side."

Pat looked at him. "He'll walk, that's how. It's not that far if you know the trails and stuff. He told us that himself."

"Yeah, but you said he's got that woman with him. Bet she couldn't walk that far. She would sure slow him down anyway."

"I said he *had* that woman with him. He wouldn't have had her for long," Pat said.

Carl stared at him. "Why not? She was still missing when we were there yesterday. That guy told us, remember? Jerry must have taken her with him."

Pat sighed and shook his head. "Because he would have killed her, that's why. Hell, I don't know why he didn't kill her right there. Maybe he fancied her. Decided he'd get himself a piece of ass to celebrate getting the stuff for himself. Maybe he dragged her into the bush, screwed her, and threw her over a cliff. Maybe he stabbed her the same way he stabbed the kid and left her there. How the hell do I know? But one thing I do know for damn sure is that he hasn't kept her with him all this time. That's not Jerry's style. He's like a kid with a new toy; fancies something for ten minutes, then he's not interested anymore—unless it's got a big payday attached. Dollar signs can hold his attention."

"Yeah, I guess." Carl nodded his head slowly, then turned to stare out at the road. The two men were on a rocky outcrop about thirty feet above the water, surrounded by the thin trunks of young trees whose crowns provided a dappled shade. Above them, screened only by a fringe of dusty leaves, a rough logging road snaked around the mountainside before it turned and descended in a straight line almost to where they stood. The steep grade meant that any vehicle would have to slow almost to a stop in order to make the sharp corner immediately in front of them and continue along to the log dump a quarter of a mile south along the shore.

"Truck coming," Carl said, pointing to a cloud of dust up near the top of the mountain.

"Okay. Keep your eyes open. He may have hitched a ride. Check every truck. It should be easy to see if there's a passenger in it. I should be back in half an hour."

"What do you want me to do if I see him?" Carl called as Pat moved away.

"Nothing. Just watch where he goes. If he's in a truck, follow it to the dump, but don't let him see you. Stay in the trees. We don't want to spook him."

▶ The logging camp was a loose collection of trailers set at the edge of a cleared patch of land. The ground was littered with wood debris, and the air held the pungent aroma of cut cedar mingled with the acrid smell of oil and diesel. Two big Caterpillar loaders, their yellow paint faded and worn, were parked above a wide log skid, their operators leaning over a big flat-deck truck, apparently inspecting a grapple crane. The only other person in sight had his head buried inside the engine of the logging truck he was working on.

Pat worked his way through the trees until he reached the edge of the camp. It would be good if he could get into the office before anyone noticed him: the fewer people who saw him, the better. If the cops caught wind of his presence on the island, they would figure he was somehow involved with whatever had gone down in Friendly Cove, and no way was he going to take the fall for that. That was Jerry's shit, not his.

Keeping an eye on the mechanic and the loader operators, he drifted across the open space to a metal shed and stepped inside. It appeared to be doing double duty as both storage area and office. Shelves, some sagging under the weight of bins and boxes overflowing with jumbled metal parts, lined two of the walls, while a third was hung with chains and belts of every size and shape imaginable. Crowded against the remaining wall, under the only window, was a scarred metal desk almost buried under piles of paper. A tiny square in the center was the only place cleared for doing work, but no one was working there. Now what?

A noise caught his attention. It came from behind the desk, and Pat moved closer and peered down. A man was bent over, searching through the bottom drawer.

"Got a minute?" Pat asked.

"Jesus!" The man snapped upright and stared at his visitor. "Who the hell are you?"

"Dave," said Pat, holding out his hand. "Dave Adams. Sorry to creep up on you like that. I didn't know you were there."

"Damn," the guy said. "You scared the shit out of me. How did you get here, anyway?"

"Got a boat down there," Pat said, giving a vague wave in the direction of the water. "I was supposed to meet a friend up at the end of the arm, but he hasn't showed. I wondered if he might have had some kind of problem and come here. His name's Jerry. Jerry Coffman."

The man shook his head. "Hasn't been anyone but the guys who are working here. You're the first visitor we've had since I've been here—at least on this tour."

"Huh. You think he could have talked to someone else here?" Pat asked. "Maybe whoever relieves you?"

"Not unless your friend has been missing for a long time. The guy who relieves me hasn't been here for close to two weeks and won't show up again until next Friday. We work three in, three out here."

"I see. Well, maybe he just got held up somewhere. I'd better get back to the boat. Sorry to have bothered you."

"No problem. Be careful in the yard out there."

Pat waved an acknowledgment as he stepped out into the yard. The mechanic and the loaders were still occupied with whatever they were doing, but he had no doubt the guy in the office would tell them about his visit. Too bad he couldn't send Carl in to take care of the problem, but he couldn't risk it. At least, not now. Once he had located Jerry, they could kill two birds with one stone. Literally.

TWENTY-THREE

▶ Dan moved the transmission back to idle as soon as they had rounded the bend and entered the narrow channel that snaked back into Tahsis Inlet. It had to be Leif's boat. From the couple of brief glimpses he had gotten as they passed, it matched the description perfectly, although he would have to check the registration number before he could be certain. But where were Sleeman and his partner? He hadn't seen any sign of activity, and it was unlikely anyone would stay inside that tiny cabin while the boat was pushed against the bank like that. That meant they were probably ashore, maybe headed to a meeting with Jerry Coffman.

"You planning to sit here for long?" Walker's voice snapped him back to the present.

"Sorry. I was thinking about that boat back there."

"You figure it's the one that belongs to that guy from Kyuquot?"

"Yeah, I do, and if I'm right, it means he was assaulted by those other two guys they were holding at Tahsis, thrown off his boat, and left to drown." Dan paused for a minute as he ran over the scenario in his head. "And it means that they're working with Jerry Coffman too, because why else would they come here?"

"So now what?"

Dan looked at him. "Now I've got to figure out how to prove all this. So far it's all conjecture."

Walker nodded. "Big word, that. Sounds like a lot of figuring.

You want to do some of that on the way back to your boat?"

"What?" The question caught Dan off guard. He had been so busy thinking about how to nail Sleeman and company that he had completely forgotten about Walker. Without his canoe, the man was basically helpless. There was no way he could do anything but sit and wait. Sitting and waiting was something Dan had always found almost impossible to do, which made him more than sympathetic to Walker's plight.

"Shit. I'm sorry. Look, how about I head back to the log dump we passed back there? I'll go up and see if they've had any strangers wandering around. Maybe talk to the truck drivers, see if they've seen anything. I won't be too long, and then I'll run you back . . . what?"

Walker was shaking his head. "Won't help you any," he said.

"Really." Dan let his irritation show. It was one thing to feel bad about inconveniencing this man he had come to think of as his friend, but entirely another to let that interfere with his job. "And why is that? You know something I don't know?"

"I know you want to find these guys."

"Yeah. I do. That's the whole point. So?"

"So the guy Jared is tracking won't be here yet."

"And you know this how?"

"Too far away. Jared figured he would probably make it down to Kendrick tomorrow morning. Maybe late tonight, if he's willing to walk in the dark, which isn't likely unless he's spent a lot of time here."

Dan stared at him. "Jared can be that sure?"

"Why not? He's walked that same route maybe a hundred times."

"Maybe the guy will take another route."

"Nope. He was heading for the road."

"Maybe he changed his mind. Took a different road."

"There aren't any other roads. Not that lead down to Kendrick, anyway. All the others join that one."

"So maybe he's not heading to Kendrick." Dan realized he was basically arguing against himself, but what the hell. If it helped him figure out what was going on, he didn't have a problem with it.

"Nowhere else to go. Can't stay on the island forever."

Dan nodded, his irritation gone. "Okay. I guess that makes sense. But then why are these guys here now?"

Walker shrugged. "Maybe they're checking the place out."

"Yeah, maybe. But I still need to find them. Make sure they're who I think they are."

"Find them later."

"They might be gone later."

"Then they'll be back." Walker's voice held no expression.

Dan sighed. Arguing with Walker was always a waste of time. The man was too logical—odd for someone who believed in two-headed snakes with weird powers and animals that transformed into men, but true nonetheless. Walker was also too matter-of-fact, and what he was saying made sense. If these guys were here for a meeting, they would either have to wait for Coffman to arrive, or leave and come back for him.

But Dan hated the idea of leaving. There were too many questions. Too many possibilities. Too many ways for things to go wrong. Now that he'd had his supposition confirmed and had found Sleeman and Rainer, or at least found the boat they had stolen, he didn't want to risk losing them. He wanted to get this thing wrapped up. Needed to tie up all the loose ends so he could get to Kyuquot and Claire.

Claire. As soon as her name brushed the edges of his consciousness, her face swam into his brain and flooded his senses. Was she still on the road, or had she already reached Fair Harbour? He could almost see her standing out in the sunlight, working on her boat. Her image was so real his fingertips tingled with warmth as he imagined running his hand across her skin, and he inhaled as if her scent was drifting on the wind. He closed his eyes and tried to force her out of his mind. He couldn't let himself think about her. Not now. Now he needed to concentrate on his job.

"You still there?"

Walker's voice jolted him back to reality again. Walker was only here because he, Dan, had asked him to come—and that would have been very difficult for the man to agree to because it meant he had to rely on Dan. It took away the hard-won independence and freedom that Walker had worked and struggled for, and that he cherished so dearly. Dan couldn't just abandon him while he went and searched for these guys.

"Yeah, I'm here, and you're right—as usual. Won't take long anyway. And you can maybe check with Jared's people again and see if anything's changed."

Walker smiled but didn't reply, and Dan started the motor and pointed the inflatable north into Tahsis Inlet. The water was calm, and if he ran flat out, he figured he could get back to *Dreamspeaker* in a little over an hour. Drop Walker off, maybe grab something he could eat on the go, and then head back to Kendrick Arm. The sun wouldn't set until around nine that night, so he would still have plenty of light to work with.

Both the tide and the current had turned by the time they got back to Louie Bay, and *Dreamspeaker* had swung her bow so that she was facing almost due north. Walker's canoe still floated quietly behind, like a well-trained horse waiting for its owner. Dan idled the inflatable up to the stern, tied it off, and stepped up onto the grid.

"I'm going to get something to eat. Trail mix or cookies or something. You want me to get some for you?"

"Nope. I like to eat real food. Might see you tomorrow."

Dan nodded and climbed up to the aft deck. He could hear Walker behind him, making his laborious way from the inflatable to the canoe by hoisting himself up onto the grid, easing himself along it, then lowering himself back down. There was a faint splash that Dan guessed was a paddle hitting the water, and then silence. Five minutes later, when Dan peered out of the wheelhouse, Walker had already disappeared, hidden against the overhanging trees on the other side of the lagoon.

With less weight in the inflatable, Dan's return trip took less time, and he was back in Kendrick Arm two hours before the sun was due to set. The shoreline was hidden in the deepening gloom of the trees, which meant he was going to need more than a brief pass to see if the boat was still there. He cruised past as slowly as he dared, noting the pale gash that marked the logging road's descent, and then he followed it along the shore until it reached the logging camp. The place was

162

deserted now, the machinery silent and the big trucks empty and parked. A single floodlight on top of a pole created a pool of light that lit the lone building and the area surrounding it while throwing the rest of the site into deep shadow. A generator hummed somewhere up near the trees, and a couple of lights glimmered from windows in a cluster of trailers set on the far edge of the clearing.

Dan nosed the inflatable into the shore beside the log dump, tied it to a boom boat tethered to the top of the log skid, and turned off the engine. He would need to move it when it got light the next morning—loggers started early—but that shouldn't be a problem. All he needed to do tonight was locate the men, and identify them if he could. Once he knew for sure who and where they were, he could go back and tie up somewhere less obvious. Maybe somewhere on the other side of Leif's boat. The bank was so overgrown they would never notice him, and he could sit and wait until it was light enough in the morning to move through the trees up to the edge of the road.

He waited a good ten minutes, sitting quietly in the inflatable and letting the sound of the engine fade into the quiet of evening while he watched for any sign that his presence had been noticed. There was none. The tick of cooling metal slowed and faded, and the chirp of birds coming in to roost in the trees took its place. A great blue heron flew in and landed on a nearby log, hoping to catch a last fish before night fell. A pair of mergansers swam past, heading home after a day on the water. Moving shadows scurried along the shore, probably minks or river otters hunting for their supper. These were all things he wouldn't have noticed if he hadn't met up with Walker again last year. Hell, he wouldn't have been smart enough to wait one minute, let alone ten, if he hadn't spent time with Walker. He would probably have powered up to Leif's boat, leaped off, and crashed through the bush. He had always been a full-throttle kind of guy, living off the adrenalin rush of the chase, and that had worked for him down in the city. But not out here. Walker had taught him that. This was a different world, and it was one he had come to cherish and respect even if it had been touched by the same evil that infected the crowded asphalt city streets.

The thought angered him, and he realized for the first time just how large Walker's gift to him had been. It was much more than just the ability to slow down, and to reach out with all of his senses to observe the world around him. It was an appreciation of the world itself, and all it encompassed. It was a nascent, burgeoning knowledge that he was an intrinsic part of this world. That he belonged to it. The awareness sang along his bloodstream and warmed his heart. He might never fit into the natural world the way Walker did. He might never know it as intimately. But it was his.

He hauled in on his tie-up line and stepped up onto the log skid behind the boom boat. The trees crowded up to either side of the skid, and in seconds he was deep into the gloom cast by their heavy branches. He stopped again and listened. Nothing. Taking each step with care, he moved back toward the place he had seen the blue boat. He stopped every couple of minutes to peer through the trees and to listen, standing as still as the silent trees themselves, but there was no movement. No sound, other than the whisper of the branches. It took him nearly an hour, and the daylight had faded into a muted, crepuscular softness before he saw it. Even then, he was lucky. He had seen the gleam of the pale rock that formed the road where it turned to climb up the hillside, and had known he was close. When he turned to look down at the shore, a gap in the trees allowed a glint of light to catch the paintwork on the hull. Another step and he would have missed it. He lowered himself to the ground, his back against a tree trunk. There was no rush. He had all night.

In the end, it was neither sight nor sound that alerted him. He had been dozing at first, allowing his mind to wander over the sounds of the night, savoring them, studying them, adding them to his knowledge. When he started nodding off, he went back through everything he had learned so far: the totem, the missing woman, the murdered boy, the theft that had taken place back in Victoria, the man he had found trapped in the rocks in Nuchatlitz Marine Park, the two men who had been held and questioned in Tahsis, Jerry Coffman. They all tied together, even if the details were missing.

Still later, as the Big Dipper wheeled overhead and Vega, the brightest star in the constellation Lyra appeared, he remembered the story his father had told him when they had been out fishing off Nootka Island. They had been lying out on deck, looking up at the stars, as his father pointed out the constellations. There was the Big Dipper, Ursa Major, with its long handle pointing down to the horizon. There was the Little Dipper, Ursa Minor, its handle ending in Polaris, the north star. When he followed the bowl of the Big Dipper out past Polaris, he came to Cepheus, the King. The story had been about Cepheus, who chained his daughter, Andromeda, to a rock beside the sea in an attempt to please Cetus, the sea monster. Cetus was very upset by Queen Cassiopeia's suggestion that her daughter, Andromeda, was the most beautiful woman in the land, but before he could devour the girl, Perseus mounted his winged horse, Pegasus, and saved the princess's life. The two were married on the spot and lived happily ever after. Dan smiled as he remembered that magical, long-ago night. The story had given him a lifelong interest in astronomy and had fed his love of celestial navigation.

When Cepheus slid behind the trees, Dan worked on his judo *katas*, rehearsing each one in his mind, flexing each muscle in turn, perfecting the transition and the flow. The katas took complete concentration, and that was good. It kept his mind from drifting to thoughts of Claire. He was halfway through his third kata, *kime-no-kata* (forms of decision), when the sulfurous smell of a match intruded into his consciousness.

TWENTY-FOUR

▶ The runners, as Jared called them, came down to meet Walker just after dusk. After leaving Dan and *Dreamspeaker*, Walker had crossed Louie Lagoon and started up a wide, shallow creek that led deep into the heart of the island. The two young men, barely out of their teens, stepped out of the trees as he passed.

"He's on the road," the first one said as soon as Walker had brought the canoe to shore.

Walker nodded. "You see what he looks like?"

The young man nodded. "Short. Kinda skinny. Black hair. Skin's a little dark. He might have some of the blood of our people, but not much." He grinned. "He's kinda crazy. Talks to himself. Keeps patting his pocket. Maybe he's got some kind of good-luck charm in there or something, but he never pulls anything out, so there's no way of knowing."

"He say anything that makes sense?"

"Too far away to really hear what he's saying, but it's probably nothing. Just rambling. Sometimes he sounds real happy. Sometimes he sounds like he's mad at someone. One time we thought he was saying something about Dzunukwa."

"Huh. He look like he's gonna walk all night?"

"Can't say. Probably not. It's gonna get pretty dark. Not much moon tonight. Easy to break an ankle on that loose rock up there, and he's pretty tired. He's moving slower than he was this morning. A lot slower than yesterday."

"So he won't be down to Kendrick till tomorrow?" Walker asked.

"That's what Jared figures. Maybe three or four hours after sunrise."

"The logging trucks will be out by then, right? He might hitch a ride with one of them."

"Maybe. But those trucks will be headed the wrong way. They'll be going up, not down. And this guy is acting like he doesn't want to be seen. He came off that main trail way early. He could've stayed on it for another couple of miles and then branched off. Would've made it way easier and put him on the old road much quicker."

"Maybe he didn't know that," Walker said. "Maybe he just got lucky when he found that old road."

The runner shook his head. "Nope. He's picked the right turn every time since he hit that first spur road. He knows this island, that's for sure. Knows what to eat too—although he's missed some stuff, so maybe he hasn't been here for a while. Or maybe he learned some things when he was younger and then left. Lot of people do that."

Yeah, Walker thought. They do. I was one of them.

"Gilakas'la," he said to the runners. "Thanks. I appreciate you coming down and telling me." He dug his paddle into the water and pushed the canoe back out into the stream.

"We found another one."

It was the second runner who spoke. Walker reversed his paddle in mid-thrust and nosed the canoe back into the shore.

"Another one?"

"Yeah. Jared changed the teams. Made them two men each so he could send out three instead of two. We stuck with the guy on the trail. One of the teams went south, toward Yuquot. The third headed northwest, then turned east. Came back down through the forest. It's slow going through there, but there's some deer trails we can follow. The guys that went toward Yuquot came back yesterday. They didn't see anyone. No tracks. No people. Nothing. Not even anyone on that white man's trail along the outside coast. The guys on the other team came back a couple of hours ago. They found another track."

Walker stared at him, his mind racing. "They see who it was?"

"Nope. But whoever it is, they're moving real slow. Stopping a lot. Hiding in the ferns. Looks like they're following a creek. Don't want to be seen, that's for sure. They already crossed a couple of the branch roads."

"They? You think it's more than one?"

"No. Just one. Someone small too. Hardly makes an imprint, even where the ground's soft."

Walker thought for a minute. "You know where that creek comes out?"

"Yeah. It crosses the main road up high and then kinda follows it down, but a bit farther to the north. Comes out into Tahsis Inlet, just past the north end of Kendrick, maybe three or four miles above the log dump."

The two runners melted into the forest, and Walker let his canoe drift back down to the lagoon. The tide was ebbing, the current running hard toward the open ocean. It swept around the eastern point and into the lagoon. It would make it difficult for him to get back to Kendrick Arm, although he knew he could do it. Just take him longer, that's all. He glanced up at the sky, lit only by the last faint glow of day in the west and the first pale glimmer of stars in the east. The runner had been right. There wasn't going to be much of a moon tonight. It was past its first quarter, and wouldn't be more than a thin crescent when it lifted above the horizon. Better than a full moon as far as the current was concerned, but not a lot, and almost useless for visibility. He had some hard paddling ahead. If he left now, it would take him maybe six or seven hours. If he waited till slack, it would still be six or seven hours, but he could spend three of them sleeping. He grinned. He still had a key to Dan's boat, and it was only a short distance away. Three hours sleeping on that big settee would be nice. Might even grab himself a couple of those snack bars Dan was always munching on—not that he would ever admit it to Dan.

▶ Walker was back in his canoe by midnight, fed, rested, and ready to go. He had slept for just over three hours, eaten some crackers and cheese, drunk half a pint of juice, and put four snack bars in his pocket. The tide had turned and the current was just starting to flood.

It wasn't going to be much help to him for another hour or two, but at least it wasn't working against him. The moon was up, laying a thin sheen of silver on the water. Not bright enough to light his way, but enough to keep him clear of the rocks, and that was all he needed.

He leaned back and gazed up at the stars, trying to fix his position. There weren't many clouds to obscure them. The Big Dipper was clearly visible, and both Polaris and Vega were bright against the blackness of the night. Flexing his shoulders, he dug his paddle deep into the water and headed north, out into the open ocean and the rock-strewn shore of Nuchatlitz Marine Park and, beyond that, Esperanza Inlet. He would figure out his options as he went.

Ten years ago, after being released from jail, Walker had decided to return not only to his village, but to his roots. While he wasn't obsessive about it, he chose to live in the traditional way of his people: close to the earth and in harmony with it. He lived beside the water because it allowed him easy access to his canoe. He used the canoe to get food from the ocean, which he supplemented with berries and plants from the shore. He took shelter in a cabin he had built from driftwood washed up on the beach. It was a simple life, and he made simple choices. But the choices for what he should do when he arrived in Tahsis Inlet weren't simple.

His first choice was to head into Kendrick Arm and find Dan so he could let him know not only the description of the man on the road, but also about the second track. The description might not be of any immediate help, but the rest of the information very well might, and the news of a second track was something Walker knew Dan would definitely want to know. Margrethe's name had not been mentioned the last couple of times the two men had been together, but Walker knew the fate of the woman was always on Dan's mind: he had seen the worry and the sadness in his friend's eyes, and this news would bring him new hope. Walker figured Dan needed that right now, because it wasn't just Margrethe who was haunting him. Whatever had gone wrong between Dan and Claire was dragging him down as well.

But even as he thought about it, Walker realized that no matter how important the information was for Dan, the plan simply wasn't feasible. Dan would be holed up somewhere, watching for the two men he thought had stolen the boat. Walker couldn't drag himself out of his canoe and stumble his way through the trees, trying to find him. Even if he tried, it would take too long and make so much noise that the bad guys, as Dan called them, would hear him from miles away. And there was nothing Dan could do about this second person anyway, even if it was Margrethe. He couldn't be in two places at once.

That left choice number two, which was to head straight for the creek and start moving up it. With luck, it would be one of the ones he had paddled before, wide and deep enough to allow access, and without waterfalls and rapids. Once he was there, it shouldn't be too hard to find anyone who was following it down. Walker had a knack for sensing when someone was near. In his opinion, it was one of the few gifts the Creator had given him, maybe the only one, and he had worked hard to develop it. He had spent countless hours sitting silent, reaching out with all his senses, searching for the faint vibration, the slight disturbance that every living thing created in the force fields of the earth. He had become very good at it. But would it be enough? How would Margrethe—if it was Margrethe—react when she saw a Native man in a canoe? The man who had kidnapped her was likely at least part Native—and he probably looked a lot less threatening than Walker himself, with his over-developed torso and crippled legs, his long hair braided with a leather thong, and the flat, black stare that frightened almost everyone he had ever met. Would she come out of hiding when he called her, or would she run in the opposite direction? If he drove her deeper into the forest, he might be signing her death warrant. And even if he did convince her to come to him, would she be willing to get into the canoe? Dan had said she was terrified of boats.

Walker shook his head and focused his eyes on the dark water. He was overthinking things. He was a simple man, and he liked simple solutions. He would go to the creek and look for Margrethe. All he could do was his best. The rest was up to fate—and the spirits.

▶ A little over six hours later he found the mouth of the creek. The sun had been up for more than an hour, but it was just now appearing over the tall peaks of the Coast Mountains, spilling a warm, golden light down the steep slopes and into the inlet. Its slanted rays shone deep into the forest and caught the ripple of the moving water as it tumbled toward the ocean.

Walker turned the canoe and headed into the creek, using his paddle to lift and push the tiny craft over the shallow gravel estuary and into the main channel. It narrowed a little as he ducked under some overhanging trees, but then widened out again, and he entered a different world. Even the early light on the inlet was cool green here, colored not only by the trees but by the moss and ferns that lined the banks. Other than an occasional burble from the water flowing past, he could hear only the soft morning chatter of birds.

He steered the canoe toward the northern bank, where low branches and exposed roots provided a handhold he could use to anchor himself as he reached out into the forest with his eyes, ears, nose, skin, and spirit. The air smelled green and fecund, full of new growth and rich earth. Small butterflies fluttered between newly unfurled leaves that whispered in the slight breeze, and a pair of bright yellow warblers darted through the branches. After five minutes he moved on, using the same branches and roots to pull himself silently forward against the weak flow of water. He had sensed nothing out of place, no movement, no smell, no sound other than the scurrying of small animals starting their day. Nothing.

He stopped again after another few minutes, watching, listening, sensing. Again there was nothing except the normal comings and goings of the forest residents.

Again he moved. Stopped. Sensed.

Nothing.

Again. And again. And again. Still there was nothing.

The loud snap of a broken branch and a shuddering movement in the undergrowth pulled him instantly to a stop, but then he caught the wet-dog scent of a bear and moved forward again.

An hour passed. Then two. Still there was no sign of a human presence. The steep bank disappeared as he rounded a bend, and the creek widened as it swept around a gravel bar. The trees were not quite as close together here, perhaps because the gravel was less conducive to growth, and Walker saw five shapes slipping through the shadows between the trunks. Wolves. Probably off for a day of hunting. There were more of them since the logging companies had started work. Lush grass grew in the clearings the loggers left behind, and that had allowed the deer to flourish. They in turn provided food for the wolves. He had seen several wolf packs on his previous visits to the island, but this one looked different. One of them was pure white.

The sun climbed to the middle of the sky, peering down at him through the canopy, and still he had found nothing. He rounded yet another bend and for the first time heard the sound of fast-running water. Rapids. They were still some distance ahead, but they were there, and there was a good chance they would block his passage. He pushed on. He would go as far as he could and then wait. Perhaps the woman had not made it down this far yet.

A flock of birds erupted from the forest perhaps fifty yards ahead and fifty yards to his right. Walker grabbed a loose root that was sticking out of the eroded bank and brought the canoe to a halt. Seconds later he heard a flurry of movement in the undergrowth as animals ran in panic, and a deer and fawn burst out of the forest and splashed through the creek ahead of him. It had to be her. Jared's men walked quietly. So quietly that the birds and animals ignored them. They were part of the forest. This was an intruder.

He pushed off and guided the canoe to the opposite shore, then used the bank and the trees to pull his way upriver. The forest had become still and silent. The sound of the water seemed louder in the hush. When it came, the crack of a twig breaking sounded like a rifle shot. Walker waited to see if it came again. It didn't.

"Margrethe?" he called. "It's okay. My name's Walker. I'm a friend of Sanford. I've come to take you home."

▶ TWENTY-FIVE ◀

▶ Dan figured it was around four-thirty in the morning. It was still too dark to see his watch, but he knew the sun rose a little after five at this time of year, and the first pale glow of light was staining the eastern sky, throwing the jagged crests of the mountains into sharp relief. He also knew where both of the men he was tracking were: the match flare, and the brief argument that had followed it, had shown him their location. They weren't far away from him, perhaps only a couple of hundred yards farther up the hill and a few yards off the road, hunkered down in the bush as he was. Too close for him to move, but too far away for him to make out what they were saying.

Their presence confirmed his suspicions about both the ownership of the boat he had seen tied to the bank down below and what had happened to Leif Nielson, but it told him nothing about the reason they were here. He had assumed they had set up a meeting with Coffman, which meant they either had some way of communicating with him or had been involved with everything from the start, including the murder and the kidnapping. But now he wasn't so sure. If they were meeting Coffman, then why were they hiding? Why wouldn't they just wait on the boat, which had to be more comfortable than the rough, damp ground that Dan also was forced to lie on? So maybe it wasn't Coffman's trail Jared had located—in which case Dan's whole theory went out the window.

He flexed his shoulders and worked the muscles in his arms and legs, aware that every sound he made might attract attention. The judo katas had been finished hours ago, and new constellations had appeared above his head, each following the other until the stars disappeared altogether. He hadn't planned on being here this long—hadn't planned at all, if he were to be honest. As usual, he had simply acted. Followed the scent like a damn tracking dog without a master to guide him. Maybe he should go back to the city and rejoin the squad. Regular hours—at least for most of the time. A lieutenant and a staff sergeant to assign duties. Support personnel to handle the grunt work. A team to work with rather than this lone-wolf stuff. And he could go home at the end of the day to his own bed . . .

An image of the house he had shared with Susan rose unbidden before him, and he squeezed his eyes closed to hold the memory back. He wouldn't think about that. It was over. He had put it behind him. Moved on. He couldn't go back. Now he had Claire . . . He clamped his jaw shut on a groan. No, he didn't have Claire. He had screwed that up too. What the hell was the matter with him?

"He ain't coming."

The sound of a voice snapped him back to the present and pulled him out of the bog of self-pity he was wallowing in. The men were moving. Dan pushed himself lower into the bushes and twisted his head toward the rustle of branches.

"Yeah, he is. And I bet he'll be here long before Stephanson shows up."

"I dunno, man. This whole thing is fucked. With our luck, Stephanson's already been and gone."

"Jesus! Give it a rest, will you. The man is coming. All we have to do is watch that road and we'll see him. Now get down to the boat and see if you can find something to eat, and then get back out here. We need to take care of that little bastard before Stephanson gets here."

The men passed within twenty feet of where Dan lay hidden. Two of them, one tall and heavyset with dirty-blond hair, one small and dark. Rainer and Sleeman for sure. But if Coffman was the guy on the trail, who the hell was Stephanson?

Dan watched as the two men moved away from him and Rainer disappeared from sight, then listened to the sounds of their voices as they continued their conversation. Only when he was sure Sleeman was no longer moving did he carefully push himself up into a crouch. He needed to call in some help—would have done it earlier if he'd been able to—and then find himself a better place to hide. If he stayed where he was, they just might fall over him when they left the boat again.

Moving slowly, he made his way back toward the logging camp. He had to stay hidden in case the men left the boat sooner than expected, which meant staying low and working his way through the bush. He had barely made it halfway when he heard doors slamming and a generator starting. The logging camp was waking up. Maybe an hour, hour and a half, for breakfast, and then there would be traffic on the road, first the vans and pickups taking the loggers to the cut block, and later the logging trucks and the machinery operators. If Jerry Coffman hadn't already made it here, the vehicles would probably push him back into the bush and slow him down. That might give Dan breathing space, and maybe enough time to get some backup in place.

He moved out onto the road as he neared the camp. If either of the two men happened to be looking, he was far enough away to be mistaken for one of the camp occupants. As he neared the trailers, the tantalizing aroma of bacon and pancakes drifted out to greet him. The cooks were already at work. His mouth watered, and his stomach growled. He was hungry. He hadn't eaten since that damn granola bar yesterday afternoon. Maybe he could grab a couple of slices of bread, make a bacon and egg sandwich, before he went back to his surveillance. If that wasn't possible, at least he knew where to go when the time came: the loggers were stumbling out of their trailers, all drawn as if by a magnet to the source of that smell.

The friendly babel of voices died as he entered the eating area, and in the ensuing silence, a dozen men all turned to stare at him. After a few seconds, one of them stood up and made his way toward him.

"Who the hell are you?"

Dan smiled and held out his hand.

"Dan Connor. I'm with the RCMP."

The man took the proffered hand, but there was no answering smile.

"Bob Mackay. I run the camp. Haven't seen you around here before. Who are you with?"

"Victoria," Dan answered, silently cursing the fact that he had no ID. "I'm working on a case with the North Island Division. You're welcome to call them."

Bob Mackay nodded slowly, then inclined his head.

"You'd better come in. You can join us for breakfast if you like. There's plenty to go round."

"Thanks," Dan answered. "I could really use something. I've been up all night. But first I need to call my boss. There are a couple of guys here on the island that we need to pick up."

"These guys some of yours? RCMP?"

"Nope." Dan shook his head. "They're on the other side. They've all done some time, and are maybe headed for more. We're looking at them for a couple of pretty nasty crimes."

"This anything to do with that kid that got murdered over at Friendly Cove?"

Dan shook his head. He had forgotten how efficiently the gossip network worked in these remote areas. "I can't answer that," he replied. "Right now, we just need to pick them up and ask them some questions. You got a phone I could use? I need to get some guys here as quickly as possible—and then I need to get back out there."

"Yeah, sure. Got one in the office." Bob started toward the door, then veered over to the food counter. "Hey, Lee," he called to someone in the kitchen. "Can you put together a bacon and egg sandwich for this guy? We'll be back to get it in five."

"You got it." A female voice drifted out along with the kitchen smells.

Bob led the way down to a metal shed that sat in the middle of the cleared site. "Gonna have to build a bigger office if we keep getting visitors. We had another guy here yesterday. Said he was looking for his buddy."

Dan looked at him. "Another guy? He give you his name?"

"Yeah. Said he was Dave . . . something. Can't remember now. He was supposed to meet up with some other guy to go fishing, but his friend didn't show. He figured the friend might have had some kind of problem and come here."

"You remember what he looked like?"

"Didn't really look that hard, but he had dark hair, I remember that. Not skinny but slight, you know what I mean? Looked kinda like a city guy to me. Wouldn't make it as a logger, that's for sure." Bob paused. "You think he might be one of these guys you're looking for?"

"Maybe. You know how he got here?"

Bob shrugged. "I asked him that. He said he had a boat."

"You see it?" Dan asked.

"No. I just figured it was down at the skid. It's the only place to tie up."

Dan nodded. "I'm tied up there myself right now. Am I going to be okay there for a couple more hours? And my guys will come in by boat too. They'll need to tie up somewhere."

Bob frowned. "You can stay there till the trucks start coming down, but once they start dumping, you're going to have to be someplace else. I can have the boom boats pull you out to one of the booms and tie you up there. They can bring your boat back when you're ready to go. That work?"

"Yeah, sure. And thanks. I'd better make that phone call."

Bob pointed to the radio phone on his desk. "No problem. I'll go and get that sandwich while you make your call." He turned to go, then turned back. "Oh, I don't know if it helps, but I do remember the name of the guy he was asking about. It was Jerry. Jerry Coffman."

Dan was in the process of picking up the phone, but as he heard Bob's words, he carefully replaced the receiver in its holder.

"Jerry Coffman?" he asked. "You're sure about that?"

"Yeah," Bob answered. "I guess the name stuck in my mind because I used to go to school with a guy called Jerry Hoffman. Weird, huh?" He looked at Dan. "You know this guy? Coffman?"

"Yeah," Dan answered. "At least, I know *of* him. He's one of the ones we're looking for. He's not someone you want to mess with."

He reached for the receiver again, then stopped as another thought crossed his mind.

"You get a call from the RCMP to watch out for a blue boat—probably with a couple of guys in it?"

Bob shook his head. "Nope. Call probably went to head office, and those jerk-offs never bother to tell us anything. They probably figured we don't have a wharf or a float anyway, so what are we going to see?" He paused. "You thinking that guy that was here might have been in that boat?"

Dan shrugged. It was too late to worry about it now. "Maybe. You might want to tell your guys to watch out for anyone on the road. Tell them if they see someone not to pick him up but to call it in right away."

"They'd do that anyway, but I'll tell them. Back in a minute."

▶ Gary Markleson was still in bed. "This better be damn important," he said in a voice still clouded with sleep.

"Found Nielson's boat," Dan answered. "It's tied to some trees just north of the log dump in Kendrick Arm. Those two guys you had in custody were in it."

"Who? Sleeman and Rainer?" Sleep had left Markleson's voice.

"The very same."

"So we've got them for attempted murder?"

"Maybe. If they're smart, they could say they found the boat somewhere—at least, they could if Nielson doesn't make it. But we've got enough to pick them up—especially as one of them came to the logging camp yesterday looking for Jerry Coffman."

"You're shitting me! So they're in this jewelry heist with Coffman?"

"Yeah, but I can't figure out where the woman fits in. You hear anything on her yet?"

"Not a trace so far. It's like she vanished into thin air. We've got the search and rescue guys out checking the beaches, but they haven't found a damn thing, and the chopper people say the heavy bush and that rain a few days ago make it almost impossible to get a heat signature, let alone find anyone. They got one hit yesterday, but it turned out to be a bear."

"Okay, well, we'll have to figure that out, but right now I need you to send me some backup. I overheard Sleeman and Rainer talking a while ago, and they're expecting someone called Stephanson to show up, so if Coffman arrives too, we'll have four guys here, and there's only one of me."

"Stephanson? Who the hell's Stephanson?"

"Beats me. Guess we'll find out when he gets here. Meanwhile, I've got a bunch of loggers moving around, one guy who we know has already killed someone, another two who tried to kill Nielson, and all I've got is a goddamn service revolver. I need some help here."

"Jesus. The Tahsis boat's up in Kyuquot—went up yesterday. I can get somebody out from Gold River, but it's probably going to take a couple of hours for them to get there."

"Well, get it started, and tell them to move it. Have them come to the log dump. I'll have the manager here tell them where to go."

"You got a radio?"

"Just a handheld VHF. Call the logging camp if you need me. I'll check with them if I can."

Dan hung up just as Bob returned carrying a sandwich in a plastic bag.

"Thanks. I'm going to head out again. Keep the traffic normal, but don't have anybody wandering around on the road on foot. There's going to be an RCMP boat with a couple of guys coming from Gold River in a couple of hours. I told them to wait here till I come and get them, but if you hear any shooting, tell them to get to the corner down there as fast as they can."

"Damn. This is really weird. Kinda like a movie or something, but it's real." Bob looked out the window as the harsh sound of a logging truck starting its engine assaulted the quiet of the morning. "Can't say I'm too comfortable about sending the guys out."

"They'll be fine in the trucks. Just make sure they don't stop for anybody or anything."

TWENTY-SIX

▶ Dan's return to the corner was a good deal easier than his walk to the camp had been. The sun was higher, making it easier to see the roots and branches that lay in wait for the unwary, and the sandwich the cookhouse had sent over had given him some much-needed nourishment. He kept to the brush on the high side of the road, not because he was worried about being seen crossing the open area of the camp—there was plenty of normal activity happening there now anyway—but because he wanted to be able to move higher up the road if he had to without having to risk exposing his presence by crossing the lower section. He had no way of knowing whether Sleeman and Rainer had returned to the same place they had been during the night, but it seemed likely. Dan hadn't heard the sound of a boat engine, and from the little he had overheard, it was unlikely that Sleeman would trust Rainer to do anything on his own. So. Both of them, probably in much the same place as they were before, waiting to see if Jerry Coffman would appear.

A logging truck rumbled past, sending a spray of rocks and dried mud into the trees near the verge as it made the sharp turn and geared down for the climb up the mountain. The engine noise faded briefly as the transmission disengaged, then surged again as the gears meshed and the driver accelerated. Dan used the noise to clear a comfortable space for himself in the middle of a clump of low bushes and settled himself down into the hollow. Just by turning his head he had a good view of both the forest across from him and the road stretching up the mountain. With no load, the truck's ascent was quick, and the engine sound diminished as the big vehicle moved up into the trees. It was replaced with the familiar sounds of nature: birds calling, gulls screaming, insects droning. They were interspersed with the occasional clang of metal or whine of a power tool at the logging camp.

"This is bullshit, man. How long we going to stay here?"

It was the same voice he had heard the previous night, and it was coming from the other side of the road and a little closer to the water. Dan peered through the bushes, trying to locate the source, but couldn't see anything other than trees and brush.

"Keep your voice down, goddamn it. He'll hear you."

Dan figured that was probably Sleeman talking. The other voice fit the profile of Rainer: not too bright but good with a blunt instrument.

"He ain't coming." Rainer again. "I already told you that. And we're screwed anyway. We don't even know where the stuff is anymore. What the hell are we going to tell that guy when he shows up?"

"I'll deal with that if it happens." Sleeman's voice sounded tense and angry. "All you have to do is watch that fucking road and let me handle the rest."

There was silence for a couple of minutes, and then Rainer started up again.

"So what you want me to do if he does come? You want me to take him out?"

"Jesus! No, I don't want you to take him out. We need him to tell us what he did with the stuff. He can't do that if he's dead, can he?"

Silence fell again, although now it carried within it a brooding resentment that coiled through the air like something palpable. Dan gazed back and forth between the trees across from him and the bare slash of road spearing up the mountainside, but still nothing moved, and after half an hour he found his attention straying. He had always hated stakeouts—had never been able to deal with the boredom they brought. Patience had never been his strong point, and while the dark of night had helped him pass the time by looking at the stars and rehearsing his katas, the light of day offered both too much distraction and too little to hold his interest.

As he looked out at the endless greenery that lined the road, he wished, not for the first time, that he had Walker's knowledge of nature. Walker would know the names and uses of each tree, while Dan could only recognize the cedar and hemlock for sure; the others he was not certain about. Tamarack, maybe, and perhaps some fir or spruce. No pine, that was for sure. He'd read somewhere that pine didn't grow where there was a lot of rain. And most of the bushes looked like wild roses—there were still some rose hips on the branches—and some other kind of berry bush, probably salmonberry or huckleberry. He remembered both of those from when he was a kid. And those low, big-leafed ones would be blackberries. They always seemed to grow at the edge of something—a road, a fence, a forest—where they could be easily seen by a kid passing by, and where the huge, lush berries could tempt him to try to reach them even as the sharp thorns kept him out.

"What time is it, man? I'm hungry. Them stale crackers we found weren't worth shit."

Again a voice called him back, and again it was Rainer, and this time the petulance was loud and clear, even if the volume was a little lower than before.

"It's nearly nine." Sleeman spoke in a hiss that was barely more than a whisper but which carried clearly across to Dan where he sat in his hiding place. "Keep your eyes open. He'll be here any time now."

"Yeah, right." The words were an aside, barely loud enough to hear, but Dan heard them and wondered how much longer Sleeman was going to be able to keep his partner in check. If the two men decided to leave, Dan would have to decide quickly whether to follow them or continue to wait for Coffman to appear.

The snap of a twig somewhere in the trees a little higher on the mountain caught his attention, and he turned his head toward it. Walker had tried to teach him to reach out with all of his senses, but that still didn't work for him. He had to rely on logic and deduction.

It was certainly not uncommon for a tree, or even a single branch, to fall without apparent cause, but then there would be the telltale scrape of its passage down to the ground and at least a quiet thud as it hit the ground. He hadn't heard either of those sounds.

It could be an animal—a deer, perhaps, or even a bear—but it didn't seem likely. Deer moved through the forest in complete silence, and bears caused much more noise and disturbance than a single branch snapping. There were no cougars on the island, but Dan had heard there were wolves. He hadn't seen any, but if there were, they also moved silently, and they would never come so close to an active logging camp. That left raccoons and minks and otters, which were all too small to have broken a branch, and humans, who were notoriously careless. Humans often stepped on branches and broke them, but what human would be out here in the bush? No logger would be wandering around, and no tourist. That left Jared and his team, Margrethe, and Jerry Coffman.

According to Walker, Jared's men were like the deer and the wolves. They moved silently. They were also on the other side of the island—or, at least, well away from Kendrick Arm. The possibility that Margrethe had not only survived but also found her way to this particular location was so slight as to be miraculous—and Dan didn't believe in miracles any more than he believed in coincidence, although it would be one miracle he'd be very willing to pray for. That left Jerry Coffman. Things were heating up. It could get interesting.

The sound of a boat engine swelled from the south, came closer, and then stopped. It was the right direction for someone coming from Gold River. Dan risked a glance up at the sky. Had it been two hours? Yes, it had. He had left the logging camp just before seven, so the boat was probably bringing the backup he had asked for. The knowledge was reassuring. If he was right about Coffman having arrived, then there were already three men to deal with, and there might still be a fourth. Stephanson had yet to make an appearance.

▶ "Hey, Pat! Carl! You boys waiting for me?"

The voice rang out from farther up the mountain, piercing the morning air, startling the birds into silence. There was still no one visible on the road, and Dan couldn't see or hear any movement or disturbance in the forest, but it had to be Coffman, and the guy obviously knew how to handle himself in the bush: Dan hadn't heard or seen a thing since that one twig snapping, and he'd thought it had come from a different direction.

"Hey, guys, I know you're there. Aren't you going to talk to me? It's your old friend Jerry. The guy you left behind in Gold River for the cops to pick up."

The voice was loud, nasal, taunting. And Coffman had just confirmed that he was involved with Sleeman and Rainer, although it seemed there had been a falling-out among thieves. Too bad he didn't have some way to record this, Dan thought. It would be nice to have it all on tape.

"You boys been over to the cove lately?" The words were followed by a high-pitched giggle. Coffman sounded like he might be more than a little crazy—not a good thing when he was also known to be quick with a knife. Dan fought the urge to pull out his weapon. He didn't want to make any movement that might cause Coffman to mistake him for Sleeman or Rainer, both of whom had so far remained completely silent. That suddenly changed.

"Jerry?" Sleeman stepped out onto the road almost directly across from where Dan was hidden. "Damn, it's good to hear your voice. We were worried about you. Those damn cops were right there when we left the house. We had to move real fast or they would've caught us."

"Right there, huh?" It was Coffman, and he had moved again. "Funny; they weren't around when I left."

Sleeman shrugged and spread his hands. "Guess they must have been following us. Carl and I lost them down near the old mill site. Guess they didn't know you were there with us. Where the hell are you anyway? What are you hiding for?"

"Never mind where I am. Where's Carl? He waiting around somewhere to bash my head in?" The voice had turned sulky, the inflection oddly childlike.

"What? That's nuts. You're our partner, Jerry. Carl's down at the boat, waiting for Stephanson to show up. Come on down and join us."

The reports had been right, Dan thought as he listened to Sleeman talk. The man was smooth, and quick on his feet. No doubt he was the brains behind any plan this group had come up with.

There was no answer from Coffman, and for a minute Dan wondered if he had moved again, perhaps trying to get nearer to the boat to see if Rainer was really down there, but suddenly the man stepped out onto the road. He was maybe thirty feet above where Dan was hiding, a small, dark figure on the pale gravel.

"You ain't got a boat, Pat. Don't pull that bullshit with me. Carl ain't down at no boat. He's right there in the bush with you."

Sleeman smiled and shook his head. "Come on, Jerry. We're partners, for chrissake. We're in this together. We've got a boat. How the hell you think we got here? We took it from some old geezer in Tahsis who doesn't need it anymore. It's right down there, if you want to take a look." He turned and pointed to the water, then started walking back into the trees. "I'm going to go back down and join Carl. I need to be there when Stephanson arrives. You're welcome to join us."

Dan watched Coffman as he watched Sleeman disappear into the bush. The man seemed to be talking to himself—at least, his lips were moving, although Dan couldn't hear any sound. He was also jerking his head from side to side as he patted his thigh with his right hand. Crazy for sure. And dangerous.

After a few minutes Coffman started down the road, stopping every couple of steps to peer into the forest. Sleeman was still moving down the bank, making no attempt to be quiet. In fact, Dan thought he might be working hard to ensure he made enough noise for Coffman to easily follow him. He was also moving slowly, wandering openly between the tree trunks so that Dan, still hidden in his rough blind, had no problem seeing him.

Coffman paused briefly when he reached the point where Sleeman had left the road, then stepped in after him. He was obviously nervous, his head swiveling back and forth as he crept cautiously from tree to tree. Looking for Rainer, Dan figured, as well he should. There had been no sign of Rainer since Coffman announced his presence. Either he had gone down to the boat while Sleeman and Coffman were talking, or he was still out there, waiting.

The answer wasn't long in coming. When Coffman had moved a few steps into the trees, there was a sudden motion in the brush, and

Rainer burst out onto the road. He was four or five yards from where Coffman was standing, brandishing what seemed to be his favorite weapon, a baseball bat.

Dan fought his way out of the bushes, straining for balance as he pulled his gun out of its holster.

"Freeze. Police!" he yelled, wishing he hadn't told the backup guys to wait at the log dump. "Drop your weapon."

Another death was not what he needed. If Rainer took Coffman out of the picture, they might never find out what had happened to Margrethe, and Sleeman might get away altogether. Dan moved out onto the road, where he could plant his feet firmly. He had aimed the gun at Rainer, but he switched to Coffman as he caught movement and saw a glint of metal appear in the man's hand. A knife was a much greater threat than a baseball bat in close quarters, and Coffman was much quicker on his feet than the lumbering Rainer.

The two men stared at him, immobile with shock, but Dan figured it wouldn't take long for them to make a move. It was two against one, and they were already in the forest. Time to call in his backup. He raised his arm and aimed his gun up the road, feeling his finger tighten on the trigger. One shot was all he needed.

TWENTY-SEVEN

A shot rang out, but it was not fired from Dan's gun. And whoever had fired it knew what he was doing. Dan's hand was hanging uselessly by his side, his finger still hooked on the trigger of his own weapon. The bullet had come out of nowhere and had hit him just below the shoulder. The force of impact spun him around. Pain blossomed and flared, freezing his muscles and tendons, and he could feel the liquid warmth of blood coursing down under his shirt sleeve. In the brief second before his brain registered where the shot had come from, Dan thought it might have come from his backup, but then he realized it had to have come from somewhere below him, down near the water, not from along the road.

He threw himself forward and sideways, twisting his body as he fell to try to cushion his landing. A bullet tore the air overhead, slicing through the leaves and twigs and showering him with debris. Shit! He was a sitting duck. He scrabbled forward, using his good arm and his feet and legs to burrow deeper into the vegetation. He didn't care about the noise he was making. As long as the guy couldn't see him he had a chance, but it wasn't a good one. The shooter only had to walk a few feet down the road and he would see where Dan was lying. His only chance was if the guy thought he had scored a direct hit.

Dan willed his body closer to the ground, trying to sink deeper into its embrace. He could hear his heart thudding as it pumped the blood that was pulsing out of his wound and pasting his shirt to his body. Moving would only make it flow more freely, and the noise he would create would only make him easier to find, so he lay still and braced himself for the next shot.

It never came. Instead, he heard the sound of someone crashing through the bush, and then the whine of a boat engine starting. Goddamn it, they were going to get away.

Ignoring the pain that stabbed down his arm, Dan pushed himself up and stepped back out onto the road. There was a movement to his left, a little farther up the road. Snapping his head around, he caught a glimpse of a man disappearing into the forest. Coffman. No point in following him. There was no hope he could catch him now, but he would damn well find him later. He would lock down the island if necessary.

He turned back toward the water. The blood had reached his hand now and was dripping off his fingers onto the ground. He needed to staunch the flow somehow, or he could be in trouble, but first he had to find out who had fired that shot. He pushed into the trees, weaving and dodging as he tried to see down the bank to the boat. Behind him he heard feet pounding down the road toward him. His backup. Too late to help. A root caught his foot, and he pitched forward, biting back a scream as his arm jarred against the forest floor. The engine revs picked up. They were leaving. Dan pushed himself back up and staggered on. There was a sudden surge of noise as the pilot cranked the gas, and the old inboard howled in protest. Dan caught a flash of churning white water as a seething wake boiled up behind the boat, and then a flash of blue as it leaped forward, heading north toward Tahsis Inlet. There were three men in the cockpit, Sleeman and Rainer and a man who stood staring back up at the land, one hand resting on the coach roof and the other holding a rifle. He was tall and angular, and his white hair shone as it reflected the sunlight. Stephanson. Also known as the Reverend Steven.

Dan let himself slide to the ground and sat waiting, cradling his arm across his knees as he listened to the footsteps approach and slow.

"Down here," he called, his voice taut with pain.

The backup guys approached cautiously, their weapons drawn.

When they were close enough for Dan to see them clearly, he recognized them from the cove: George and Parker. The two constables from Gold River.

"Hi, guys," Dan said. "We meet again. I think I need a little help this time."

▶ Things got a bit hazy after that. He remembered the two of them coming down and checking him over, and he thought it was George who sent Parker back to call for the rescue chopper. One of them unzipped his jacket and eased it off, and then Dan blacked out as something was pressed onto his wound. He must have come to when they lifted him onto a stretcher, because he was aware of being loaded into the bed of a pickup truck for the short ride to the camp. He didn't know how long he waited there, but somewhere in the dim recesses of his mind he heard the beat of helicopter blades. After that there was only blackness.

▶ He came to again in a hospital bed. A nurse was standing beside him, holding his wrist. Beside her, a metal stand held two plastic bags, one half full of what he assumed was blood and the other containing some kind of clear liquid. Tubes led down to his arm. Heavy bandages wrapped his shoulder and upper body.

"What time is it?" he asked.

"Glad to see you're awake," she answered. "We were quite worried about you. You've been asleep for several hours."

Dan shook his head. "What time is it?" he asked again. "How long have I been here?"

The nurse let go of his wrist and scribbled something on a chart. "It's almost five o'clock. You came in this morning just before eleven. Are you hungry? I'll go and see if I can get you something to eat."

She disappeared, closing the door behind her. Dan didn't want something to eat; he wanted to get out of there. The hours since he had been shot might be blurry, but the events leading up to it were crystal clear. He needed a phone. If he could call Markleson, he could get him to send someone out to check the marinas, and seal off the island. He looked around the room. It was bare and functional. Other than his bed, there was a metal tray on wheels, a metal cabinet, and a single metal chair. Some kind of instrument panel occupied the wall above his head, and a cord led down from it to his pillow. There was no phone. A small window beside him appeared to look out on open sky, so he guessed he was on an upper floor. It was like a prison cell, but white instead of gray. He needed to at least know where he was, but there was nothing that would tell him. The name of the hospital would probably be on his chart, but the nurse had hung that on the end of his bed, and he couldn't reach it without disconnecting the IV, an impossibility because it was attached to his good arm and the other one was immobilized. Shit! Shit! Shit!

Dan twisted his head to the side and saw a towel and washcloth hanging on a metal rack on the side of the cabinet. He reached out and pulled them off. At least he could wipe his face. As he lifted the washcloth, he saw the words CAMPBELL RIVER HOSPITAL printed on the white terrycloth. So. One question answered. Now he had another one. He dropped the cloth and fumbled for the call button. The same nurse reappeared.

"Your meal will be here in a few minutes," she said.

Dan ignored her. "Do you still have a patient named Leif Nielson here?" he asked.

The nurse frowned. "I have no idea," she said. "He's certainly not on this ward."

"Can you find out?" Dan asked. "It's important."

She looked at him for a minute, her face wavering between concern and annoyance, and then left without saying a word. Five minutes later she returned, carrying a metal tray covered with plastic plates and bowls.

"I managed to snag you a meal off the cart," she said as she slid the tray in front of him. "The doctor says you can eat whatever you want. The more the better."

He stared at her. Was she going to ignore his request completely?

She lifted the cover off what appeared to be a bowl of soup and handed him a spoon. "Mr. Nielson is down on the second floor. He's due to be discharged tomorrow morning."

Dan grinned. The man had made it. He would be able to testify. "Any chance I could get a phone?" he asked. "I need to make some calls."

▶ "You find out anything about the Reverend Steven?" he asked Mike between mouthfuls of some unidentifiable soup-like substance.

"Yeah, I did," Mike answered. "Took me a while to figure out who the man is—Steven isn't his real name—but we got it sorted out. Rosemary ran him through the system yesterday."

"I don't suppose his real name is Stephanson, is it?" Dan asked.

"How the hell do you know that?" Mike's voice was incredulous. "It took us three days to track him down."

Dan grinned. "Pure luck," he said. "He's the guy who shot me. I heard Sleeman say they were waiting for someone called Stephanson, and then I caught a look at him when they took off in that boat they stole from Nielson. It was the same guy I saw on the wharf at Esperanza. The Reverend Steven."

"Son of a bitch. That really is a bit of good luck."

"Depends on your point of view," said Dan, wincing as pain shot through his shoulder. "I guess it's lucky he isn't a better shot. I didn't see him coming."

"Yeah. So how are you doing? They patch you up okay?"

"Guess so. They've got me hooked up to an IV, and they're replacing the blood I lost. I hope it's better quality than the food they're feeding me."

Mike laughed. "You must be doing okay if you're bitching already. You know when they're going to let you out?"

"I'm aiming for tomorrow morning. I've got things I need to do. Those guys aren't going to hang around for long."

"Don't do anything stupid, Dan. Markleson's got this thing covered. Those guys have got nowhere to go. They'll have them by tomorrow morning."

"It's not those guys I'm worried about. It's Coffman I want." Dan watched as a different nurse appeared. She frowned at the phone, walked over to the IV, injected a vial of something into the tube, smiled, and left.

191

"Markleson's got that covered too." Mike was still talking, urging him to rest. "The Marine Division has a boat out there now, and they've put a dog team in. They'll get him."

"Yeah," Dan said, although he wasn't as sure about that as Mike was. Coffman was a slippery little bastard, and he knew his way around the island. "Any sign of that missing woman yet?"

"Nothing. She seems to have completely vanished. We got her husband to give us some of her clothes and we're going to put a dog on the trail, see if it can pick up anything, and we've put out an APB in case she left the island. I'll let you know if we get anything. You look after yourself. Spend some time with Claire."

Claire. Dan didn't want to think about Claire right now. She had said she would call him. Had she tried and been unable to reach him? How would she react to the news that he had been shot? He had to call her, but not right now. He couldn't gather his thoughts together properly. He wasn't sure if he could come up with the right words. Didn't know if he could face her reaction. Was certain he couldn't handle her rejection. Maybe tomorrow, after he had had a good night's sleep. Yeah, sleep. Even the word sounded good. Whatever the nurse had put in his IV must have been pretty powerful stuff. He could already feel it working, feel his body relaxing. His shoulder was not throbbing anymore, and he felt like he was drifting. He let his head fall back on the pillow and closed his eyes. The phone slipped out of his hand as he smiled at Claire. She was laughing, the wind blowing her hair as she held out her hand to him.

TWENTY-EIGHT

▶ Walker sat quietly, the canoe bobbing gently as he held it steady against the stream. There had been no further sign of movement, but he knew the woman was still there. Her unseen presence was as real and solid as a rock in a river, changing the flow of the air as it moved around her, altering the molecules of the earth beneath her, bending the invisible lines of electrical current that connect all living things. He didn't know how he could convince her to come out of hiding. He wasn't good with people—didn't spend much time with them. He didn't have the gift of words, couldn't tell the stories like some of his people could, and his physical appearance was more likely to send her running than draw her in. But he did have instinct, and his instinct told him that patience and stillness were what was needed. Those he had plenty of.

"You might remember me," he said in the soft voice he would use to talk to the deer and otter that wandered into the cove where he had built his cabin. He didn't look at the bank, but kept his eyes focused on the water, watching the swirls and eddies dance toward him. "I visit Sanford sometimes. My sister married his brother. They live in Tsaxana, over by Gold River."

He let some more time pass, feeling the rays of sunlight move across his body as the sun rose higher in the sky. The muscles in his arm were growing tired from holding the canoe to the bank, and he flexed them slowly, easing the tiny craft into a slightly different position in such a way that the change could not be discerned. "Sanford told me you like his designs. Said you use them in your weaving." He nodded gently to himself. "I'd like to see that. I like his designs too."

There was a shimmer of movement on the bank above him, and two pairs of bright, inquisitive eyes peered out through the ferns. Walker smiled. "There's a couple of raccoons here to see you," he said. "You must be a good friend to the animals. They only come to people they trust."

He sensed rather than heard her shift her position. Felt rather than saw her eyes looking out at him. Slowly, and still without looking at where she was hidden, Walker raised his free hand and pointed at the pair of masked faces looking out from the green fronds. "They're hungry. They're looking for breakfast." Then, for the first time, he turned his head toward her. "You must be hungry too. I've got some food here you're welcome to." He slid his hand into his jacket pocket, pulled out one of the bars he had taken from Dan's boat, and laid it on the thwart in front of him. "It's good. I got it from Dan Connor. He's a friend of Gene and Mary at the lighthouse."

Some branches moved, and between the leaves a face appeared.

"You know Gene and Mary?" The voice was faint, quavering, a little rusty from disuse and attenuated by fear, but the words were clear.

Walker smiled. "Yeah. They're good folks. They've been really worried about you."

The face tipped up toward the sky as the woman tilted her head back, and she took a shuddering breath. "Oh God!" she sobbed. "Oh God!"

▶ "Sanford told me you are afraid of the water."

Walker had moved the canoe over to the opposite side of the creek, turning it so it was facing downstream and holding it in place by hanging on to yet another protruding root. Margrethe was crouched on the bank above him, eating the second of Dan's granola bars. She was filthy, her hair matted, dulled by dirt, and tangled with twigs and debris, her skin scratched and blotchy, and her clothing torn and stained, but her eyes were what held Walker's attention. They were huge in her gaunt face, wet from the tears that still streaked her cheeks, a startling blue that reminded him of the campanula that bloomed in the clearings in summer, or the wild lupines that carpeted some of the old village sites each spring, but they were also strangely calm as she looked steadily down at him.

She nodded. "Yes," she said.

Walker looked back at the creek, the water flowing steadily past him on its journey down to the ocean. It would take him an hour or more to paddle over to the logging camp on Kendrick Arm, where he might be able to find somebody with a powerboat who could come and pick Margrethe up, but he was not sure that a powerboat would be any better than a canoe when it was the water she feared, and it would mean bringing at least one stranger back with him. Another stranger might be enough to scare her back into the forest. If he could call the lighthouse and get Gene to bring Jens over, it would be better, but that would take time and he didn't know how long she would wait. He had seen the tremor that ran under her skin, the clenched muscles in her jaw, the constant flexing of her fingers. Her eyes might be calm, but her body was near breaking point.

He looked back up at her, reading the contradictions written in the language of her body: the still, unflinching stare and the trembling limbs that were poised for flight. Their eyes locked and held.

"Will you come with me?" he asked.

She didn't blink, didn't move, didn't answer. Just sat there, looking straight at him. He wasn't even sure she was seeing him. He thought she might be lost somewhere, her mind wandering, gone somewhere safe where dark-skinned men and deep, restless water played no part, but he didn't know how to bring her back.

In the end, he didn't need to. She smiled.

"Yes," she said.

▶ "You'll have to come down. I can't come up." Walker gestured to his legs, twisted in the bottom of the canoe. "Take your time. You can use the branches and roots to help you."

She leaned forward and looked down at the bank. He wasn't sure she had the strength to stand—she had obviously been slender to start with, and the ordeal of the last few days was written on her sunken flesh and prominent bones, which looked as if one slight tap would break them. He pulled the canoe in closer to the bank and wrapped the bow line around the root to hold it in place while he reached up, ready to brace her, to guide her feet if she needed help. She twisted around until she was lying on her stomach and then slid one foot downward. It found a niche in the bank, and the other foot followed. Slowly, inch by inch, one foot following the other, she edged down toward him, sliding more than climbing, showering rocks and gravel onto him, but he didn't care. A few rocks didn't matter. She was coming down.

She turned when she reached the bottom, lying back against the slope, feet braced against the flatter lip of the creek, and he held his hand out to her. There was no hesitation this time. She simply reached out and stepped into the canoe.

"You might be more comfortable facing me," he said as she bent down to sit on the forward seat. "That way you won't have to look at the water so much."

"No," she said, her voice a little stronger. "I'm fine."

Walker leaned out and released the line, dug his paddle in the water, and felt the little boat move into the current.

▶ They had just entered the narrow northern opening into Kendrick Arm when Walker heard the shots, two of them, close together. Sounds carry well around the water, and the sharp reports were unmistakable, even at a distance. They sounded too close to be coming from the logging camp, but far enough away that there was a long delay before the echo arrived. Maybe two miles by Walker's calculation. He looked at Margrethe, sitting quietly in front of him, her hands braced on the sides of the canoe, but he couldn't detect any sign that she had even heard them, let alone been bothered by them. Perhaps they meant nothing anyway. The people at the logging camp had been known to fire shots at inquisitive bears, hoping to keep them away from the kitchen, and deer were sometimes hunted out of season. But he thought these shots had come from somewhere away from the camp, yet close to the water, and that didn't make sense.

He had been keeping the canoe in close to the Nootka shore, where it was out of the main flow of the ebbing current and where the proximity to land might allow Margrethe to feel safer, but now he thought about moving farther out, maybe even crossing over to the other side. It seemed paranoid, with nothing to go on but the sound of two rifle shots, yet somehow those shots troubled him. Perhaps that was because he knew Dan was out here somewhere, looking for that boat and the two men who might have stolen it, or perhaps it was because of his concern that nothing else should trouble Margrethe's fragile state of mind. Whatever the reason, he was bothered by them.

The waterway widened as soon as they had passed the entrance, which meant a longer crossing but less current. Walker twisted his paddle to steer the canoe out into the channel, and immediately Margrethe's back tensed and her fingers tightened on the gunnels.

"I think it's better for you when we are closer to the shore," he said, moving the paddle back to the other side.

Her voice drifted back to him, so faint he could barely hear it. "It doesn't matter," she said. But it did, and Walker steered back in.

They traveled another mile south. Margrethe appeared to be lost in her own world, staring ahead. Her back was straight, although not as rigid as it had been, and her fingers had relaxed their death grip on the sides of the canoe. Walker watched the wooded banks as they slid past, and the slopes behind them. The forest had been quiet ever since the shots rang out, which meant that whatever had caused them was still out there somewhere. Even the birds were silent.

A ripple of movement traced a path through a patch of slender saplings that had filled in a clearing near the water, and Walker followed its course by watching the shudder and sway of the branches. Something was moving through them, traveling fast, not trying to hide its presence. As it came closer, he heard the sound of twigs snapping, and then the thud of feet on the forest floor. Two feet, not four. It was a man, and he was running.

Walker glanced at Margrethe, but she was still staring straight ahead, oblivious to what was happening around her. The footsteps continued on, heading north, the sound diminishing as they went.

They were followed by a brief blur of motion, and five pale shapes streaked between the trees, four of them gray and one pure white. It was the wolf pack he had seen on the other side of the island, and they were hunting. Walker smiled. Thunderbird had spoken. He had sent He'-e-tlik to take care of his people. Another totem would be carved. Margrethe would be safe to continue weaving her designs.

Walker kept paddling. The forest returned to normal. Birds were now visible in the trees, darting between branches, calling to others in their flock. The bushes along the shore signaled the passage of small animals. An otter slithered down the bank in front of them and slid soundlessly into the water. Insects flew in the sunlit air. It was going to be one of those days the Creator gave the world as a gift, a day that helped the people understand their relationship to the earth and all that was in it. The abrupt scream, when it came, barely lasted long enough to register on his brain. Even the birds continued their song uninterrupted. Balance had been restored.

TWENTY-NINE

▶ The doctor arrived shortly after nine o'clock in the morning and found Dan sitting on the edge of his bed. The nurse had removed the IV sometime during the night, but had given him a shot just before bringing him breakfast, and had left two pills in a tray on top of the cabinet.

"You releasing me this morning?" Dan asked.

"I wasn't planning on it," the doctor replied. "I think you should take advantage of our hospitality for at least another day so we can make sure no infection develops."

Dan shook his head. "I need to get out this morning. Right now, if possible."

The doctor looked at him, then flipped open the chart. "You're a cop, right? You guys always make the worst patients." He looked at Dan's bandaged arm and chest, clearly visible through the hospital gown he had wrapped around himself. "When that pain shot wears off, that's going to hurt like hell."

"I'll manage."

"That's what they all say, until the meds wear off."

"I'll manage," Dan repeated.

The doctor looked down at the chart, then back up at Dan.

"Okay, here's the deal," he said. "Right now, you're looking good. I'll get the nurse to bring your clothes. If you can dress yourself, I'll sign a release and give you prescriptions for antibiotics and painkillers.

The painkillers are going to make you a bit sleepy, so don't be doing anything stupid while you're taking them. If your arm gets worse instead of better, and you end up back here, I'll tie your ass to a bed for a week."

Dan smiled and held out his good hand.

"Deal," he said.

▶ It took him much longer than he had expected to get his clothes on. He had to get the nurse to change the dressing so his arm wasn't bandaged to his chest, and even then he had to ask her to cut off the sleeve of his shirt because it wouldn't fit over the bandages. When he finally had the shirt on, he found he couldn't handle the buttons using just his left hand. He asked the nurse for help, but she just grinned at him, so he left it open. The jacket was even harder. At this time of year he might not even need it for warmth, but it would give his shoulder a bit of protection and perhaps make him look a little less obvious. In the end he simply draped it over his left arm—a challenge all by itself. By the time he was ready to go, the shot was wearing off, and the pain was so bad he was sweating, but he was damned if he was going to let it stop him.

"Done," he said to the nurse, who had left him to struggle on his own for a while, then returned just before he slid his feet into his shoes. "I'm outta here."

She reached into her pocket and pulled out two plastic bottles, flipped the lid off one of them, and held out two white tablets. "You might want to take a couple of these now." She put them into his hand and then offered him a glass of water. "And keep taking them every four hours. You have enough for four days here. After that, get to your doctor."

He put them in his mouth and swallowed them. "Thank you," he said.

▶ A police helicopter was waiting for him on the roof. He had called Markleson right after the doctor left, and Markleson had come through.

"Kendrick Arm?" the pilot asked.

"No," Dan said. "Friendly Cove—as fast as you can get me there."

Markleson had told him that they had found Nielson's boat abandoned on the beach at Boca del Infierno, just north of the cove, and had a dog team in there tracking. Another team was out at Kendrick Arm, and there was a helicopter with heat-sensor equipment flying over the island. Dan figured the main action would be at the cove. He would leave Coffman to the dog team and the helicopter boys and deal with him later.

It was a fast trip, and the chopper put him down on the landing pad at the lighthouse. Mary came down to meet him.

"My God, what happened to you?" she asked as she took in his empty sleeve and bandaged arm.

"One of the guys we're looking for took a shot at me," Dan answered.

"You were shot? But that's terrible. Shouldn't you be in hospital?"

"Don't worry. It's not as bad as it looks," Dan answered. "I was just at the hospital. The doctor bandaged me up and threw me out. How are things around here?"

She rolled her eyes. "It's crazy. There are cops all over the place, and we've been told we have to stay up here, not go down to the cove at all. One of the big police boats was here yesterday, but it left, and then one of the smaller boats arrived with a bunch of guys and a dog. It's still here, and so are they. I think they used one of the cabins to sleep in, but I'm not sure." She pointed down at the wharf. "And the coast guard stopped by as well. Looked like a circus for a while." She grinned. "Haven't had this much excitement in years."

"How's Jens?"

Her smile disappeared. "Not good. He just sits in his house. Won't come out. I've been taking his meals down to him, but he's barely eaten anything. I saw him looking out the window when the big boat arrived, but that was it." She looked at him. "Is that why you're here? Is there any news of Margrethe?"

"No," he answered. "Nothing yet."

▶ There was a uniformed cop posted on the far end of the walkway, and Dan went out to talk to him.

"You know where the guy in charge is?" Dan asked as soon as he had identified himself. "I need to talk to him."

"I can call him," the cop answered. "See if he can come up here. No way they're going to let you out there without at least a vest." He looked at Dan's arm but refrained from saying anything else.

When he finally arrived, the guy in charge turned out to be an emergency-response-team leader from Nanaimo.

"Find anything yet?" Dan asked.

"No, but they're here. The dog picked up a scent from the boat and followed it for a way but lost it in a creek. We've split the team in two, half coming across from Boca and the rest spread out at this end. It's pretty heavy going, but the guys can handle it, and we've got the dog. We'll find them."

Dan nodded. "I'd like to be in on that."

The sergeant's eyes drifted down to the bandages and the empty sleeve. "These the guys who shot you?"

"Yeah. One of them anyway. A tall guy with white hair. The other two hit an old man on the head, stole his boat, and left him for dead."

"Nice guys." A radio crackled briefly, and the sergeant pulled it out of a pocket. "Look, I gotta get back. I can't let you come out there," he gestured to Dan's arm, "but I can get you a radio so you can follow what's happening. Soon as we have them, I'll send for you."

"Thanks. I'd appreciate that."

The radio arrived five minutes later. It was better than nothing, but not much. It allowed Dan to eavesdrop on the action, but not be a part of it. The transmissions were terse and gave no information as to exact location, but they did transmit tension, and Dan alternated between vicarious adrenalin highs and bouts of pure frustration.

At half past twelve Mary came out and met him on the lighthouse end of the walkway.

"You're going to wear the walkway out if you keep pacing up and down it like that," she said. "I've got lunch ready up at the house. It's just soup and a sandwich, but you need to eat."

He looked at her. The mention of lunch was enough to make him realize he hadn't eaten anything but a piece of toast back at the hospital, and he was suddenly starving.

"If lunch is as good as that breakfast you made me last time I was here, I'll take all I can get," he said.

Gene was already at the table when they arrived, and he pushed out a chair as Dan approached.

"That as nasty as it looks?" he asked, nodding at the bandaged arm.

"Nope. Hurts like a bitch when I forget the pills, though," Dan answered, pulling out the bottles the nurse had given him. "He caught me when I wasn't looking, but it missed all the important stuff."

"That the same guy you figure took Margrethe?" Gene spoke around a mouthful of soup.

"No. He was there, but he ran off into the bush. One of his buddies did this. They're who the guys are looking for out there." Dan nodded back toward the cove. "Once we've rounded those three up, we'll go back over the other side and find him. I plan on having a serious chat with him." The smile didn't reach his eyes.

He was back out on the walkway when he heard the dog start to bark, and the radio came to life with shouted commands and directions. With nothing to see except the stolid back of the constable posted at the end of the walkway, all he could do was try to put the pieces together in his imagination. It didn't work well. It was like a movie that he should have had a role in, played on a small black-and-white TV with lousy sound.

The dog quieted, and the chatter on the radio calmed down. A group of four ER guys appeared on the path that led from the old cemetery to the wharf, but they had no one else with them. They turned off after they passed the church and moved across the clearing behind the house, toward the trees on the other side, and then stopped with their weapons drawn. Another group emerged from the bush in front of them, led by a dog handler and his dog. Behind him came four more cops, surrounding three handcuffed men. One of the men had white hair.

The radio chattered briefly, and the constable turned and walked over to Dan.

"Sergeant says you can go down now," he said.

The ER team, all eight of them plus the leader Dan had spoken to, had come to a stop at the head of the wharf.

"This the guy who shot you?" the sergeant asked when he arrived, nodding toward Stephanson.

"Yeah, that's him. I saw him over at Esperanza a couple of days ago. He was calling himself the Reverend Steven then, but I think his name is Stephanson."

The sergeant nodded. "Okay. We'll take all of them back to Nanaimo and hand them over to the detachment there. They'll probably want you to go over there and make a statement." They started down the wharf toward the police boat.

"You searched them yet?" Dan called after them.

The sergeant turned. "Yes. One rifle. Should be able to match the bullet they took out of your arm with that. And one baseball bat." He shrugged. "That's it."

"You might want to check with a guy called Leif Nielson about the bat," Dan said. "He was discharged from the Campbell River Hospital this morning. Probably back in Kyuquot by now."

The sergeant looked at him. "We'll do that. You look after yourself."

Dan lifted his hand in acknowledgment.

▶ The emergency-response team left with their boat, and the dog handler and the constable left with theirs, leaving the wharf empty once more. Dan used the lighthouse phone to call Markleson and bring him up to date, then asked for transportation back to Kendrick Arm. Markleson said he would see what he could do, but it might take a while. The Tahsis police boat was already over at the logging camp, along with a fast inflatable they had borrowed from the marina. There was nothing else he could send.

"I'll let you know when they find him," he said, and Dan had no choice but to be content with that.

He spent an hour with Gene and Mary, but he couldn't relax. Coffman was still out there, and Margrethe was still missing. So was a half-million dollars' worth of jewelry. The jewelry didn't bother him too much. Chances were it would turn up somewhere, and if it didn't, insurance would cover it, but Margrethe needed to be found.

"I'm going to take a walk," he said. "Maybe head to the cemetery. I didn't get a chance to look at it before."

The gravel path curved up along the side of the clearing, skirted the church, and then led along the top of a cliff. A narrow beach hugged the base, and beyond it, surf crashed against a barrier of black rocks that stood firm against the vast power and reach of the Pacific. The day had grown warm, the sun high overhead in a forget-me-not sky sprinkled with cotton-ball clouds. A breeze brought with it the fresh salty smell of the ocean as it rippled the young grass filling the bowl with the burgeoning green of new life. There weren't many idyllic spring days on this temperate, rain-washed coast, and each one was a gift to be cherished, but as Dan stood beneath the Welcome Pole, its outstretched arms reaching out on either side of him, he barely saw it. There was too much he still had to do.

▶ THIRTY ◀

▶ The sun had traveled a considerable distance by the time Dan made it to the cemetery. Long rays slanted over the old headstones and slid between the pickets of the fences surrounding each grave. Each stone told its own story: a single name, and two dates that bracketed the span of one life. Nothing else. Many of those who lay under this soft earth had not survived past childhood. Most had lived only two or three years.

He moved slowly from grave to grave, reading each name, looking at the personal objects those left behind had added, each a treasured belonging no longer needed by its owner: a rusty wagon; the head of a doll, its body disintegrated by weather; a cooking pot. And then he saw the totem pole and stared at it in disbelief. It was on one of the oldest graves, and it was small, perhaps only four or five feet tall, but that wasn't what bothered him. It had been damaged in exactly the same way as the one down in the cove—the beak of the thunderbird hacked off, the bear's snout gouged and torn. Even the ground around it had been dug up, the surface of the grave itself disturbed. It had to have been the same guy, but why? Could he have been looking for something?

Dan went back and checked the other graves to make sure he hadn't missed anything there, but they were all untouched. He moved on, skirting the one with the damaged pole, and started to check out the three he hadn't looked at yet. They were all old. All deep under the trees. They all carried one name and two dates. Someone had left a pair of tiny shoes, wrinkled and twisted but still recognizable, beside the headstone on one of them. Another had a rusty sewing machine. It looked very much like the one Dan's mother had used when he was a kid, an old Singer treadle machine. He leaned closer to see if he could still read the nameplate. It was hard to see because the wooden cross that had served as a marker had fallen on top of it. He moved around to the other side to try to get a better look. This was the shaded side, the side the sun never reached, protected by the towering cedars that stood sentinel on three sides of the graveyard. Moss had grown here, and lichen clung to the fence posts. Ferns had sprouted in the grooves of the wood, and wild strawberries carpeted the ground. Even the air seemed green. A deep, soft green that spoke of time and peace and eternity. Perhaps that was what made the gouge of raw scraped earth so obvious.

Dan straightened up, blinked a couple of times, and looked back down, but he hadn't imagined it. The gouge was still there, and it was fresh. It was maybe six inches deep where it disappeared under the base of the sewing machine, and the top inch was dry. He looked back at the damaged totem. Why hack up a pole and leave an old sewing machine intact? The machine hadn't even been moved, and as far as he could tell the wooden grave marker had been left untouched.

He bent down and tried to peer under the machine, but the light was too dim to see anything. Now what? Once again he wished Walker were there. Walker would know exactly when this gouge had been created. Without him, Dan could only use his common sense and his logic, and both were telling him that this must have happened very recently, probably in the last four or five days, which meant it could very well be linked to Coffman's visit and maybe even to Margrethe. Which meant he had to check it out.

But it didn't seem right to just reach in. Even though the hole wasn't dug into the grave itself, checking inside it would still be a desecration, an invasion into the privacy of death. It would help if he could talk with the people who lived down at the house. They were members of the same band, maybe even the same family, as the occupants of the cemetery. But they were still away, perhaps out fishing, perhaps still visiting relatives, but probably waiting for the cove to return to its former peaceful existence. In any case, they were not in residence. So no permission to be had there. No dispensation. No forgiveness if he was wrong.

He took a deep breath, offered up an apology to whatever entity watched over this lonely site, and stretched his arm down over the fence. He couldn't even come close. If he could hang on to the fence it might be possible, but that would require two functioning arms and he only had one. His best chance, probably his only chance, was to sit down and stretch his good arm through the old pickets, and that meant reaching across the grave.

Whispering a silent explanation to the occupant of the grave, he lowered himself to the ground and sat as near to the fence as he could. The sewing machine was still too far away. The tips of his fingers barely reached the start of the gouge. He would have to lie down, and that was not going to be easy. Getting up again would be even harder.

A disturbance in the branches of a nearby cedar tree drew his attention. A raven was peering down at him with bright, black eyes. Feeling more than a little foolish, Dan looked up at it and asked himself if there was any way it could be some kind of emissary—Walker belonged to the Raven clan. Of course the whole idea was ridiculous—but on the other hand, it couldn't do any harm to check. After all, there was no one around to hear him make a fool of himself.

"If you've got any ideas, now would be a good time to share them," he said.

The answer was a harsh squawk.

"Yeah. That's what I thought."

So much for that idea.

He let himself fall backward. He was still too far away, and now the angle was wrong. He grabbed a post and, using his heels to assist, hitched himself forward. Pain flared as his bandaged arm bumped along the ground, and he closed his eyes and clenched his teeth as he waited for the worst of it to pass.

He reached out again, stretching as far as he could, pushing hard against the fence, and felt his fingertips touch something soft. Fabric? Maybe a cloth bag or pouch of some kind. He could feel a ridge that might be a cord closure. Doubt froze him. Was he robbing a grave? Was this some gift or offering? A medicine pouch? Hell, he didn't even know if such things really existed. Maybe they were just something he'd read about, or seen in the movies. Another thing to ask Walker about when he saw him again.

But whatever this was, it felt new. He could feel the threads, feel where they intersected. They were thick and slightly rough, textured in some way. Not fragile. Not disintegrating. He hooked a nail under them and edged them toward him. They moved an inch, then slipped off. He tried again and managed maybe a half inch. Not enough. He turned his hand over and hooked the fabric from above, felt it move. Tried once more and felt it graze the fleshy part of his thumb as he closed his grasp. He had it. Now to get it out. It was heavier than he had expected, and an awkward shape that seemed to catch on the ground as he pulled. To make matters worse, his arm was wedged between two pickets, which left him little room to maneuver.

Inch by inch, he worked it closer, until finally he had it clear. He pulled it over the grave until it was close and left it lying there while he worked his way back into an upright position. He should have taken some more of those pills. His arm was throbbing, pulsing with pain, and he was sweating with the effort of sitting up, but he forced himself to reach out and draw the fabric through the fence. It was a drawstring bag, made of some kind of woven material, and even before he managed to get it open, he could feel the curving shapes inside. It had to be the jewelry.

Some of the guys he had worked with had worn rings, or maybe a gold chain or a cord with a medallion, even a bracelet, but he had never been a jewelry kind of guy. Sure, he had bought a couple of necklaces for Susan, but they were just ornaments. Pretty things that looked good on her and that he knew she would enjoy. This was nothing like that. Even peering down into the dim interior of the sack he could see the difference. Gold and silver shapes gleamed with an inner life, some three-dimensional, others incised. An eagle stared up at him, its silver eyes unblinking beside a curving beak. The fin of an orca plunged into a sea of gold. They looked alive, expectant, watchful. Perhaps waiting for him to release them back into the light. He shook his head. It wasn't like him to be so fanciful, but these were beautiful. These were works of art.

A shadow moved across him, and he looked up. The raven had moved, and it now perched on one of the fence posts surrounding the grave, no more than ten feet away. Dan had never seen a raven this close. The bird was huge, much bigger than a crow, its beak thick and heavy, and its feathers a rich, lustrous black. It was watching him, tilting its head from side to side as if to get a better view, and then it arched its neck and lowered its beak as if it too wanted to see what was in the sack. Well, why the hell not? He had already talked to it.

Moving slowly so as not to startle it, Dan reached his hand inside the sack, extracted a gold bracelet, and held it out for the bird to inspect. The raven's eyes moved from Dan to the object he was holding and fixed on it. They stayed that way, man and bird frozen in place, for what seemed to Dan like long minutes but could have been only seconds, and then, with an odd, bell-like call, the raven lifted off and disappeared.

Dan shook himself and glanced around to make sure he was still alone and still where he had been, sitting on the grass beside a small grave, high above the cove. What the hell was happening to him? Was he going crazy? Maybe he had simply imagined the raven. There was certainly no sign of one now. Perhaps it was the pills he was taking. Quickly he replaced the bracelet and tightened the drawstring. It was time to get back to the lighthouse and see if his ride to Kendrick Arm had arrived yet.

▶ There was a boat at the wharf, but it wasn't his ride. It belonged to two wildlife officers who Gene said routinely visited the island to monitor the size of the deer population and discourage the out-of-season hunting that spiked during the summer months. Gene introduced them as Mary poured coffee and set out a plate of scones, hot from the oven.

"Help yourselves," she said, loading up another plate. "I'll be back in a minute."

She went out the door and Dan watched her head down to Jens's house. If bad things happened, Mary would be a good person to have around.

"Nice job you guys have," Dan said, turning back to the table.

"Nice now. Not so great in winter," one of them answered. "You ever been out here in a winter storm?"

Dan shook his head. "No, but I've heard it can get pretty rough."

"Rough, hell," the guy answered. "It's goddamn insane. Wind can blow over seventy knots, and that's steady, not just the gusts. The gusts are even higher. You can hear it howling even when you're four or five miles inland, and the waves—" He stopped and they all turned to look out the door. "What the hell was that?"

A high-pitched shriek had split the air. It was followed by yelling and pounding feet, and then Mary burst into the doorway.

"She's here," she yelled, half laughing, half crying. "It's her. Margrethe! She's back." She turned and ran back outside. The four men all followed her.

Dan saw her when he was halfway across the walkway. She was sitting in the front of a canoe that was approaching the beach. She was smiling as she watched her husband race toward her, her arms outstretched in greeting. Walker was sitting behind her, paddling. He was smiling too.

▶ "How the hell did you find her?"

Dan and Walker, together with Gene and the two wildlife guys, were sitting on driftwood logs on the beach. Jens and Margrethe had made their way up to the house, and Mary had gone with them to monitor the radio.

"Jared told me where she was heading." Walker shrugged. "I went there. She came out of the bush."

"Just walked right up to you, I suppose," Dan said.

"Yep."

"And stepped right into your canoe."

Walker smiled. "Yep."

Dan shook his head.

"Who's Jared?" Gene asked. "One of the cops?"

"No. He's just a guy I know from Esperanza," Walker answered.

"From the mission?" Gene sounded puzzled. "I know most of the guys there. Don't think I've met Jared."

"Jared doesn't like to meet people," Walker replied.

"Too bad he can't tell me where Coffman is heading," Dan said. "Be nice if that asshole would just walk right up to me when I get over there."

Walker looked at him. "No need to go over there. Coffman ain't walking anywhere."

"Wish that was true," Dan said. "But he's still out there. He ran off when Stephanson shot me."

"Didn't run far," Walker said. "The wolves took care of him."

"Wolves?" four voices chimed in unbelieving chorus.

"What the hell are you talking about?" Dan asked.

"What wolves?" one of the wildlife guys asked. "Don't have many wolves here on the island—just two small packs. More than enough deer to support them. I've never heard of them attacking anyone."

"Pack of five," Walker answered. "Four gray and one white."

"White? No. Not possible. No white wolves here. Never seen one anywhere, although I've heard one or two might exist up north. Must have been something else you saw."

Walker smiled. "You should get a dog team out there. Shouldn't be too hard to find what's left of that guy."

THIRTY-ONE

► "You were serious, weren't you? About the white wolf."

The two men were standing out on the wharf, waiting for a water taxi to pick Dan up and take him back to *Dreamspeaker*. The police boat that had been sent out had been diverted to Kendrick Arm when the dog team there found Coffman's body about a mile and a half north of where Dan had last seen him. When Markleson called Dan to update him, he said the dog handler figured Coffman had been killed by some wild animal, but they couldn't figure out what: his throat was torn open, but there was no other sign of injury and no tracks.

"Yes," said Walker. "I was."

"Did you actually see it?" Dan asked.

"Saw him twice here," said Walker. "The first time was over on the other side, 'round Louie Bay. Guess he was waiting for the right time, or maybe he just wanted to let me know he was on the job." He smiled. "I've seen him twice before, too. Once over near Gold River a while back, and another time up by Nimpkish River, maybe six years ago."

"Couldn't have been the same wolf," Dan said. "The Nimpkish is over on the other side of Vancouver Island. And those wildlife guys said white wolves are very rare."

"Not rare enough."

"What's that supposed to mean? There's something wrong with them?"

Walker shrugged. "Nothing wrong with him. Something wrong with why he's here."

Dan shook his head. "You're not making sense, Walker. Why shouldn't there be a white wolf here? You just said you've seen one four times—which means they can't be as rare as those wildlife guys think."

Walker looked at him. "The time I saw him at Nimpkish River, a kid from the band there had been murdered. Police didn't know who did it, but two days after I saw that wolf, they found a body up in the bush. Said it was some guy out hunting. Must have got lost. Said the body had been ravaged by animals. Not sure if they ever identified him."

"You're saying this is some spirit animal?" Dan could see that Walker was completely serious. "An animal that takes revenge on anyone who murders a Native kid?"

Walker shrugged again and pulled a snack bar out of his pocket. "Not saying anything. That time in Gold River, it was right after a young girl was raped and murdered. She was from the Muchalaht band. Only ten years old. Just had her birthday a few days before she went missing. They found her body in a ditch down behind the school. I came over about a week after it happened. Saw the wolf up at the top of the hill as I was coming into town. Next day some loggers found a body. Took the cops a while to figure it all out, and I had left by then, but they said it was the guy that did it. My sister told me. The newspaper report said they thought maybe a cougar had got him."

"Son of a bitch," said Dan. The story was so far-fetched it was almost impossible for his brain to accept. Almost, but not quite. He had dismissed Walker's stories before, only to find out they were true, and there were a lot of things here that sounded real. Not only that, but the way Coffman had died would fit right in. Still, a spirit wolf?

"I had a raven come down and sit right beside me up there at the cemetery," Dan said.

"Yeah?" Walker smiled.

"Yeah. I was feeling kind of bad about reaching into the grave site, thinking it was sort of a desecration or something. I kinda thought . . ." Hearing himself talking about it, it sounded foolish, but he had started, so he couldn't very well stop. "I sort of sent up a prayer. Not sure who to, but I said I was sorry . . . Hell, I don't know what I said. It just felt like I was going to do something I shouldn't be doing." He shrugged. "Anyway, this raven squawks at me. He's sitting up in one of those cedar trees right above my head. So I reach in and find the stuff, and this shadow flies right over me. When I look up, that damn raven is sitting right there on one of the fence posts. He was so close I could almost have reached out and touched him. Anyway, I got this idea that maybe he wanted to see what was in the sack, so I showed him. Just reached in and pulled out a bracelet, and it was like he looked at it. Just sat there for—seemed like a long time. And then he flew off."

He shrugged in embarrassment. "Crazy, huh?"

Walker burst into laughter.

"What the hell's so funny?" Dan asked.

"Better be careful, white man. You're beginning to think like us Indians. Gonna have to give you a proper name pretty soon. Take you to the Hamatsa."

"Fuck off, Walker," Dan said. "It just seemed . . . weird. I even talked to it. Asked it a question. Thought maybe you sent it. You did tell me you are from the Raven clan."

"I am, but I didn't send him. U'melth doesn't serve me. He's pretty powerful. Gave us the moon, and the sun, and the tides. Gave us fire and salmon too. But he's a trickster. He can transform himself into any creature he wants to." Walker paused for a minute, his face thoughtful. "Any of that jewelry have Raven on it?"

"I don't know. There's an eagle for sure. And an orca. I didn't look at all of it, and I can't recognize all of them anyway." Dan had borrowed a briefcase from Gene and locked the bag into it.

"Huh. Well, sounds like he was looking for something. Or maybe he just wanted to check you out. Let you know you did a good job getting the stuff back."

"Yeah, well, whatever it was, it was kind of cool," Dan said. "Never seen a raven close up before." He looked at Walker. "Hey, is that one of my snack bars you're eating?"

"Wondered when you'd notice," Walker said as he pulled the wrapper off. "Not bad for fake food. I took it from your boat a couple of nights ago. Pretty good couch to sleep on too." Walker reached into his pocket. "Here's your key back."

"Gee, thanks. Anything else I should know about?"

"Nope. You might be short a few more bars, but I left the radio on the table."

Both men turned as the sound of a boat engine came from behind the point.

"Sounds like your ride's here," Walker said. "Stay safe, white man."

"You too, Walker. You heading back home?"

"Yeah. Might see you up there again sometime."

Dan watched as Walker grasped the top of a ladder that led down to the beach and used it like a pommel horse to swing his legs around. His body slowly disappeared, swinging from side to side, until only his head was left, and then he stopped and started up again.

"Forgotten something?" Dan asked as he watched and marveled at the strength Walker's movement required.

"Nope. But I think you did." Walker nodded at something out beyond the wharf, and Dan turned to see a big Boston Whaler drifting up alongside. As he walked toward it, the door to the wheelhouse opened, and Claire stepped out. She jumped down, tied up the lines, waved to Walker, and then turned toward Dan, her eyes taking in his bandaged arm.

"I guess this is what comes with being involved with a cop," she said. "Gonna take some getting used to." She smiled as she lifted her face up to his.

ACKNOWLEDGMENTS

I would like to gratefully acknowledge the help of several people during the writing of this book. They include Jim Tipton, Victoria Schmidt, Antonio Rambles, Bob Drynan, Margie Keane, Mel Goldberg, Janice Kimball, David Bryen, Carol Bowman, Pam Harting, and Lynne Stonier-Newman, all of whom helped guide and shape the final copy.

Thanks are also due to my editor, Linda Richards, and to Taryn Boyd and the entire team at Touchwood Editions, without whose skilled and careful attention this book would not exist.

For information on ocean current drift rates, the Canadian Coastguard provided invaluable assistance, and I am indebted to J. (Jason) Fidder, Sergeant, of Nootka Sound Detachment, for his input on RCMP structure and operational procedures in the area of the west coast of Vancouver Island, and to Ward Clapham and Chris Stewart, both retired RCMP officers, whose vast knowledge of that policing force has helped flesh out not only this story but also Dan Connor and his background. Barb McLintock, of the BC Coroner's Service, is owed thanks for her advice on the possible effects of immersion on a body, and Ed and Pat Kidder, former lightkeepers at the Nootka lighthouse, provided invaluable background on both life at a remote light station and the reality of living on Nootka Island (as well as great stories and cold beer).

Ray and Terry Williams, Cecilia James, Rose Jack, Michael Jacobson-Weston, and many others in many Native communities have done their best to educate me in the rich and complex traditions of their culture, and any errors or misrepresentations that appear here are entirely attributable to me. Thank you to each of you for your efforts and your generosity. Gilakas'la.

I was also assisted by the many stories and photographs provided by my mother- and father-in-law who spent their early years at the Nootka cannery and lived there from 1928 to 1937.

Lastly, Sanford Williams, a brilliant master carver whose work can be found not only in his studio in Yuquot but galleries and private collections around the world, generously allowed me to use his name, for which I am most grateful. Some of his work can be seen on his website: www.sanfordwilliams.com.

R.J. MCMILLEN has spent over thirty years sailing the Pacific Northwest on a thirty-six-foot sailboat she and her husband built, visiting the remote coastal communities where her family worked in the early 1900s. *Black Tide Rising* is her second mystery. Find out more about the Dan Connor mystery series at www.rjmcmillen.com.